WIND THERAPY

Sacred Hearts PNW Chapter - Book II

A.J. DOWNEY

SACRED HEARTS
MC
PACIFIC NORTHWEST

COPYRIGHT

DEDICATION

To the survivors. You made it; it was awful. Now it's time to move on and instead of just surviving, it's time to start thriving. You can do it.

CHAPTER ONE

*M*averick...

The ride was long and dusty; the sun punishing and the wind hot. I hated Eastern Washington in the summer. Everything was rolling golden-brown hills and scree, sun-scorched grass and baked rock. Inhospitable, barren, and it happened almost immediately as you got through the pass and it never let up.

I was much happier on the other side of the Cascades where it was green, blue, and the mountainside was a *cool* and inviting gray. The rock on this side of the mountain range was darker somehow, more like an iron gray; the color difference enough that it even *looked* hot to the touch. In the summertime, you could see the heat distortion rising from the rock and shale, the shimmer persisting from the asphalt of the interstate as you redirected your attention back to the roadway.

I wanted back on the other side of the mountains something *fierce*, but that wouldn't go down until tomorrow at the earliest.

There weren't enough men left of the Eastern Washington chapter of the SHMC to run it. Almost all of them had been locked up on charges stemming from some dirty dealings unrelated and unbeknownst to the club at large. Personal greed had overwhelmed their loyalties and the price would be steep even though, as of yet, it was undecided what that price would be. I did know some motherfuckers would be out bad before it was all over.

That would come in a few weeks' time when the club at large made the run out to the annual National Meet at Lake Eversong. It happened once a year, and wasn't something that was required to attend yearly, but this year – we had to be there. All of us. From Western Washington, Idaho, and Western and Eastern Oregon.

The Eastern Washington chapter had put the entire region of clubs in jeopardy and needed to answer for it. Worse, they needed to answer for what they'd done to the people we were on our way to help now. As far as I was concerned, the pigs could deal with the rest.

We were loaded with all kinds of prescription drugs from up north over the Canadian border. Lifesaving drugs such as insulin and a variety of cardiac meds and even antibiotics. The only thing we *didn't* run was narcotic painkillers. There was plenty of that shit flooding the market down here in the states as it was readily available without our help.

We were riding for the Gregson Family Orchard and Farms outside Yakima. There was a permanent camp there for migrant workers and their families. Some of them weren't even migrants anymore. The permanent structures became permanent residence to a few families that weathered things out year-round on the farms. Those few families sticking around maintained the greenhouses on the property when the orchards weren't going anymore.

It was a sad sort of place, reminiscent of the old Japanese internment camps, only on a slightly nicer scale. While drab and a little shabby, the buildings that comprised the homes were in good repair for the most part.

We rode carefully down the dirt and gravel track to what we affectionately called the 'town square' which was comprised of a ring of some of the original homes. More a cul-de-sac with squared off edges, if you'd like. There was no pavement, just gravel, and the homes here were essentially all mobile homes – rundown and rudimentary but again, kept in as best repair as could be afforded; which considering how hardcore these people relied on us said something about affordability.

Visually, it was appealing; usually kept freshly painted, which was honestly just a lot like putting lipstick on a pig. It was when you got up close that you realized just how badly some of their shit was falling apart. Gutters held up in places with zip ties and penny nails. Washing lines strung up between units while the busted old dryer sat out front rusting with flowers planted in it, growing out the front.

I mean, at least they tried to keep it pretty and looking nice, but there was only so much you could do out here with so very little to do it with.

The residents, mostly older women, and young kids, came out of the mobile homes onto the rough plywood front porches and steps when they heard the bikes approach. Some of the men who were injured would come around. Sometimes, a truck would come from the field with more – but the one we needed to talk to was the camp doctor and the one who held the purse strings.

She was a formidable old lady for sure. We considered her the camp matriarch. The queen of them all, she was respected enough, revered enough, that whatever she said went. I couldn't help but think that she ruled this place and its people with a modicum of fear because while the respect was there, so too was something else. An inability or unwillingness for some of them to look at her directly, which was sort of a riot.

She couldn't be more than five foot. Obese, probably with diabetes herself, she was by far not exactly the healthiest among them. Yet even the strongest of the fieldworkers bowed to her will. They called her *Abuela*, or grandmother, and I got the impression she was just that. Some sort of grandmother to them all, a strange dichotomy of good will – willing to feed everyone and giving the occasional sweet to the kids, while simultaneously containing a hardcore iron will. A woman who shouldn't be trifled with and who held a ruthlessness to her unmatched by any man here.

That included me and my guys, in her eyes – but if she only knew. Still, she held the purse strings and hadn't crossed us yet. So, we let her illusion live and thrive that she had any kind of clout over us. No reason to destroy a perfectly good symbiotic relationship over what would end up tantamount to a dick-measuring contest.

After we'd ironed out the mess that Rebel and the majority of his crew had made of things with these people, we'd been good to go since, and now it'd grown apparent exactly how much fuckery that Rebel and the officers of his chapter had been up to. Some of the members, too. It was only a few of them that'd tried to reach out from behind bars or who were *still* out and hadn't let themselves be swept up in his bullshit.

It was giving me headaches. Headaches I didn't need, but that were on my mind being the closest chapter with the wherewithal to deal with it. Idaho was no help, even though their territory bordered on Eastern Washington's. They were a smaller outfit than even mine and were fending off an encroaching club from Montana. Idaho was holding their own with that just fine but didn't have it in them to stretch themselves any thinner and I understood how that went.

So, it was up to me and mine. Eastern Oregon was doing what it could to alleviate things from the southern border, but the truth of the matter was, there wasn't enough chapter left in Eastern Washington and there weren't enough members outside of cabinet members in the rest of the Pacific Northwest territories' chapters to make migration enough of a thing to bulk or recreate Eastern Washington on even a temporary basis until shit could get sorted out.

Eastern Washington was on the verge of collapse and truth be told; Western Washington was ready for that eventuality. We were ready to absorb what members were left in good standing and to make this taking up of the slack a permanent thing if need be. We'd just have to see how the proverbial cookie out here continued to crumble.

Besides, it wasn't up to me. It was up to the mother chapter. Hence, why the upcoming Lake Eversong Run was a run the remaining chapters of the Pacific Northwest territory were all going to make. We just had to hold out for a couple more weeks now. Labor Day weekend was the traditional date and this year was no exception. Now it was just a matter of figuring out who all was able to make it versus who would stay behind. We didn't all *need* to go, but that was for church in the next week – no decisions needed to be made right now.

Right now, it was what had become business as usual. I cut the motor to my bike and the rest of my guys did likewise.

"Welcome." Abuela sat in an aluminum framed folding lawn chair up on her little front deck, to the side of her open front door. To the other side was one of the *only* reasons I enjoyed coming here. Her granddaughter was a sight for sore and road-weary eyes.

Slender yet still shapely, she had long straight hair, black as a crow's wing and falling to her slim waist. She wasn't always shy about showing that body, either. Today it was a pair of form-fitting jeans. A crop top Mexican peasant blouse showed off her flat stomach, the elastic hugging her ribs, the ruffle of material off her slender shoulders making her collarbones kissable and visible begging for my lips. The white of the blouse made her dusky-tanned skin glow, and the rich red embroidery along the ruffle from shoulder to shoulder added just that little *something*.

The girl always watched us keenly, something moving just behind her beautiful brown eyes framed in thick, dark lashes. The irises kissed with a honey-golden hue in their depths when the sunlight hit them just right. I loved the glimpse of gold and was always vaguely disappointed when she put up her hand to shade them and that special golden light was snuffed out by shadow.

She was *beautiful* and there were more than a few times I ended up kicking myself because she was also so fresh faced and *young* – as in probably close to if not just barely eighteen.

Of course, I was still just barely away from the ripe old age of thirty, so it wasn't like I was in 'dirty old pervert' territory by lusting after a barely legal teen. Although, if she *were* legal and as interested as her divine stare told me she was, all bets were off. Still, it didn't do to mix business with pleasure so as I always did on arrival, I put a stranglehold on my fantasies by picturing the fat old bitch that was her grandmother buck-ass naked.

That was enough, usually, to curb my dick's enthusiasm.

"Marisol," *Abuela* said permissively and her granddaughter smiled at me and came down with a glazed earthenware pitcher and a stack of red Solo cups in her other hand.

Lemonade. Marisol had started the tradition our second time out, and it'd become almost a ritual by now. Every time we showed up, we were served lemonade, a short exchange was made, and we took our cash and rode off into the proverbial sunset.

"Many thanks, *Abuela*," I said, taking a drink of the cool, sweet but tart and totally refreshing beverage. It seriously hit the spot in the summertime.

Abuela tapped her cane twice on the plywood stoop and one of the men down here on ground level scurried forward with an envelope full of cash, handing it over to me. I tossed back the rest of my lemonade while he tracked across the dusty packed earth and handed him the cup in exchange for the cash.

I sat and counted it while my boys behind me started working the month's order out of their saddlebags and packs with the good doctor.

"Whoa, hold up boys!" I called and looked up. "You're short."

Abuela pursed her lips and her shoulders sank slightly. She looked like an angry toad sitting up there and I raised my eyebrows. We'd worked things out, the price had dropped significantly from what Rebel had been charging, we'd even given over a month and half's share of the scripts for fuckin' *free* to earn back trust but trust went both fuckin' ways here.

"My grandson, he had to go to the hospital," she said, and I nodded sagely.

"That's not my problem," I answered, and it wasn't. If I let it slide for every fuckin' sob story we'd come across, all our asses would be on the line right quick. We had bills to pay back home, too. Our coffers were still suffering from helping Dump Truck and his ol' lady, Little Bird, last September. This run was supposed to be the run to put us flush again.

"So, unless you plan on comin' with us and washin' some dishes or some shit – you'd best make some calls and find that cash." I was only half joking, but Marisol who was going back up the steps paused and turned halfway, a desperate look in those honey-kissed brown eyes of hers as she said.

"I'll go, if that's what you want."

CHAPTER TWO

*M*arisol…

The words were out of my mouth before I even knew I had uttered them. Silence rang out as everyone looked at me and I tried to do the opposite of what I wanted to do which was shrink. I straightened my back and lifted my chin.

"I can do whatever you want me to do," I said. "Work off the debt. Just *please*, my brother *needs* that medicine."

My little brother was seven, going on eight, and he was on an insulin pump. He *needed that medicine.* He would die without it, and he was the only thing I had left in this world that I cared about.

The wretched old woman who cared for us after my dad, then my mother, had died was indeed our grandmother – my father's mother, but she certainly wasn't any *familia* of mine.

"How old are you?" their leader demanded, and I raised my chin, defiantly.

"Twenty," I answered, and it was almost true. Just a couple more months.

He looked me up and down with those dark blue eyes of his, his gaze electric and raising the fine hairs on the backs of my arms and behind my neck. I didn't flinch.

"Oh, yeah? Let's see some ID," he said, and I cursed silently but produced the rectangle of laminated tough material out of my back pocket and went to him with it. His eyes connected with mine and I tried to keep the desperation out of my eyes, my heart crying out, *Please! Please take me with you!*

He gave me a sharp look, and my heart squeezed painfully in my chest. I was scared he would call me out on my age, that he would spit on the ground and call me a liar and that would be it. I could see the cold calculation in his eyes and I just wanted him to please, *please* say *yes*. Take me away from this place and these people to someplace *populated* where I could find something, *anything,* to do other than live under *Abuela's* thumb.

I wanted a better life, away from here, where I could get a place, a life of my own and eventually bring my little brother to live with me.

"I could use an extra set of hands for something for the next month," he said. "She wants to go; I can bring her back on the next run – we'll see if she can square the debt in that time."

Something in my chest loosened and I tried not to sag with relief.

"No," *Abuela* said, and I turned.

"Why not?" I snarled in Spanish. *"Why not sell me to the Gringos? It's not like I have a use for you anyway!"*

She opened her mouth. "I said, *no.*" Her tone held the sharp edge of finality and I turned my face so I wouldn't have to look at her for whatever cruelty was about to come out of her fat mouth next. "You don't want this girl. She is *nothing but trouble.* You could pick any girl here for whatever you want—"

Maverick's calm, cool voice cut her off, "I did. I picked her." To me, he said, "Go pack some shit, put on some better shoes, and make it fuckin' quick, we got someplace to be."

She tried to argue with him as I rushed to comply, handing the pitcher and cups to Frida who stood by struck dumb by what was happening. *Abuela* continued to argue with him as I swept past her into our house to go to my room and gather my things, but he was a force to be reckoned with. I stood speechless in the hall, ears straining for a mere moment as he fired back at my grandmother and waited, heart thundering, blood rushing in my ears, drowning out everything else they were saying which spurred me into action.

I rushed into my room and took up my old hand-me-down but much-loved backpack which was already packed with my favorite clothes. I did it every month when they came. It had become a ritual; I packed every night the night before they came in high hopes that were as thin as a spider's web and just as fragile.

I took out my diary from its secret hiding place in one of the floor vents, along with a bandana stuffed with my mother's jewelry I had stolen from her when I was thirteen and hidden so she wouldn't sell it for more drugs.

"Marisol, what are you doing?" My little brother stood in my room behind me as I stuffed the book and small wrapped bundle in the top of my pack. I sat on my bedroom floor, in front of the closet, and took off my wedge sandals and shoved them into the top of my pack before I cinched it closed.

"I'm going away for a while, Mateo, but don't you worry. *Abuela* will take good care of you and when I can, I will come get you. I promise," I said, shoving my bare feet into my boots, wrapping the laces around the hooks, and tying them tight.

"No!" he cried and looked stricken.

"Mateo, you have to be brave for me, little brother. I have to go. It's for the best."

"But I don't want you to!" he cried, and his little chest heaved as he took a great hiccupping sob. My own chest squeezed down painfully so, and I felt my own eyes prickle with tears. I reached for him and grabbed him, hugging him tight.

"It's only for a little while," I said. "I love you so much, and I have to do this, for *us*," I said.

"No!" he said, clinging to me.

I could only imagine how my little brother was feeling. First Dad, just before he was born, then Mom when he was three. I was the only family he had left and now, I was leaving, too.

"I love you, so much, *hermano*. You must be good for me. Promise me, okay? *Promise me you'll be good.*"

He pulled away, chest hitching, eyes streaming, and he wiped them with the back of his arm.

It was all happening so fast for him and my heart ached.

"I promise!" he wailed. "I'll be good *now*, just please don't go!"

I stood up, bag in my hand and fetched down my jean jacket from the hook on the wall by my door. I stuffed my pack between my knees and put it on, Mateo lunging, wrapping his little arms around my waist and clinging to me. I hugged him, kissed the top of his head, and tried not to cry too.

"I love you so much," I said and did the hardest thing I had ever had to do. I tore myself away from his grasp and marched away from him toward a new destiny for us.

My *abuela* had met her match in Maverick. I skipped steps and strode for him and his motorcycle that he sat astride as he held out a helmet to me.

"That all you want to take?" he asked, eyeing my pack in my hands.

"That's all," I affirmed, steel in my spine and wrapping painfully around my heart.

He traded me, taking my pack, and holding it on his bike before him as I put on the helmet, working the strap to hold it onto my head. He took off his coat and handed it to me after peeling the vest off and putting it on over his tee, the arms of which had been taken off, the holes giving glimpses of his flank through them as he swung the vest behind him and slid his arms through the holes.

He handed me back my backpack as Mateo screamed at me from the front porch. "Marisol, don't go!"

"Let her go, she doesn't care about you!" our *Abuela* cried, her cruel streak a mile wide and twice as long, as I got onto the bike behind Maverick, their leader.

I unleashed hell on her, cursed her up and down, six ways to Sunday and told her what a *puta perra* she was.

"That's not true, Mateo, and you know it! I love you, *manito*!" I cried, my own voice finally cracking as my throat grew thick with tears.

"You sure you want to do this?" Maverick asked me as he fired up his bike and I resolutely put my arms around him.

"Absolutely," I said in his ear and he made some sort of signal with his hand, wheeled us around and *away*.

Still, I couldn't breathe.

Not yet.

CHAPTER THREE

*M*averick...

It caught me off guard, but not enough for my brain to fail in doing the calculations. I had it. Enough to cover financially. There was just one thing.

"How old are you?" I demanded.

"Twenty," she answered without any hesitation, with no hint of a lie... which immediately made me suspicious.

"Oh, yeah? Let's see some ID," I said.

"Mav?" I turned on the seat of my bike, looking over my shoulder at Fenris who'd spoken. He raised his eyebrows, holding out his hands in a *'what gives'* gesture. I waved him off. The rest of my crew riding with me all looked surprised but didn't say a word.

Marisol handed me over her identification, which she'd slid out of one of the back pockets of her jeans. It was real, printed vertically, but the dates said she wasn't *quite* twenty yet. She was nineteen, but she'd hit twenty in a few short weeks.

I flicked my eyes to hers and the desperation in her gaze decided me right then and there.

"I could use an extra set of hands for something for the next month," I said. "She wants to go; I can bring her back on the next run – we'll see if she can square the debt in that time."

"No." *Abuela* shook her head and Marisol rattled off something in Spanish, clearly trying to argue the point.

"I said *no*." *Abuela* turned her attention off her granddaughter and back to me. "You don't want this girl. She is *nothing but trouble*. You could pick any girl here for whatever you want—"

"I did," I said, cutting her off. "I picked *her*." I thrust a chin at Marisol and said, "Go pack some shit, put on some better shoes, and make it fuckin' quick, we got someplace to be."

I got the distinct impression that *Abuela* wasn't happy, but not for any love of her granddaughter. There was nothing but spite on the old woman's face.

"The girl *lies*. All the time. Lies, lies, lies, lies, lies! You can't believe a word she says!"

"Duly noted, but you've got your choice. Cash or her ass, so you suddenly got the cash?" I demanded.

Her mouth thinned down again, and she turned her head, refusing to look at me.

"I'll take that as a 'no,'" I declared and called back to my guys, "Anybody got an extra lid?"

"Shit, he's fuckin' serious right now," I heard one of my boys mutter in surprise. Squatch, I think, but I wasn't mad at him. This was pretty fuckin' out of character for me – but sometimes you had to ride on instinct and mine was saying to seize the fuckin' moment, so that's what I was doing.

"I'll have her back at some point," I said with a wink as Marisol came running out of the house, an old tan, rugged but also worn and frayed canvas backpack clutched to her chest, a pair of sturdy brown ankle boots on her feet to replace the wedge sandals she'd been wearing.

Deacon walked up to me and handed me a spare helmet for her pretty head. I handed it to her with one hand, taking her backpack with the other. She'd put on a short, jean jacket but it still wasn't enough so while she worked on putting on her helmet, I shrugged first out of my cut then out of my own coat, handing her the latter. She shrugged out of her jean jacket while the guys finished off passing out the meds.

When she got done, she shoved her jean jacket into the top of her already stuffed backpack and I asked, "That all you want to take?"

"That's all," she affirmed and a kid, couldn't be more than seven, stepped out onto the front porch, face streaming with tears.

"Marisol, don't go!" he cried, and his nanna hissed at him.

"Let her go, she doesn't care about you!"

That was the first time Marisol got fired up about anything that I'd had the occasion to see. She cursed the old lady out in a string of fiery Spanish that left several people looking alarmed and several more with silent smirks that they tried to hide behind their hands.

"That's not true, Mateo, and you know it! I love you, *manito*!" she cried and got onto the back of the bike behind me. "And I'll be back for you!"

Manito, I knew. It meant 'little brother.'

Interesting.

I fired up my machine and she jumped, but put her arms around me without hesitation, holding on like she'd done this before.

"You sure you wanna do this?" I called, giving her one last out.

"Absolutely," she responded in my ear and I gave the signal and wheeled us around, the boys falling into formation behind us. We rode for Moses Lake and the halfway point to meet up with Idaho for their share.

Despite Rebel and the rest being locked up, the Eastern Washington clubhouse was still owned by the club and wasn't in any kind of default – at least not yet. Depending on the decision of the National President, Dragon, it could either be let go and the contents either divided up among the four remaining Pacific Northwest chapters, liquidated completely, and the resulting cash absorbed by the National coffers, or a new chapter rebuilt from a combination of other chapters stepping up, members relocating, or nomadic brothers settling down and moving in.

As it was, two of the remaining three brothers that hadn't gotten locked up in this mess were lookin' to absorb into my chapter if we would have them. Personally, I was on the fence about that one. They were good guys, don't get me wrong, but it was yet to be seen if they were as truly club loyal as they claimed to be.

We did the trade-off with Idaho at a different location each time in the surrounding area. We'd been over the clubhouse in Moses Lake for wiretaps and bugs and the like, and the place had come up clean – but that didn't mean we hadn't missed something and as a general rule, you didn't shit where you ate to begin with.

So, every time we stopped to overnight at the Moses Lake clubhouse, we made sure to head there clean, considering the fate of our brethren.

I sent Marisol in to use the bathroom and told her not to come back out to the bikes for at least twenty minutes while we conducted business out here. She nodded fervently and made herself scarce while we waited for the Idaho boys who had to loop around to get us back on this side.

We were at the Schrag Rest Area off I-90 Eastbound, and since our Idaho boys were coming westbound, it got a little weird. Not to mention, it got a little dicey doing any sort of shit at a rest stop. Washington State Patrol tended to roll through on the regular, which is why I did this shit. They never expected you to do shit right under their noses and it was basically like hiding in plain sight. So, we waited.

If State Patrol happened to roll up while we were waiting, we stood around smoking, vaping, and just generally lookin' like we weren't doing shit else, except stopping for a piss break and a smoke, waiting on them to either hassle us or fuckin' leave.

Occasionally, we rolled up and the little piggies were already here and we had to wait on them to leave. Once a while back, they rolled up just as we got finished with the trade and set to roll out.

So far today, we'd been lucky and hadn't encountered them at all.

We didn't do these rest stop exchanges very often because of the Staties. In fact, I couldn't remember in recent memory, the last time we'd done one, but this was also a last-minute deal. The original agreed upon location had fences go up and construction begin sometime between the last run and this planned one so this, in addition to Marisol, was totally improvised.

Speaking of the girl…

"Mav, you maybe wanna let the rest of us know *just what the fuck you are doin'?*" Deacon demanded and I turned.

"To be honest with you, Deac – I have no idea, but don't you worry. I did the math. Your cut ain't affected none."

"We're not worried about that," Cipher declared. "I ran the numbers too."

"So, what's the problem?" I asked, squinting in the direction of the restroom as the two Idaho brothers rolled up.

"Later," Fenris growled and I nodded.

We made the exchange with Hollow and Vex, Marisol rematerializing just as we finished up talkin' shit and cuttin' up. I threw her some chin, impressed that she hung back by the outbuildings and waited for me to indicate it was okay to approach.

"We'll see you happy bastards later," Fen said and Hollow, a tall and skinny motherfucker, nodded.

"Until next time, amigos," he declared and cambered his lanky ass back on his chopper with the ape hangars. Vex put a middle finger to his forehead and gave us a literal one-fingered salute. I laughed and shook my head and the two of them fucked off back to the border.

"Let's go get us some well-deserved shut-eye," I said. Riding through the hottest part of the day, and the majority of us having been up late last night, we were all tired. These were always big weekends with a lot of miles.

"Let me back out before you get on," I told Marisol and she nodded.

"I know," she said, and I smiled.

We rode back to the Moses Lake clubhouse. The accommodations there left a lot to be desired, just a bunch of couches and floor space to crash on and roll out bedrolls if we had them, but it would do for tonight.

I could tell the guys weren't all the way happy, especially with my decision to take a *woman* as payment – but that was something she and I still needed to discuss.

"Marisol." I said her name as I finished hefting my own pack onto my shoulder from where it'd been bungee corded to death to my back fender.

She looked up from where her eyes had been fixed on the ground, a fire in their depths which she quickly quelled when my eyes met hers.

"What?" she finally asked when I didn't say anything right away.

"We get in there; the guys and I are going into another room to talk. You don't bother us for anything in that room. We'll be out when we get out," I told her.

She nodded. "Before you even ask, we're clear. Crystal clear."

I smiled. "Atta girl."

We went in and the three remaining guys from the Eastern Washington chapter looked up from the table they all sat around.

"My boys and I are going to avail ourselves of your chapel for a moment. This is Marisol. She'll be accompanying us back over the mountains. For all intents and purposes, she's mine for the time being so keep it aboveboard if you don't mind."

"Cool, yeah, yeah," Goner said, tipping back his chair like some high school kid rather than the dude in his thirties, or maybe even forties that he was. Goner was short for Gonorrhea, as in he had an eye for and fucked entirely too many skeezy hos back when he was a young buck and kept coming up with the clap. As far as I knew, he kept his dick clean now, but I didn't want to chance him or anyone else thinkin' Marisol was fair use among us.

These guys, if they ended up coming over the mountains with us, still weren't from our chapter. Every chapter operated somewhat differently and ours, shall I say, was definitely more liberal than a lot of the other chapters in the area. We adhered to slightly different tenants, and I could tell my guys were dying to know what the fuck I was up to where Marisol was concerned. While we had the ability to pay for things like pussy if we wanted to, and there wasn't anything wrong with sex work or sex workers – they knew it wasn't my jam and this smacked just a little too much of human trafficking even for my liking.

Truth of the matter? I was probably projecting. The guys *were* probably curious, but that didn't necessarily mean they were thinking any kind of ill of me. They were likely just waiting to hear me out on my reasoning. Trouble was, I wasn't exactly sure my reason on this. Sometimes I just ran on instinct, and my instinct was there was a lot more to the pretty little Latina than met the eye. I had a gut feeling there was a lot more than good sex to be had, if she was on board for it that is. I didn't do shit without consent. I wasn't a fuckin' rape-o piece of shit.

I followed my boys into the chapel, Marisol wandering the edges of the room, curious eyes roaming over pictures, plaques, and other sundry items tacked to the walls. There was a wall of proudly displayed mugshots of members current and past and she let her eyes rove the photographs with their printed list of charges below them on proud display.

I shut the door behind me and my guys and turned. Fenris, Squatch, Deacon, and Cipher all looked at me.

"We're taking *girls* as payment now?" Deacon asked and I could tell he was on the struggle bus with his morals.

"It was a snap decision," I said. "Something in her eyes just about every time we rolled on up through there was tellin' me she wanted out but couldn't *get* out on her own."

"Just what do you plan on doing with her?" Cipher asked.

"I have no fucking idea. Probably have her cook and clean my place – something, I don't know. I'll figure it out. I always do."

"She's pretty," Squatch observed carefully.

"If she's down to fuck then I'd go there, but definitely not without her consent and I damn sure am planning on making it *crystal clear* that I didn't 'buy' her with that intent." I put 'buy' in air quotes where it belonged.

"Maybe she's got family on our side of the mountains," Deacon mused, pulling on his bottom lip.

"Maybe," I agreed. "I'll look into it."

"She was pretty eager to volunteer as tribute," Fenris said and the guys all glanced at each other. We hadn't even bothered to sit down or really take up any places around the table. I sat on the corner of the table, bracing one boot against the cracked and unfinished cement floor.

"Glad you noticed that," I said. "Something is off in that camp, but I couldn't tell you what and while I'll ask her, I don't really expect an answer. For now, until we get back and settled, it's tabled, but you know I'm going to bring it up."

"If anything, I hope she *can* cook or you're in for a rough month if that's what you're counting on her to do." Cipher broke into silent laughter and the guys all couldn't help but join in. Doing their best not to get too loud, lest she hear and think we were making fun of her.

"Right, anything else then?" I asked and they all shook their heads.

"We knew you were up to something," Deacon declared. "You never do anything for no reason."

I nodded carefully. "No. No, I do not," I agreed.

$\mathcal{M}$arisol…

I held nothing but disdain for the three men around the table, left out here with me – and so I ignored them.

How they weren't in jail with the rest of the men from this group of the club was beyond me. Perhaps the police didn't have enough evidence against them. Just the other four.

I knew them. They used to bring the medicine, but they also had started to charge more and more each time. Sometimes, we had to go without. Sometimes, that made my people sick. It was frustrating, and I understood why Miguel had thought to go to the police, but he was *Abuela's* man to deal with. Instead, the four men who were in jail now had killed Miguel and his whole family – his wife, Anita, and their two little ones.

It was why they were in jail now, and if they talked, it could put a stop to the medicine. I worried for my brother; was afraid he would die. We couldn't afford the medicine at the pharmacy. It was far too expensive.

I walked around the barroom, my eyes skimming the photographs of the *gringos* on the wall, their hair wild and unkempt, greasy in some photos, and their eyes bleary from too much drink. Some of the photos were Yakima County Sheriff, some were Tribal Police, and I had to think that more than a few were for riding their motorcycles while drunk.

My mind wandered to Maverick, and the men who had replaced these ones last year… He was different. They all were. Hard, yes, with their air of *don't fuck with me* the same as the men from this region – yet something was different. Their male gazes… appreciative more than lascivious.

I didn't feel *dirty* when Maverick looked at me. Unlike the fools behind me now, cracking semi-crude jokes like I didn't know that they were talking about me.

Then again, I knew when to keep my mouth shut. It was a very real possibility they didn't think I spoke English. Joke was on them. My father may have been an illegal immigrant, but both I and my brother were born here.

My mother was also Hispanic, but American like me. Her parents had immigrated like my father had.

She was a teenager when she met my father, who was in his early twenties. She got pregnant with me, and they'd married and had been happy. They were overjoyed when they got pregnant with my brother, even though they had intended to stop with me.

My brother was born, and we were happy… but then my father had his fall. He hit his head and had died before help could arrive. My mother was devastated and turned to drugs to numb the pain. She overdosed and the rest, as they say, was history. Both my brother and I were given to our *Abuela* to raise.

The door opened and the men came out of the room Maverick had called the chapel, though there wasn't any sort of religious iconography that I could see.

"Marisol," he said. "Come in here a minute, would you? I want to talk to you."

I let my gaze sweep the faces of the men who had come out, but their expressions were carefully neutral and gave me nothing.

I hitched my backpack higher on my back and gripping the straps so my hands wouldn't shake, I went forward – past the table where the three men sat and past Maverick and into the room.

He shut the door behind us, and my spine tingled, a bead of sweat sliding down my spine as I tried to turn calmly.

"You don't think much of them, do you?" he asked.

"I liked Miguel, Anita, and their two boys," I said simply.

Maverick's jaw knotted with something like regret and I frowned slightly.

"Nothing like that is ever going to happen again. We have rules, it's in our bylaws, *no women, no children*. Rebel and the rest of them fucked that up, but as far as I know, Goner and the two other guys out there? They didn't know anything about it. You know something that I should about that?" He looked at me steadily, his eyebrows going up as he pressed the pad of one thumb to his sexy bottom lip.

I swallowed and shook my head.

"Right," he said and pulled out a chair. "Have a seat. We need to discuss terms."

"Terms?" I echoed.

"Yeah, terms. What you are and what you aren't willing to do to work off this debt."

I slid the straps of my pack off my shoulders and set it on the table as he held out a chair for me. I sat down and he pushed me in. He took a seat at the end of the table at a ninety-degree angle from me and leaned way back in his seat, elbows on the arms, hands steepled in front of him, fingertips pressed together.

"I thought it was whatever *you* wanted," I said, caught off guard. "Isn't that how these kinds of things usually work?" I kept my voice measured; my tone cool.

"Surprise," he said, arching an eyebrow.

"What do you expect of me?" I asked. "I mean, what would you want me to do?"

"You cook?" he asked.

"Yes."

"Clean?"

"Also, yes… you want me to be your housemaid?"

He nodded. "It's a start."

"Sex?" I asked and he smiled.

"With your consent, if you're down for it."

I eyed him carefully and nodded slowly. "I thought that was what I was signing up for."

He gave a little blasé shrug and said, "Just wanted to be clear."

"We're clear," I said.

"There's something I'm not clear on," he said. "Why'd you volunteer as tribute like that?"

I raised an eyebrow of my own. "Do I have to talk about it?"

"Not if you don't want to," he said.

"I don't want to," I said a little too sharply and he smiled. "Just to be clear," I added quickly, a little embarrassed.

"I take it you and your grandmother haven't gotten along for a while." His dark blue eyes raked over me and I chewed my bottom lip.

"No. It's been five years."

"What started that?" he asked.

"I became a teenager?" I asked and he chuckled.

"Don't want to talk about that either, huh?"

"Not really, no."

"What do you want to talk about then?"

"I don't know," I said. "A month is plenty of time to figure it out."

"That's true," he said, nodding slowly.

"So, will I be living with you?" I asked after the silence drew out for a time, though the silence wasn't uncomfortable, surprisingly enough.

"Yes," he said. "You'll be sleeping with me, too. I've only got the one bed."

"That's alright," I said with a crooked smile. His smile was slow, an echo of mine and I said sarcastically, "I mean, *oh no, the hardship!*" I even put the back of my hand to my forehead and he laughed outright.

"Point taken. Fucking you is going to be fun; I can already tell."

"We'll see if you..." I cleared my throat, "measure up."

He leaned forward and put his booted feet to the floor, saying

"Once I rail that sweet ass, you'll never look at another dick the same way again."

His confidence made me smile and made my pussy clench.

"We'll see," I murmured.

"Just wait until we get home."

Home. Now that was something I didn't have anymore. Something must have made it to the surface, flitted across my face, because he lost the easy smile and searched my eyes with grave concentration, nodding slowly at whatever he found there.

"You hungry?" he asked, and it wasn't quite what I expected but I'd take it.

"More thirsty."

"Well, you need to eat. Come on. Let's get us all fixed up."

He got up and I rose with him, taking up my pack again.

"Where are we staying tonight?" I asked.

"The pool table," he answered, and I laughed. I thought he was kidding.

What was for dinner was decided, food was ordered, and the men raided the bar for beer, whiskey, or whatever their poison was. It looked like we were in for the night, and I was alright with that. Although, I was beginning to come to grips with the notion that Maverick hadn't been joking about sleeping on the pool table.

"What are you drinking?" Maverick asked me from behind the bar, and I thought it was nice of him to serve his men. I didn't know many leaders that did that… although, for as many faults as my *abuela* had, I suppose her cooking all day on Sundays after church to feed the village was something like the same thing.

It was the one place she and I managed to find some harmony – the kitchen. She was a patient teacher in the kitchen, almost kind to me. I think that was going to be the only thing I would miss, if I were being truthful with myself.

"Um, you have a Coke back there?" Mav smiled and opened a cooler or something hidden by the bar and lifted out a Coke in the glass bottle, the kind from Mexico made with real cane sugar. I smiled as he pried the lid off with a bottle opener.

"Thanks," I murmured, sliding up onto one of the bar stools.

"Sure, you don't want something harder?" Derringer, one of the men from the Eastern Washington group, asked. I looked his way. He was a big redneck. The kind that if he drove a pickup, you would expect it to be painted in hunter's camo with a variety of rifles in the back window. He was a fat guy. The kind of guy who had *always* been heavy from the time he was a kid, but also the kind of fat that was deceptive. He was a good ol' country boy and there was muscle under that fat. The kind of muscle that would make cracking an opponent's head like an egg child's play for a man like him.

He smiled at me, his teeth a little too perfect – probably dentures despite the fact that he was still relatively young. He didn't seem the type to have grown up with a family who could afford braces.

His blue eyes sparkled under the brim of his John Deere trucker hat, and I knew he was prematurely balding underneath. He kept his hair shorn short, but when the stubble was long enough, it was enough to know he was a brassy kind of dishwater blond.

"No, thank you," I murmured. "I'm not twenty-one."

He cracked a wide grin and chuckles swept through all the men. Even Maverick smiled from behind the bar where he tossed back something amber in a short glass.

"Contributing to the delinquency of a minor is the least of our worries out here, darlin'," the one called Deacon said.

I liked him. He was the epitome of a silver fox – well-kept and easy on the eyes. His beard was carefully groomed and edged; his hair gelled into place. He smelled nice, too – his cologne subtle and woodsy, slightly spicy. It reminded me of cedar and church incense and there was something comforting about the smell, even though I wasn't, by any means, a devout Catholic girl.

"I'm good," I said, and held still, despite my wish to shift uncomfortably on my seat.

"You're all good, *sladkiye glaza*."

I frowned and demanded, "What did you just call me?" The men all chuckled and smiled at me like I was adorable, which just pissed me off more.

Maverick took another drink from his refreshed glass and with a wry smile said, "Too familiar, I get you. Wasn't anything bad, I promise."

"Do they know what it was?" I asked, looking at each of them in turn.

"None of us speak Russian," Fenris said, knocking back some of his beer.

"Eh, Slavic is useful for some ciphers and codes," Cipher declared and Squatch groaned.

Squatch looked exactly as his name implied – unibrow, pronounced brow ridge, but not *un*handsome if he could only tame his wild growth of hair.

Cipher, by comparison, was fire to Squatch's darkness. His copper hair and beard were kept neat, while long on top, and slicked back, his hair didn't reach past his collar. It was shaven underneath on the sides and the back, probably to keep cool as his hair looked thick.

"Do you know what he said?" I asked.

Cipher shrugged and I tried not to go mad with worry.

"Relax," Maverick said, which was easy for him. "Nothing bad, you've got nothing to worry about."

Yeah, right, I thought to myself.

"Girl, it is way too easy to wind you up and watch you go," Derringer said, laughing to himself.

"Derry, let the woman alone. Jesus," the third and final man from the Eastern Washington group had finally spoken. Skeeter, the vice president, had been released from jail. Word was he had been arrested on a warrant for assault, and the police had tried to leverage it against him for the other four that were still in jail. He hadn't given the police anything but had called Maverick which was why there had been no interruption in the medicine supply. For that alone, I was grateful to Skeeter, but only because of my brother.

A knock came at the clubhouse door and Mav thrust his chin at Derringer, who heaved his big ass up out of his seat and hitching his deep tan carpenter pants up in the back, marched for the front door.

He opened it up and spoke with someone outside, taking bags from him.

"Alright, thanks now," he said and let the door swing shut behind him.

"Food!" Fenris cried with enthusiasm.

"Alright!" Cipher echoed.

I stayed put, but I was interested in what might be in the bags. I was hungry.

"Hope you aren't vegetarian," Goner said to me and I frowned and shook my head. "Good, 'cause we got burgers, burgers, and more burgers over here." He tossed one of the foil-wrapped burgers in my direction. I caught it with both hands and turned to the bar to unwrap it. It was that weird foil that was paper on the inside, and I was pleased to see it was a *good* burger – like flame-grilled and double-stacked dripping with cheese and all the toppings, not some form pressed soggy piece of caca from a fast food place.

"Toss one here," Mav said and held up his hands. A silver foil-wrapped missile arced over my left shoulder and landed square in his hands in a catch that would make my old high school team quarterback jealous.

I smiled and carefully took a bite of my double stack, over the wrapper to catch the tomato juice and watered-down mayo that dripped free.

"Napkins?" Deacon asked and I nodded and took the ones he offered.

I let myself zone out a little, while they all talked here and there over their food, but I could tell, they were all tired. They probably would have bantered much more if they weren't.

Maverick hovered, but didn't try to make conversation with me, for which I was grateful. I was starting to feel like the day was catching up to me, a deep exhaustion taking over my faculties – not physical, but emotional with a side of mental. I felt bone weary, if your thoughts and emotions could be such a thing seeing as they didn't have bones.

"You get the fights on that thing?" Fenris asked, turning to the large-screen television at the back of the room and the ring of couch around it. A huge, great sectional that rung the outer edges of a big black throw rug on the concrete floor. It could easily sleep three men with room to spare, which I think was the intent.

"So, you guys coming back the other side of the mountains with us?" Cipher asked.

"We welcome?" Skeeter asked point blank and my ears perked, even as I schooled my face into careful lines of, *I'm not listening.*

"Until we get out to the Eversong meet, that's in the air but you swear on your mother's life you ain't have nothing to do with what went on out here, we could maybe take you so you don't have to go nomad," Maverick said. "It's a discussion for another time, though, if you catch my meaning."

I glanced at him as he tipped his head in my direction.

"Talking about the Vargas family? It's no secret, at least not to me," I said after washing down a bite of my burger with a swig from my Coke. Mavericks lips thinned, and a muscle ticked in his jaw.

"I understand that you knew them, but on this side of things it's club business, which is to say, it *ain't* none of yours."

"Noted," I said.

"Better make that note in Sharpie, little girl," Cipher said, and I looked at him, eyes narrowed. I didn't like his tone. "Big block letters," he said and moved his hands, thumb, and forefingers three inches apart and sweeping out from the middle for emphasis.

I fought not to roll my eyes. I didn't want or need to disrespect them. As far as I had been able to gather, disrespect is what got a person's ass beat faster than anything with these men.

I didn't say anything, just returned to polishing off the last of my meal.

The television came on and Goner scrolled through the channels, a caged fighting ring coming up on the screen with a woman bowed at the waist, trapped in a hold while the other woman threw a knee up into her middle.

It was something to distract, to concentrate on, while the men talked about other things.

CHAPTER FIVE

*M*averick…

She was more tired than she let on, sitting silently, almost miserably, shoulders hunched and still wearing my jacket. I couldn't decide if she was cold, which I couldn't imagine. Even though the building had air conditioning and it was on, it wasn't set to arctic chill or anything. I had to imagine it was more out of self-consciousness, though not around me but around the other guys. She finished her burger, crumpled the wrapper into a little ball, and I held out a hand for it. She handed it over and I ditched it in the trash behind the bar.

She watched the fights with mild interest at first, eventually her eyes glazing with a lack of concentration while she disappeared way away inside of herself. While she made a show of watching the screen, and most of the rest of the guys were glued to the action on it, too, I watched *her*.

I spoke perfect English. Had been born here, but my origins were decidedly more… Slavic. I spoke at least four languages fluently, and though I hadn't intended to offend, the little nickname *honey eyes*, for the golden-amber cast she had to hers, had just slipped out in my original Russian. Her reaction had been fiery, to say the least, and I thought back to what her grandmother had said about her. About how Marisol lied and was a liar.

Something didn't *feel* right about that. I think it was more a case of Marisol wasn't *believed*. She had the air of a girl who spoke hard truths freely and doing so wasn't apt to earn you many a friend. I got the distinct impression it had earned Marisol the opposite. I wasn't sure if it was at school, at home, or some combination of both where she had been bullied but she certainly had a chip on her shoulder as a result.

The very second she thought we were having any sort of laugh at her expense, fire had sparked in her eyes, and she looked a hairs breadth away from turning into a full-blown Latina hellcat.

I know the fiery Latina was a bold stereotype, and in a lot of ways unfair, but stereotypes became stereotypes for a reason and there was nothing wrong with a little fire if she knew how and when to properly unleash it. Looking at her beautiful profile now, I could see trouble radiating off her like the heat patterns off the highway coming in. I was betting some time and distance from her family would do something to cool her off, though. If not, I was in for a wild ride with her, so long as it wasn't too much drama.

I wouldn't be able to get her full measure until it was just her and I alone and I could get over, under, or just plain *through* some of the heavily guarded walls she had up around her. Even though she'd volunteered for this, her defenses were up, and she seemed to be on red alert. It was going to be a lot like approaching a wounded wildcat to get close.

I expected to get clawed a time or two in the coming days or weeks. I was getting ahead of myself, though. Right now, we just needed to get through tonight so we could head home.

I came around the bar and heaved myself up onto a stool behind Marisol and let myself get lost in the fight for a minute. All of us were chill, laid back, and little better than armchair critics making a chess match out of the brutality going down on the screen.

Occasionally I would glance at Marisol and finally, Deacon looked back over the backrest of the couch to say something to me but whatever it was didn't make it past his lip. He quirked an eyebrow and asked instead, "You want me to do something about that?" and gestured to the girl.

I felt my eyebrows go up, got to my feet, and came around her side to find her fast asleep on her seat.

"That's impressive," I commented. How she hadn't come unseated off the stool was a mystery, but so long as she could maintain while I made up a pallet for us, I was good.

"Like I said," Deacon said, a twinkle in his eyes. "Need a hand?" he asked, and I shook my head.

"Naw, I got it, man. Just gimme a few."

I went to the pool table and pocketed the balls off its surface. Hard? Yes. Not the most comfortable? Also true, but it would allow me to keep her close tonight as it was easily big enough for the two of us. I went back by the front door and grabbed my bedroll. It was just a couple sleeping bags rolled together, good enough to lay down for a base and throw the other over the top of us.

Deacon got up and helped me, anyway, in making up the table into a makeshift bed. Fen threw some couch pillows our way for our heads. I was unsure at first, touching her shoulder lightly not wanting to just go for it and scare the shit out of her. She jolted away, and I took the weight of her pack with my hands.

"Come on, beautiful. Your bed awaits."

She yawned, pressing the back of her hand to her mouth to cover it as she stretched, and she was like a sleepy kitten. I smiled and she let me have the bag. I passed it to Deac without looking and he pulled a chair from one of the regular tables over and set it in it next to the pool table so it would be at hand for her.

"Up you go," I said, turning her back to the pool table.

"I thought you were joking," she said, voice thick with sleep.

"When I joke, you'll know it," I promised her. She hoisted herself up onto the table and feet dangling, finally shrugged out of my coat. I laid it over the arm of the chair beside her bag and she went to settle.

"Keep moving over," I said and gestured. She scooted to the other side of the table and I hoisted my own tired ass up onto it and laid down, raising an arm so she could tuck herself into my side. She hesitated, but finally did, turning onto her side, resting her head cautiously on my chest.

Deacon flipped the top sleeping bag over us, and I propped my head on the couch pillow, my other arm up under the back of my head.

I watched the rest of the fight and let her sleep. It was going to be a long ride tomorrow, and she was far more tired than I'd thought earlier on.

I woke when she shifted against me, pushing herself up onto her hip sometime the next morning. The rest of the guys were racked out in one spot or another around us.

"You alright?" I asked, voice rough with sleep.

"Yeah, just have to pee," she said frankly.

I smiled and said, "Bathroom is through those doors there," and pointed at the doors past the bar to the left of the entertainment center where Squatch, Fen, and Deac were passed the fuck out on the sectional. Cipher was nowhere to be seen, but I didn't worry about that.

"Who dat?" his voice came from under the pool table Marisol and I were on when her booted feet hit the concrete floor. I closed my eyes and tried to suppress my laugh, but it was hard.

The Eastern Washington boys had apparently fucked off back to their respective homes at some point last night, which I couldn't say I blamed them. I would damn sure take a real bed over this bullshit if I had the option. A penny saved was a penny earned, though. Why spring for a motel in what was essentially hostile territory and invite suspicion and trouble?

Fucking Rebel, I thought dispassionately. He just had to make shit difficult for nothing other than his own fuckin' greed.

Marisol disappeared into one of the small bathrooms that had only a toilet and sink, shutting and locking the door behind her.

"Are you seriously *under the table*?" I asked Cipher.

"Yeah, you drank me here, don't you remember?" he asked and without realizing it, I walked right into it.

"No."

"That's because you drank me here."

I rolled my eyes, Fen cracking up from over on the couch, sitting up and shaking his head.

"Cipher, you're a fucking nut," Deacon declared, from where I couldn't see him, still lying down in the bend of the 'U' shape the sectional made.

"Fuck," I muttered and laid back, pressing the heels of my hands into my eye sockets. My eyes felt gritty and tired from a combination of allergies and shitty and insufficient sleep. I wanted to go the fuck home, take a hot shower, fuck the shit out of the hot woman that'd be sharing my home for the next month and finally, sleep for like the next three days. In. That. Order.

The bathroom door opened back up, and I breathed deep before sitting up forcefully and asking Marisol, "You know how to make coffee?"

She made a face at me like I was stupid or something and said, "Yeah." Without any further lip or preamble, she went behind the bar and started rooting around to get the coffee maker in the back corner going.

She was somewhat of a self-starter, good to know. I got into my jacket pockets and pulled out this prescription bottle with the label peeled off. In it was a mix of shit. Some MDMA or Vitamin E for personal use, some 24-hour decongestant allergy pills, a few ibuprofens, and a couple of Captain Cody's or Tylenol with Codeine from up over the border.

I kept the shit I took relatively low-key. I stayed the fuck away from the hard shit like meth, coke, and opioids. Hardest I went was MDMA, weed, and if I was really feeling froggy? Maybe some Alice Boomers – what the old hippy motherfuckers called magic mushrooms.

I also kept my shit to myself and didn't share, unless it was with Dahlia and I *never* rolled on any E around her. Molly got me way too in the mood to fuck, so it was only around club girls or a readily available bitch willing to put out that I let myself get high on that shit. Still, it was usually only when I was super stressed and needed to check out for a few hours that I hit the Vitamin E. Molly tended to mellow me the fuck out like nothing else when I came down off it and with how long I was in the throes of the effects? Yeah, well, weed was my usual go-to, let me put it that way. Also, weed was legal in these parts so it was safer to have it on me on the regular.

The two Molly I had on me were from Goner and were headed straight for my stash at home. If she got curious, I would indulge her, but I wasn't one to pressure anyone into trying something that wasn't their thing.

I shook out one of the decongestant allergy pills out onto my palm and sealed the bottle back up, stuffing it back into my pocket. I sighed and went to swing my legs over the side of the table so I could get down when a glass of water appeared in my field of vision.

"Thanks," I mumbled, taking it from Marisol's hand. I looked up and her countenance was cool, calm, and collected. The look in her eyes sharp as she gave me a sharp nod. I popped the pill and washed it down, watching her return around the bar to finish getting the coffee going.

I drained the glass and got up, my own bladder experiencing some urgency now that I was awake.

I took myself in to drain the ol' lizard and to splash some cold water on my face. I would kill for a fucking shower, but this would have to do for now. I could kind of only imagine how Marisol would feel by the time we got off the road.

It was a solid three hours from here to my place, just off Delridge edging into West Seattle. I was going *straight* home, too.

I felt like I was just completely assed out mentally. Like, I needed a fucking break. The wheel was spinning, but the hamster was dead as far as I was concerned. I just didn't have two thoughts to rub together anymore.

Of course, there was no rest for the wicked, and the distant rumble of bikes pulling up out front was an all too *loud* reminder of that right now. I straightened up, grabbed for some paper towels, and dried off my face, feeling both slightly more awake and refreshed.

I stared at my reflection in the mirror, mussed hair temporarily tamed and slicked back from a high forehead with the water I'd brushed through it with my hands. It'd turned my already dark brown hair to mahogany. I had a five o'clock shadow just starting to invade the hollows of my cheeks, and goddamn did they look *hollow*. Didn't help that I had these high, pronounced cheekbones that could cut fuckin' glass.

I had an angular jawline, and a narrow-ass chest, trim, though I was by no means *weak*. I just wasn't as bulky as some of the other guys. Shredded, yes, and I *looked* wimpy, but what I lacked in pure brawn, I made up for in speed and it was handy to be underestimated. Made it the last mistake a motherfucker ever made more often than not.

I took after my mother in body and looks, much to my father's disappointment. He was a real chip of the ol' eastern bloc. Must be strong! Like bull! Unfortunately, strong like bull almost always equated to dumb like ox, and I preferred using brains over brawn.

He hated me for that, and truth be told, I was alright with that. The feeling was beyond mutual. I hated my father's guts with the fire of a thousand suns and had zero fucking regrets about it.

He had his little criminal enterprise, and I had mine. We mostly stayed the fuck out of each other's way. It suited us.

I went back out to the front and Marisol brought me a steaming mug of coffee from the pot.

"Cream or sugar?" she asked.

"Nah, black is fine," I said and sniffed, my nose starting to run and the sinus pressure starting to dissipate. I took the mug from her, wrapping my long fingers around the heated ceramic and blew across its surface, my eyes following Marisol as she went back behind the bar. I couldn't wait to have her naked and underneath me, to where I could blow across the smooth surface of her skin and see if I could get it to pebble with arousal beneath my touch.

I sucked down some of the bitter brew, wincing, and looked toward the door and the remaining Eastern Washington boys coming through.

Skeeter looked about as rough as I felt, and I could tell he was a good man, running interference with Goner and Derry, who probably didn't enjoy feeling like outsiders. I felt for them, I really did. I mean, I was pretty sure I trusted they were solid members still in good standing, but it wasn't up to me. It was up to *us*. All of us in the Western Washington chapter to decide if we wanted to grow by three seats. Then it was up to National to give us blessing to do it.

Bylaws were bylaws, and we needed to follow them. Sometimes, it felt like trading one 'man' for another, but still, this life was a life played by our own rules for the most part and I would take that over society's bullshit rules any day.

"You guys comin' over the mountains with us then?" Fenris asked, and we were met with three somber and weary nods.

"Was up all night talking about it," Skeeter said.

"Feels like we're all starting from square one." Derry sounded unhappy.

"Watch yourselves," I reminded them and gave a side-eyed glance to Marisol.

"Who's she gonna tell?" Goner asked.

"You need to ask that, you're missing the fuckin' point," Skeeter answered him in a growl and there was the crux of it.

Derry and Goner looked to Skeeter for leadership. My chapter already had leaders. Me, and Glass Jaw respectively. I raised an eyebrow at Skeeter who caught my eye and nodded. Good, he understood where I was coming from and to be fair, his comment could have been interpreted one of two ways.

"Nine and I have got some room at our place for at least one of you comfortably," Squatch said. "Been looking for a third housemate."

"I'm a bit off the beaten path but my pops and I got room," Fenris offered up.

"For how many?" Derry asked.

"For you, country boy. My pops turned to goat farming of all the fuckin' things after he retired. Looks like you know your way around a farm."

"Baby goats?" Marisol said and perked up.

Fen smiled and nodded. "Usually around January and February, but yeah. We got a kid or two running around the place right now on the edge of being all grown up."

"Awww!" It was the first crack in that hard, placid surface of hers that I'd seen since the one she'd formed in the face of her brother crying and I had to say, I much preferred this one.

"Dairy or meat?" Derringer asked casually.

"What do you think?" Fen asked and Derry nodded.

No sense in putting it out there these goats were being raised for slaughter. Why dash Marisol's happy just as soon as she'd expressed it? Girl was clever, and figured it out for herself, her smile slipping into an expression of *really guys?*

"Pops rents a bunch of them out for briar patch control. It's a full-time business and he ain't getting any younger," Fenris said and Marisol's hard look receded as though she hadn't considered that.

Fen and Derry talked about maybe working something out while Derry looked for work doing what he usually did, which was plumbing or electrical or some shit. I don't know, I stopped paying attention.

Deacon and Skeeter were working something out, and it looked like Goner was headed home with Squatch.

That meant everyone was sorted for the time being until they could get places of their own, which was pretty sweet. Meant I had less shit between me and my own home and bed with the sexy woman behind the bar.

"Breakfast or just home?" I asked the guys and apparently it had to be put to a vote. Breakfast won, goddamnit, but that might not have been such a bad thing. I mean, there was a distinct possibility I was so damn grumpy because it was an actual case of hangry. I wasn't always the best at keeping my ridiculously high metabolism fed.

You would think, edging the line of thirty it would start to slow down some on me, but it didn't look like that was going to happen.

We cleaned up, took out trash and closed up shop here at the Moses Lake clubhouse. Marisol actually did most of it, pointing out things that we didn't honestly even think of when it came to closing up a building for any kind of extended period of time.

She was cool about it, too. Making it into innocuous suggestions or asking simple questions like 'aren't you going to do...?' and when one of the guys stopped to ask why would they? She was always ready with an astute answer that never preached and was phrased in such a way to keep the boys from feeling dumb.

I didn't know if it was a natural talent on her part or a learned behavior. Maybe it was a bit of both. In any case, she was a mystery to me in a lot of ways, a puzzle, and I think that was why she appealed to me even more than her earthly beauty.

She had on the same pair of jeans and boots from yesterday, but she'd changed her top to something a touch more modern. Simple, black, and fitted; it had long sleeves and a keyhole cutout at her chest above her breasts and at the back that gave tantalizing glimpses of her rich, golden sun-kissed skin. She'd undid her hair from its braid from yesterday, the long tresses falling down her back in kinked waves, and had only bothered pulling half of it up to keep it out of her face using a cheap, drugstore, plastic hair clip – the kind with the metal spring action hidden beneath the decorative part.

She'd washed her face and had redone her subtle makeup and she was beautiful. Natural, earthy, with an underlying edge of badass that if she were Norse? I would compare her to one of Fen's Valkyries.

Truth was, there simply wasn't any comparing her to anything. Marisol was just uniquely Marisol in my eyes. Quietly defiant is how I would have described her the first time I had met her. I could see the cool appraisal and intelligence in her eyes the moment she'd locked them on me the first time I'd rode into her little village of fruit growers.

Wise beyond her years was a close second that I would apply to her – and I couldn't chalk it up to her simply living underneath *Abuela's* roof. While that woman was somewhat clever, she wasn't as smart as she thought she was. She simply made up for her lack of intelligence with cruelty.

Not so with Marisol, and I wanted to know, *why*? What made this beauty tick?

I certainly wasn't going to find that out hanging around here.

I sighed and looked the place over, swinging my keys around my index finger and catching them in my palm, the metal teeth biting.

"Until next month," I said and was the last one out, locking up the doors, effectively temporarily rendering this clubhouse inert. Whether it would be permanently mothballed remained to be seen, but I sincerely hoped it wouldn't. If it was, it would be the end of an era — for sure.

CHAPTER SIX

*M*arisol…

We stopped and ate breakfast at a Denny's. Maverick, however, didn't care to sit with his men. Instead, he had us seated, just me and him, at a two-person table some feet away from them. I hid behind the menu while I made my decision and then hid behind it longer while I decided what exactly he wanted to talk to me about that was so important it couldn't wait until we were over the mountain range.

I set the menu down and looked up into his disquieting indigo stare.

"So, what's the deal?" he asked. "Why was *Abuela* so hard up to keep you right where you were?"

Ah, so it was about *her* and not necessarily about *me*. Or, it could be. Maybe he just wanted to know what I was supposedly a liar about. Apparently, he hadn't been listening when my grandmother had said *everything*.

"Probably didn't want me giving away family secrets, which I won't," I said, raising my chin defiantly.

"Loyalty or something else?" he asked, and I gave him nothing. Nothing with my eyes, nothing with my face whatsoever, my voice mute in my throat.

He nodded slowly, gaze calculating, and asked me, "I make a mistake taking you on?"

I shook my head slowly. "I say no," I said, "but how could you believe me? According to my grandmother, your friend, I am a liar."

Maverick laughed and it made him beautiful, the way the Japanese drew men in their romantic Manga's.

"Your grandmother and I aren't friends. Don't get it twisted, beautiful." He shook his head and raked a hand through the top of his hair, resting his elbow on the table, rolling his eyes to pin me with his gaze as he considered me and he looked predatory, dangerous…

"I'm not stupid," I said with irritation. "I don't want to die. Not like Anita. Not like her boys. I won't do anything to put my brother in danger, which means I won't tell you anything about them, and I damn sure won't tell them anything about *you*."

I stared back, mostly in an effort to convince him on this, there was no lie.

His mouth thinned down into a grim line and he nodded.

"You can keep your family secrets," he said, and I scoffed. He sat up and cocked his head. "You won't get to learn any of ours," he said. "Club business is club business. I tell you to get lost, you do it. You're there to cook, clean, and occasionally, if you're down for it, to fuck but that last one? That's always *your choice*," he said, and I felt my brow wrinkle in a frown.

Yeah, right… I thought to myself.

His eyebrows went up and he nodded slowly, as if something had just been confirmed and I rolled my eyes. He shouldn't automatically assume that he knew *anything* about me that didn't come straight from my mouth.

Something in his expression softened and he dropped things for now. I shifted in my seat, uncertain, but kept my mouth shut. I'd learned quickly, and a long time ago, it didn't do to ask questions. Asking questions got you in trouble and you didn't always want to know the answer.

The same thing could be said for speaking the truth. People didn't care. Didn't want to hear it. You never had to take back anything you didn't say. Never had to go into further explanations. Silence was, for the most part, the safer option.

We ate in silence, but it was a tense one, at least for me. I felt as though Maverick was trying to take my temperature. That he was trying to feel out my motives, and I thought a little less of him for it. I mean, wasn't it obvious? Everything I did, I did with the intention to leave that place. To leave that place and to get my brother *out* so that he could leave *with me*.

I just wanted a new life. I honestly didn't care how I got it as long as I got far away from here, *with my brother*. After that, I would figure it out. This was as good a start as any in finally accomplishing that goal.

Maverick paid for everyone's tab and we left. The ride toward the mountains had me low-key excited. I'd lived on this side my whole life and had only had the occasion to cross over them once when I had been small, with my papa.

It was one of my favorite memories of him. I missed him every day. It was like once he was gone, all the happiness had gone, too. Like he had taken it to heaven with him.

I let the wind wash over me, sitting up on my seat, letting go, face tipped into the sun, arms flung wide as we skimmed over the highway. I loved to ride. One of the boys back at the grower's village had a dirt bike. He would take me back and forth to school my junior and senior year. We'd been friends. He didn't care about what they said about me. That I was a liar. Although, I don't think he believed me either. No one did.

I let the wind be my therapy, chasing the bad feelings away, leaving them behind me as I tried to make room for hope, but it was hard. I felt like I was racing into the unknown… and the unknown was as scary as it was exhilarating.

Maverick sat up some when I leaned back and put one hand atop his thigh and we just rode… comfortably, in sync, each trusting the other not to fuck this ride up and send us spilling along the pavement in a bloody tragic smear.

The ride was *much* longer than I anticipated, but I was buzzing with excitement the whole way. The brown gave way to green, the green to gray and a bit of snow holding onto the mountain peaks stabbing their way into the great blue sky.

Somehow, *even the sky* was a more pleasing blue and as I held onto Maverick as we climbed the westbound approach to the pass, I wondered about what it was going to be like having a man like him between my thighs.

I mean, he was *experienced* for one. I somehow doubted there would be awkward fumbling from him, but it was *other* things I wondered about. Was he a demanding lover? Did he give as good as he got? Did he rush things, or did he take his time? Was he rough, or would he be gentle with me?

These thoughts were paramount in my mind coming out of the pass, and the vibrations of the bike were so not helping in any way to curb my mounting arousal.

Maverick made some sort of hand signal, and midway back in the pack, Fenris changed lanes and dropped back. Derringer followed suit, and they took an exit for Highway 18 and peeled off from our pack.

I turned back around and put my arms around the corded muscles of Maverick's trim waist, and we rode on. For another hour we traveled, the urban taking over, nature thinning out as we passed through a place called Issaquah.

More hand signaling, and several more broke off and took the Interstate 405 exit. I watched them as they took the ramp heading south toward Renton. I checked and it was just Deacon with us now. Maverick checked off to our side. Checked again, and I held on as he twisted the throttle. The bike snarled and we swept into the next lane over, Deacon with us still, even as we poured on speed.

I gasped as we came over the rise as the bridge resting on the water came into view. It was cooler on this side of the mountains, and the breeze off the lake kissed my face with the scent of freshwater. I knew this was the floating bridge over Lake Washington, but this lake wasn't like any other I had ever seen. While you could see across it side to side, it was so long north to south you couldn't see it end to end.

It was so *blue*. Not like you see out of pictures from someplace like

Hawaii, but more a deep, beautiful, indigo blue, as though the night sky were trapped in the depths.

I hugged Maverick tighter around the waist, almost cuddling against his back. It was impossible to thank him in words over the roar of the bike and the rushing wind, but it was the best I could to. My sentiment of gratitude for him bringing me this way, so that I could see this… well, there weren't really words anyway.

When we reached I-5, Deacon waved and split off going north while Maverick turned south. He put his hands over mine where they rested on his stomach, pressing them against his hard body, and I held on tighter. The reason for it became clear as we started to go over steel expansion joints in the freeway surface. Set at regular intervals, I remembered them being nothing in my father's pickup truck but on a motorcycle? They were a completely different experience and were more than a little nerve-wracking.

He took the exit by the old Rainier brewery for the West Seattle Bridge. Unlike the I-90 floating bridge, this one was *high*. Like *really high*, and I was relieved when he took the exit for Delridge Way and we descended the off ramp back down to earth, stopping for the light at the bottom. After close to three hours, I was ready to be done.

"Almost there!" he shouted over the chug of the engine, as though he'd read my mind.

I nodded and we turned left, up the hill. At some point, we turned off Delridge and onto one of the little residential side streets. He slowed and turned again, then once more down a back alley that had deep ruts that he carefully walked us around to pull in behind a small, rundown house. He killed the engine on the concrete pad, back beneath a ramshackle, hastily erected carport, and I hopped off. Straightening, my hands on the back of my hips to aid in a deep stretch, I felt bones in my spine crackle and pop, and it left me sighing in satisfaction. Tired and sore, I longed for a decent hot shower and hoped his bathroom wasn't excessively gross or old and falling apart.

"Come on," he said and went up the back step. He keyed open the lock on the back door and I followed him, cautiously. If he were the type to hurt women, now would be the time to do it. Beautiful didn't equate *safe,* and I knew the personal cost my being here could wring out of me. I knew it, and I was *still* willing to pay it.

The back door led right into the kitchen which was an odd sort of shape. There was a long closet behind the door with that slatted sort of doors that slid along a track. I figured it was a pantry or something, but there was a bit of a jut in the wall and then another set of white slatted sliding doors. I didn't know why two sets, but I could explore later if he let me.

Though tight, the kitchen was new-ish. At least, newly remodeled. There were two doorways – well, maybe doorway wasn't the right word. I mean, there were no *doors*, just open archways. Both were in line and straight across from the back door. They appeared to lead straight through the dining room and into the living room.

The kitchen was retro black and white with all modern, stainless-steel appliances, and it made me smile. I could really cook in a kitchen like this. I made a mean tamale and there could be tamales for *days* coming out of this kitchen if I were allowed free rein and the money for the ingredients.

"This way," Maverick said, shutting the door behind him and I jumped slightly when he brushed past me. He slowed, but didn't comment, and I followed him through the archway, through the dining room with its heavy dark wood table and modern straight-backed black leather chairs, and through the intersection between the short hall into the rest of the house and the living room.

The living room had nice furniture – black leather, a modern couch, recliner, and a love seat with a big screen modern television against one wall. The leather furniture was accented by a glass coffee table and three end tables all shiny, modern, and new, but that's where the nice newness ended. The carpet was threadbare and dingy and the paint on the walls cracked. It was dusty in here; the curtains and rods didn't look like they worked overtly well, and they also appeared as though the curtains were always closed. Cobwebs hung in the corners and from the ceiling and I felt my brow wrinkle at the state of the room.

"See the desk?" he asked and to one end of the room there was a messy glass desk with an open laptop on a leather blotter. Papers stacked at random on its surface, a window covered in dusty venetian blinds behind it.

"Yes."

"Leave that alone. Don't go near it," he said flatly.

"Okay," I said, already planning to defy him to get at those dust-coated blinds. The thick layer of fuzzy gray I could see from here on their surface driving me crazy already. I would leave the desk itself alone, but those dust bunnies would be mine. That was disgusting.

After the mishmash of old and new, dusty, and relatively clean of the living room, I started to worry about the state of the rest of the house, specifically the bathroom.

Maverick turned right down the short hall which held three closed doors—one to either side of us, and one straight ahead. He opened the one on the right.

"Spare room," he said, and I cringed. It was full of a jumble of junk on a canvas drape laid out in the middle of the floor. Bare wires capped with those colorful little plastic caps hung out of the center of the ceiling where a light fixture belonged. There was a paint-spattered aluminum ladder standing up in the middle with a bunch of other random shit like five-gallon buckets, paint cans, toolboxes and other things piled up at its base haphazardly in the room. It was a nightmare disaster zone and I did not like it! What was I supposed to do with that?

"Don't worry about this room for now," he said, and I nodded, eyes still wide with my disbelief.

"Bedroom," he said and popped open the door straight ahead. Hardwood floors, but they weren't nice. They were scratched, scuffed, and tired—in need of a deep refinish. Again, this room had dirty paint on the walls, cracks, and even some splintered trim along the edges of the room at the floor.

The bed was large, but just a mattress on a frame with some shabby but comfortable looking black bedding. The dressers, unlike the rest of the house's furniture, were rundown and looked like they'd come from a secondhand store or from a yard sale.

I think there was more laundry stacked on the dresser tops than there was in the drawers, but the room was otherwise somewhat cleaner. It certainly wasn't as dusty and unused like the living room.

"Take this off," he ordered and took the weight of my pack from my shoulders. I relinquished it and slid my arms through the straps. He set it on the floor, just inside his bedroom door, leaning it up against the side of the dresser along the wall just inside and to the right, across from the foot of the bed.

I was in a deep dread about what lay behind door number three by now, not knowing what to expect. He turned to the door on the left and I steeled myself, but I apparently didn't need to. At least not as much as I thought I did, quite the opposite in fact.

The kitchen had been refurbished, but this bathroom had been completely ripped out and redone and was *beautiful.*

It had that retro vibe, much like the kitchen, but held a modern flair. The tub was a big, beautiful, and *deep* claw foot. It had a shower curtain that wrapped around on a free-standing rod, but I didn't see a showerhead. There was, what looked like a square chrome vent set in the ceiling above the tub, but I hadn't ever seen anything like it before.

The toilet, like the bathtub, was old-fashioned. It had one of those tanks separate from where you sat, high up closer to the ceiling with the old pull chain with a wooden handle to flush.

The sink was one of those beautiful old white porcelain pedestal sinks that perfectly matched the tub and toilet and I loved it. The floor was the old retro white ceramic square tiles with the black diamond tiles set at the corners where they met, but that was the last *old* thing that was in here.

The walls were painted a deep charcoal gray from about midway up. There was a band of narrow cooler lighter gray glass tile in narrow horizontal strips surrounding the room, and from that sort of chair rail band down to the floor was cool, wide slate colored tile, though I believe it was ceramic and not the actual stone. It was this funky mix of modern and old that didn't look like it *should* work, but it totally did.

My first emotion upon seeing it was relief, my second one was abject dread at the potential work involved in keeping it *clean...*

although it didn't appear that Maverick was having any trouble doing so on his own.

"Panel for the shower is right here," he said softly, and I turned around. Sure enough, just inside the door to the left as you came in was a touch screen panel. To the right of the door was the set of light switches.

"I don't understand," I said, and I didn't. I looked back at the tub, which had its usual faucet for drawing a bath, but I still didn't see a shower.

He tapped the button at the bottom of the screen to wake it up and showed me how to use it. Gentle rainfall started from what I assumed was a vent in the ceiling and fell into the tub.

I felt my mouth drop open in surprise.

"Want to try it out with me?" he asked softly.

It took me a second to realize what he was asking, but I was surprised that the answer was *yes*… I really would like to shower with him. It would be a pleasant introduction to his body.

There was a single window in the bathroom that faced out over the front yard. It was the old-fashioned kind that you lifted, but rather than clear glass, this was frosted and pebbled, allowing light in, but also keeping unwanted eyes out.

Maverick touched another button or two on the touch screen and music started—easy listening old 70s rock ballads. I knew the song, but I didn't know the name of it or the band who played it.

He stepped up to my back, edging into my personal space and I kept my arms down to my sides, unsure what he wanted.

He was easily six foot to my five foot four, his lips hovering just to the top of the back of my head, his breath slightly stirring my hair, his proximity stilling the breath in my lungs.

The reality was better than the countless fantasies I'd had about this very beautiful man doing this very thing as he hooked his long fingers into the collar of his coat and began to undress me.

I let him take the coat, which he dropped into a pile on the floor. His one hand at my hip, drawing me back into him, his other hand sweeping my hair out of the path of his lips which he rested lightly over the jumping pulse in the side of my neck.

"Fast," he whispered against my skin. "Like a little rabbit's."

"Mm." I gave a throaty little laugh and leaned back against him.

He put his lips against my ear and whispered, "Are you afraid of me, *Zaychik*?" he asked, and my heart skipped a beat at the language I didn't know.

"What is that?" I asked, pulse thumping so hard I could feel it throbbing against my own spine from the inside.

"*Zaychik*?" he asked.

"That, too, but the language," I said, voice raspy with desire as he slipped the hand at my waist beneath the hem of my shirt, fingertips light and gentle, the barest kiss of a touch against my skin at my stomach. I wanted to know it all, everything about this man.

"It's Slavic," he said. "For 'little rabbit.' Do you like it?" he asked and leaned back slightly, switching sides, his other hand sliding against my ribs, over my shirt. I closed my eyes, heartbeat echoing in my ears, breath squeezing out of my lungs at his tantalizing touch.

God, girl! He is playing you like a fucking violin! I thought to myself, and just on the heels of that thought? *Just like you want him to.*

I wanted to feel good, and the promise in his touch to do just that almost made me let my guard down for real.

The hand that rested over my shirt slid down my front and dipped below the waistband of my jeans. I'd been about to answer him, that *yes*, I liked the sound of that, but my brain short-circuited as he buried his nose in my hair and breathed me in deep. One hand going low, the other, under my shirt, rising to cup my breast and pinching my nipple through my bra.

I found my own hands at my belt, undoing it, unfastening my jeans for him, lowering the zipper to give him better access.

He hummed against my ear in satisfaction, his fingertips touching my sex with a light little electric jolt, a single long digit sliding against my clit, dipping between my folds to find the wetness of my arousal there.

He moved his other hand across my body to my other breast, his arm across my body, pulling me tightly back against him as he played with my pussy. His touch was light, teasing, so sexy and stimulating. I threw my head back and gasped as my excitement mounted and he turned his head, capturing my mouth with his own, tongue plunging past my lips even as his hold on me tightened. The pressure from his fingers against my pussy increased, and he began to rub at my clit with fervor.

I cried out and twitched against him, the sound from my mouth muffled by his kiss as he held me fast, determined to make me come on my feet, the music soft, the shower fall gentle, and us standing there still mostly clothed but having sex standing up, nonetheless. I mean, there was obviously no penetration happening here, but I was eager for it. I wanted this, was suddenly desperate not only to reach that climax but I wanted him inside me, fucking me, when I got there.

There wasn't enough time. He was going to make me come with his hand, and I felt helpless to stop him. It skirted that edge of fear, having him do this to me. Having him hold me like this, keeping me from engaging much beyond reaching behind me and gripping his hard cock through his jeans, rubbing it through the thick material even as my other hand gripped the top of his thigh to hold on, to keep me grounded as the pleasure mounted and prepared to ride me.

He tore his mouth from mine. "That's it, *Zaychik*. Come for me, baby. Come for me."

With a high, thin wail I did just that, my knees going weak with only Maverick there to catch me and hold me up.

CHAPTER SEVEN

*M*averick...

Oh, fuck yes, that was good. She was so hot, so beautifully responsive and her pussy felt so nice against my hand I couldn't wait to get my cock involved.

Jesus, *fuck,* she was wet, and any misgivings I had about whether she might actually want me or not were dispelled right then and there.

She leaned back heavily against me, her chest heaving with deep and rhythmic breaths as she tried to recover from her orgasm. I loved each and every little aftershock twitch I wrung out of her as I intermittently tweaked and teased her oversensitive clit, enjoying the hot satin slickness of her arousal against my fingers. I could play in it, with her body, for *hours* and I intended to at some point – just not right now.

Right now, I wanted a shower with her, to fall into bed with her, and to *sleep*.

She turned around slowly and put her arms around me, cuddling against my chest and I put my arms around her, kissing the top of her head as she came down from me rocking her world. There was no little sense of satisfaction in what I'd accomplished with that.

She looked up at me and I smiled down into her beautiful face and said, "Shower, bed, sound good?"

"What about you?" she asked startled.

"Oh, I'm gonna get mine," I assured her. "I'm tired, and it can wait. What can't wait is getting cleaned up. I'm not getting into a clean bed feeling this filthy."

I began to undress her while I talked and she let me at first before she seemed to catch up to herself and what was going on and reached for me. She undid the buckle of my chaps. I smiled, and we worked on each other's clothes. Carefully, piece by piece, item by item, until we were both nude, our clothes mingling in a heap by the door.

I unclasped her hair last, tossing the clip back among our discarded clothing as she stepped over the high lip of the tub to stand beneath the hot rainfall of water from the showerhead. I stood with her, hands lightly resting on her hips as I tipped my face into the gentle fall of water.

God that felt good…

The hot water worked some magic on the both of us, relaxing sore and tensed muscles as we worked the rest of the knots and tension out of each other with soap-slicked fingers and hands.

"How do you turn it off from here?" she asked gently, and I smiled.

"It's on a closed circuit," I said, then called out, "Shower off!" The rainfall ceased and she blinked up at me.

"Seriously?"

"Yeah," I said and laughed and reached out of the enclosed shower space and opened the linen storage in the corner and pulled out a couple of warmed towels. I handed her one.

"For real?" she asked, surprised as her hands met the warm, soft material.

"Ride out in the cold and the wet as much as I do, you appreciate the finer things. Bathroom was the first thing I did when I bought this place."

"How long have you owned it?" she asked as I stepped out of the tub and onto the black bathmat.

"Two or three years?" She frowned slightly and I chuckled. "I like doing as much of it as I can myself," I explained and she nodded thoughtfully, her brown eyes kissed with amber honey roving my face, as though perhaps, her initial assessment of me was changing or evolving.

Whatever the case may be, I liked the look in her eyes, the subtle changes being made in the expression on her face, so I left her to her thoughts and hitched the towel around my waist, holding out a hand gallantly to help her out of the tub.

She stepped out carefully after wringing her long, waist length hair between her hands and I asked, "You want another towel for your hair?"

"No, it's okay. Do you have a hair dryer though?"

"I do," I said and went to the storage cabinet beside the sink and got it out for her.

"Thank you," she murmured.

"Need your brush out of your bag?"

"Please, um, it should be in one of the front pockets."

"Sure." I went and got it for her.

"Take your time, come to bed when you're done," I said and she nodded, covered from just above her breasts to just below her knees by the large bath towel I'd handed her.

I let my eyes flick over her and added, "Don't even think about putting anything on."

She gave me a smile that was more an unsurprised twist of her lush lips, and started the dryer, directing the hot air onto her scalp. I chuckled and left her to it.

I fell asleep so fast, I don't even remember lying down in the first place. I jolted awake to the warm and sensual slide of her skin against mine as she cuddled up to me.

"You want me now, or later?" she asked, voice husky with desire and I chuckled lightly, holding her close.

"Sleep now, fuck me awake later," I said, and she laid her head on my shoulder.

"You got it."

I passed the fuck out, slept like the dead, and I think she slept too. I couldn't be sure, because it felt like a blink of an eye later that I woke with her mouth on my cock, lush and soft, hair tickling my thigh as she worked me, sucking me with enthusiasm.

I lifted my hips and strained not to thrust down her lovely throat. My hands hovering over all of that beautifully thick, black-raven hair.

"Oh, *fuck*," I heard myself whisper and her lips twitched around my dick in a smile as she blew me and blew my fuckin' *mind*.

I fought to hold still, but it was hard and as enthusiastic and eager as I was to come, I liked a lot of edging, so I gripped her upper arm and ordered gruffly, "Stop. Stop a minute, I don't want to come yet."

She drew her mouth up my shaft and let my head slip from her lips with a soft little pop and a loss of suction.

"Sorry, you said to fuck you awake, but you twitch and talk in your sleep a lot and I didn't want to get hit or something. At least this way, I could throw up an arm or something, you know?"

I chuckled and said, "I didn't know I did that. Sorry. You uh, mind grabbing a condom off the top of the dresser over there?" I asked. I didn't need to worry about knocking anyone up. I'd had a vasectomy in my mid-twenties. I didn't want any accidents running around and fuck these club bunnies and any of them thinkin' they could get me in a child support trap.

She smiled, the sultry little minx, and all thoughts of any of that shit fled my mind. She slipped off the bed, fetching the foil packet and returning to me. She did the honors, opening it up and rolling it down my length. I couldn't help but arc into her touch and my breath coming like I'd run a damn marathon, I reached for her, urging her up here to ride me.

Her sweet little pussy was *tight,* and she felt so fucking good around me. Hot, slick with her own desire, and more than willing and ready to take control. She put my hands on her body, guiding my touch over her skin as my cock plunged deep, stroking into her wet satin depths, her pussy gripping me lightly, rhythmically, as I watched what few inhibitions she did have fall away.

Her face grew lax, her eyes slipping closed, her head tipping back as she rose and fell over me, riding me, taking her pleasure from me and all I had to do was lie back and enjoy the erotic subtleties that played across her soft features as she lost herself in the sensation of my cock deep inside of her.

Shit, that had to be one of the most gorgeous sights I had ever laid eyes on. The way her attitude, ever present and worn like a shield, just seemingly *fell away* in this moment as she rolled her hips and moved me inside of her, touching off the subtle glow of pleasure like the sun, just beginning to peek over the horizon.

The sensations played across her face, communicated in the sound of her gentle, gasping moans as she worked herself up, and I loved it. I couldn't stop touching her, hands skimming lightly over her soft flesh as she grew so wet with her pleasure.

I let my eyes close, just concentrating on the feel of being inside of her, the feel of her wrapped around me, of her hot, slick walls pressing tightly against my shaft, milking me, begging me to fill her up until her cup ran over. I bit my bottom lip savagely to try and hold off, but goddamn, it was hard, and this was going to be way too quick.

I knew I had better do something about it, or I was going to come first and that was just plain unacceptable. So I licked the pad of my thumb, delving it between our bodies, and teased at her clit.

She sucked in a sharp breath, cried out in surprise, and lost her even cadence for just a moment. I felt my balls contract, tightening up, that familiar pressure building at the base of my shaft, like it was going to come from the base of my spine, that first blush of warning, of pleasure, curling up from my belly in a wash across my chest as I got close and closer still.

"That's it, baby," I whispered as her mouth dropped open, working in a silent gasp as she got tighter around me. Tight and tighter still, I almost couldn't take it until with a final shout, a shocked and surprised little cry, she jerked above me, collapsing over my chest as her orgasm shook her.

I thrust up into her hard as my own release overtook me, and I rode the waves of pleasure that ensued. Both of us gasping, both of us washing up onto the other's shore, motionless and weak except for the involuntary muscle spasms that rocked each of us to our very cores.

I put my arms around her and held onto her, as much to protect her in this vulnerable moment as to protect myself. I held her down tight to my body while the pleasure wracked us both and I held on for dear life.

We came back from the brink, each of us on our own personal journey, and we took our time doing it.

"Wow," was the first word she managed to utter between the warm, panting breaths that swept my shoulder.

I laughed, a short expression of sound between my own panting deep breaths and stroked my hands over her skin.

She went to sit up, but I held her fast.

"Not yet," I declared, and she tensed but after a time, slowly, her muscles unclenched, and she allowed her body to drape beautifully over mine.

I couldn't see her beautiful face, her head turned and nestled on the pillow beside mine. I loved how her soft, lush form pressed me back into the softness of my bed. I kissed her shoulder lazily and kept running my hands lightly over her exposed skin, pleased when she shuddered against me, her delicate little pussy twitching light little aftershocks around my cock.

"Can I get up now?" she asked stiffly after a few minutes more and I couldn't tell you how disappointed I was.

"Sure," I answered, not about to hold her against her will or anything.

I sucked in a sharp breath as she got up, letting me slip from her body.

"Mm." She closed her eyes and froze as she kneeled beside me, savoring the sweet sensation between her legs, that final blush and glow of pleasure as we parted.

I knew, because I was doing the same damn thing over here.

"Fuck, you're hot," I said, and her eyes flicked open, wide, and deep, the brown kissed with that edge of sweet honey turned in my direction to take me in.

"You too," she said after a moment and I almost felt like that *surprised* her somehow.

"Yeah?" I asked.

"Uh-huh," she murmured.

"Can I get a kiss?" I asked.

She didn't hesitate, just kneeled up beside me and brought her lips to mine and I smiled against them.

"That's my girl," I whispered against her lips and when we parted and I looked, her face was shuttered, stony, and unreadable.

I made a mental note that something about that bit of praise bothered her and vowed to change it up.

"Now come here," I ordered gently, pulling her down into my arms, tight up against my side. She settled and while it was wary, it was also eager in the way she did it. She smoothed some of her long hair behind her ear before resting it on the upper swell of my chest – or what passed for it on my slender frame.

"Now what?" she whispered, and I smiled.

"Now, we sleep."

CHAPTER EIGHT

Marisol...

I woke to a gentle sweeping touch along my nude back. I sucked in a startled breath and hugged the pillow to my chest out of reflex, my head coming up and turning on my neck to take in Maverick, fully dressed and sitting on the edge of the bed framed in the daylight pressing in at the edges of the bedroom's window's blinds.

"What time is it?" I asked, my voice coming out sultrier than I intended as I chased the cobwebs of my lingering sleep out of my head.

"Not too late," he answered. "At least by my standards."

I pushed myself up and he sucked in a sharp breath. I froze.

"You do that, I might get undressed to fuck you all over again," he declared, his voice rough with need.

"Don't threaten me with a good time," I teased gently. "Seriously though, did I miss something? Do I need to get up?"

"Only if you want to come with me. I figured I would give you the option."

"Where are we going?" I asked, not wanting to be left behind. At least, not today. I was sure I would want some alone time at some point, but not yet. I didn't know how I would feel left alone in Maverick's house so soon.

59

"The club," he answered. "I have paperwork and shit to do."

I nodded slowly and pushed myself up again into a sitting position. This time, it was met with just a rakish curve of his lips, an appreciative smile filled with lust.

"I have time for a quick shower?" I asked softly.

"That you do. You drink coffee?" he asked.

"Um, yeah."

"Good deal, I'll get some going."

I showered swiftly after clipping up my hair to keep it from getting wet. It was a bit of a challenge given the rainfall feature of the shower, but I managed. When I got out, Maverick was moving around the kitchen. I skirted around the doorway and back into his room where my pack lay.

Dressing swiftly, I pulled my hair up into a high ponytail, smoothing things out when he ducked around the doorway with a travel mug in his hand.

"Thanks," I murmured, taking it from him.

"Gonna have to bring it on the bike, I got shit to do," he said, and it wasn't unkindly, wasn't terse, it was just sort of matter-of-factly stated. My curiosity about the man deepened as I nodded and followed him through the house and back out to where his bike was parked.

We didn't have to ride very far, maybe just a couple miles over cracked and weathered streets through poorer neighborhoods that were showing signs of major gentrification. I felt my heart sink, knowing what that meant for the poorer demographic. How many of them likely ended up priced out of their rental homes? It'd never happened to us or our family, but it'd happened to some of the other workers. Hard workers who ended up seven or eight deep in a one- or two-bedroom home.

He pulled up in front of an old wrecking yard full of bikes, having me hop down so he could back his beastly iron horse in line with the rest. Across the street was a heavily graffitied building, another man from the Sacred Hearts smoking on the little wood platform for the back steps, thumbs moving swiftly as he tapped out a text.

"We're going on a trip," Maverick said, and it was loud in the wake of his bike's engine ceasing. I turned my attention back to him. He stood beside his parked bike, helmet off his head, swinging from one of his handlebars, his hair tousled and long enough on top it tangled in front of his eyes.

Those eyes were intent, intense, where they were fixed on me. Their color made brilliant in the morning light, their color contrasting behind the thick tangle of his dark hair. I swallowed hard and nodded.

"Where?" I asked.

"Doesn't matter," he said. "You go where I say you go for the next month."

"I know that," I countered. "I was just curious."

"Yeah, well, around here – curiosity killed the cat. Remember that, *Zaychik.*"

He was different now than he had been back at his house. Harder somehow, like he had something to prove, and maybe he did.

"C'mere," he ordered, and his tone had gentled. I went to him and he guided me to the front door of the salvage yard's building and pushed it open.

I went through and he stopped me, a hand on my shoulder. A brunette woman looked up from behind the counter and smiled.

"Hi, Mav," she said. "Who's this?"

"Little Bird meet my little *zaychik*. Marisol, this is Little Bird. Your personal shopper today."

Little Bird laughed as Mav held out a big wad of bills past me over the counter to her. She took the money and slid off her stool.

"What're we shopping for?" she asked him and he gave her that crooked smile that tended to make my heart skip a beat. The back of my neck prickled with jealousy and I frowned.

I had better not be getting attached after only one night. That would be crazy of me to do!

"Road gear, head to the toy store and get her outfitted for at least a couple to three weeks. Also, get her some regular shit to wear. Whatever she wants."

"Where are we going?" I asked, bypassing his generosity in favor of the bigger picture which was a likely cross-country trip.

"Later," Mav said. He raised his eyebrows at Little Bird who swept her jacket off a peg as she came around the counter.

"Come on, it'll be fun," she said with a warm smile and I nodded. I knew better than to argue.

The great mountain of a man that sometimes rode with Mav on his Eastern Washington trips got up and limped around the low wall. Little Bird went to him happily, and they shared a kiss that would have had my *abuela* screaming at them in a string of Spanish about being obscene in front of the children. That in and of itself made me smile.

"Be careful. Call me if you run into any trouble," he grunted like he wasn't happy about it and let her go.

"Always," she said softly and turned and raised her sleek dark eyebrows at me.

I gave a careful nod, took a drink from my steel tumbler, and followed her out the front door. Mav looked up from his phone as I went to pass and caught me by my arm. He leaned in and brushed my lips with his. I blinked a little in surprise and he winked with a slightly promising curve to his lips – a promise for later.

I softened. He was this strange dichotomy of hot and cold, all sharp jagged edges with a gentle, soft touch.

"Stick with Little Bird. She'll get you everything you need, then come back here," he ordered.

"Your wish is my command," I said lightly and followed her out the front door.

She smiled.

"Is he always like that?" I asked.

"Mm-hm. You get used to it."

"Be nice if I knew where we were going," I said.

"Now, or what you're getting the gear for?"

"Both?"

She laughed and hit the key fob, the lights flashing on a nearby 4Runner, the locks giving a soft thump as they disengaged.

We went shopping, she explained things – except where the fuck I was meant to be going. I tried to play it cool and gain some trust before I asked again.

Our first stop was the Harley-Davidson store in Renton. A bubbly blonde woman was happy to pour me into all the skin-tight leather I could want.

While I tried things on, Little Bird explained how she had learned some things the same way I was now from a woman named Dahlia.

I liked Little Bird. She was… nonthreatening. Nice, in that way that said she hadn't gone through a whole lot of shit to make her hard yet. That, or she was one of those people who could do that thing where they never got hard from life. I wasn't one of those people, and I sometimes seriously envied the ones that so effortlessly were able to forgive or forget and live their life happy without the burden of shame I felt every day.

"What's Dahlia like?" I asked, in part to keep her talking but mostly to keep her talking about anything but *me*.

"Intense," she said after a moment of quiet from the other side of the dressing room curtain, the word followed quickly by a nervous laugh.

"So, a total bitch," I said pragmatically.

"Oh, no. I wouldn't go that far. She's just very… particular. Comes in, takes the world by storm, that type of thing. She's one of Maverick's best friends. I get that they've known each other a long, long, time. Like since they were kids."

Interesting.

"So, do you know what all of this is for?" I asked, handing some items out from behind the curtain. She took them from me and thrust something else into my hand. I blinked and rolled my underwear-clad self in the mirror. *More?*

"These guys take riding safety extremely seriously," she said.

I dutifully tried the things she handed to me on and decided they didn't look half bad —the jeans fit like a dream and were definitely keepers. I wasn't sure what to do with the leather that was supposed to go over them.

"I don't know what to do with this," I said holding it out.

"Can I come in?" she asked.

"Sure."

She helped me and didn't make it weird, and I was grateful. My walls incrementally easing down, still cautious but not nearly as scared.

I felt like I was somehow making a new friend and the impossibility of that task at home had been insurmountable… but here, maybe all things *were* possible.

"Do you know why he has me buying all this stuff? Like, I get safety but, girl, you got a *pile* going over there."

"My guess is he wants you to have enough gear for the two-week run coming up."

"*Two weeks!* Where the hell does he think he's taking me!?"

She hesitated and finally erred on the side of caution. "If he plans on taking you anywhere, he's the one that should really be the one to discuss it with you and he absolutely will. Mav is always ten steps ahead of the rest of us – and I don't mean by strong-arm tactics or anything. He's just got things all figured out before we do. He's super smart, and he's not the type to make you do anything you don't want to do. He just likes to be prepared."

Her words did little to comfort me but at the same time took the jagged edge off my concern – for now anyway.

"Just to be sure, which pile is 'keep' and which pile are we putting back?" I asked and she smiled.

"That's up to you. This pile is the one you didn't say anything about or make any noises. This is the one that you sounded like you liked." She touched one pile hanging up on one side then the other smaller pile with the other hand.

"Shit, okay, guess I'd better try all this on again and whittle it down more?"

"You really don't have to. Mav is gonna expect you to have enough gear for a two-week run and I don't want to go back and have him disappointed."

"Why? Does he get mad easily?"

She laughed. "Not at all. He'll just send us right back here to get more and maybe will come with next time and have you model the entire store."

"You sound like you speak from experience."

She shook her head. "Dahlia told me, and I believe her."

"Kind of can't wait to meet her," I said and blew out a breath dubiously. Either we would get along great or we would hate each other. There was no happy medium with me.

I was just naturally inclined to believe the latter because that was just about always how that seemed to work out.

"I think you have a good plan though," she said, standing back so I could get a look at myself in the mirror. "These chaps look great on you with these jeans. Like one pair of the chaps and at least two pair of the jeans for sure."

I nodded. "If you say so."

She wrinkled her nose adorably and exclaimed, "I do! Trust me. You won't regret it."

I smiled and more of the tension riding me loosened.

I decided that I really did like Little Bird. Her smile and lighter than air, easygoing personality were starting to lift my spirits too.

CHAPTER NINE

*M*averick…

I sighed and sat back in my seat and asked, "Not to put too fine a point on it, but two weeks with any of our number away is a big fuckin' deal right now. So, let's hear it. Who wants to stay and who wants to go?"

I ran my eyes over each man in turn sitting around my table and sniffed, waiting to see who would speak first.

"As much as I would fuckin' love to do an Eversong run, my leg ain't worth shit for the long rides lately and I got rehab and doctor appointments out the ass to get it rehabbed some more. I'll stay." Dump Truck sighed and didn't look happy to be saying it and truthfully, it was a kick in the balls. He was solid and I wanted him with me, but not enough to set him back any more than he had been already lately. It was a hard four days' ride there and back again and no telling if his broken wings and officer's status would net him a room in the lodge this year.

From what I gathered, this was shaping up to be one hell of a Lake Run – with just about every chapter making an appearance and some guest clubs, the number was climbing into the high triple digits on headcount. Something like seven or eight hundred signed on to attend.

Bikes and tents as far as the eye could see kind of a deal. It was making for some headaches this year according to Data from the mother chapter. Even taking into consideration that not everyone who signed on to attend would or could make it.

I think it was wise for D.T. to sit this one out.

"Fen, that means you're on deck?" I asked.

"Fuck yeah, I'm going. You know you ain't going nowhere without at least one or the both of us on your wrecking crew." He planted his fist in his opposite palm and cracked his knuckles loudly.

I nodded.

"I'd like to go, I got the time," Glass Jaw said. I nodded.

"Dump Truck is more than capable of handling the home front," I declared.

So, there was three.

In the end, I had Glass Jaw, Fenris, Tic-Tac, Nine, and Cipher ready to rock and roll and ride to Eversong with me. The rest decided to stay back and handle personal shit – or just couldn't get the time off from their cover jobs, which was fine by me. The bigger the pack, the more likely for the pigs to try and hand out fast-riding awards like confetti, hauling our asses over as we were passing through to try and jam us up.

In addition to Glass Jaw, Fen, Cipher and Nine, we would have the Eastern Washington crew, or what was left of it. So, Skeeter, Derringer, and Goner.

That was plenty big enough. Only time would tell if we'd be coming back plus or minus any of our retinue.

I dismissed the church meeting and let the rest of them get back to it and fuck off to whatever they had going on the rest of the day. Glass Jaw sat with me awhile, mostly while I stewed in silence. Brooding. Just yet one more service I offered aplenty.

"You good, man?" he asked when I'd been marinating in my thoughts just a little too long for what was probably his comfort. I could give a fuck.

"Yeah, man. Just kicking myself for being impulsive back in Yakima."

"Then why were you?" he demanded. "It's not like you, for one thing. Ain't you got enough on your plate?"

"I do, and I honestly can't tell you why, except for everything about the situation called for it. Sometimes I do shit, and I don't even know why I do it," I said. I sighed. "Not once has it ever been the *wrong* thing to do, though. Every time, shit becomes clear in its own time and it's like…" I groped for how to explain it in a way that made sense and didn't sound like a bunch of mystical bullshit – because it wasn't like that. At all.

"You trying to tell me you started runnin' on intuition now?" he asked and laughed some.

"It's like that and it's not. It's like subconsciously, I got the lay of the land, right? But it's like my conscious brain hasn't caught up to it yet, you know? Like the chess pieces are all laid out on the board and I wanna make the move but everything about it is screaming it's the wrong one and that I should make this move over here even though on the surface it's the wrong move to make, you know?"

He laughed at me. "That's like, exactly what intuition is."

"Except it's really not. It's like I've run the calculations and I know shit ain't adding up, and I am always right."

"Okay, Mav." Glass Jaw shook his head. "You don't gotta explain any of it." He grunted and got to his feet calling back over his shoulder, "You ain't steered us wrong yet, man."

"Don't plan on making it a new thing, either," I muttered, losing myself back in thought.

I tried to keep my thoughts on the problem at hand, which was immersing Marisol into this life as opposed to the one she'd come from at quite literally the *worst* possible time for me – but I couldn't. Instead, my mind kept wandering back to last night.

That girl had a body made for fucking. Perfect. Lush. Golden tanned skin smooth under my touch, raven hair cascading around her face as those perfect youthful tits of hers bounced. The perfect palmful for each of my hands, low hanging fruit for real.

She wasn't scrawny, she wasn't skinny; she was the perfect woman, all slender and sleek curves that begged for my hands to sweep

over them appreciatively. Her sleek frame a better ride than my bike –
which was fuckin' saying something.

I was getting hard just thinking about it, which perfect timing. She
and Little Bird were coming down the hall from the front of the club,
hands loaded with shopping bags. Quite a few, I was pleased to see, the
majority of them emblazoned with the Harley-Davidson logo.

"Put 'em in the office," I called out and Marisol turned from where
she looked behind herself at Little Bird who was saying something I
didn't catch.

Marisol's honey-toned eyes drifted immediately to mine and held
them, her gaze calm, and her intelligence sparkling from those eyes of
hers as I rose. I came around the head of my table, drifting along the
wall and shoving chairs out of my way, pushing them in the rest of the
way beneath the gleaming wood and resin as my boot tread fell heavy
on the cement floor.

She stopped, Little Bird nearly crashing into her back, and I
smirked. I could see my effect on the girl from here – if she only had
any idea of what she did to *me*.

"Go on, first door there on your left," I said, and she stepped past
me slowly and crept into my office. I didn't like it. Didn't like how if
she'd been a dog, or a cat, her tail would have been tucked firmly
between her legs in fear. Again, that prickling sensation of I knew what
I was looking at, I just couldn't seem to find the *words* for it.

My intuition if you will.

I stepped out in front of Little Bird and held out my hands for the
rest of the bags she carried. She smiled up at me and said, "Go easy on
her, Mav. Seems like things might be a little… intense for her."

"She tell you something I should know about?" I asked, raising an
eyebrow.

Little Bird smiled gently. "Call it women's intuition," she said and
again with that word.

"Gotcha," I said. She went to get into her purse, and I shook my
head.

"Just give it to her the next time you see her," I said.

"You sure?"

I gave her a look and she smiled and nodded saying, "Right. Forget I asked."

"Your man's waiting for you," I said and she nodded and turned, heading back out front, a prolonging look over her shoulder, her big, deep brown eyes lingering on the empty but still open doorway of my office tinged with worry. Nothing to set me off overtly, making me want to demand answers – but whatever it was? It was there. There was no mistake. I'd seen it and there was no taking it back.

I turned and followed Marisol into my office and kicked the door shut.

Marisol was looking through a couple of the bags she'd brought in with her, having set them on the floor in front of the filing cabinets.

"Maybe it's in one of these," I said and held out the bags to her.

She took them from me and set them down, and curious, I stood and watched her.

"Ah ha," she murmured and came up with a gray Henley. It was a man's shirt, and she held it out to me.

"Thought this would look good on you," she said, and her gaze was steely. She was trying to gauge my reaction.

I smiled and said, "You bought me a present with my own money?"

"Thought you'd look good in it, and no, I used my own money for this."

I cocked my head to the side and swept her up and down with my gaze. She didn't have a lot of money. She couldn't have. She came from poverty the like that shouldn't even be on American soil by my estimation. Brand name shit from the Harley store wasn't cheap. This meant something. What, I just didn't know. Not yet.

"Thank you," I said, taking the gift. She was right. It was right up my alley and with how hard I was getting in my jeans; I was about to be right up hers.

I shut the door and tossed the shirt she'd bought me up onto my shoulder.

"Turn around, hands on the desk. If you're up for it, I'm going to eat your pussy then fuck you into next week."

Her eyes widened and she sort of just froze. *Like a little rabbit.*

"Because I bought you a shirt to say thanks for getting me out of that shithole?" she asked.

I smiled and knew it was a bit feral.

"A man needs to know when to show his appreciation – the how of it is personal to him. Welcome to the life, *Zaychik*. I can either fuck you on my desk, here and now, which is my preference… or out on the pool table out there in front of the guys." I was only throwing that option in to get what I wanted. My hard-on was starting to ache already. At the slight edge of utter fear and panic on her face, I backpedaled. "Although, I suppose, if I must, I could wait until I got you back at my place but where's the fun in that?"

She swallowed hard, and I watched the calculations formulate and play out behind her eyes.

"Here," she whispered and turned around, putting her palms flat to my desk's top, sticking out that gorgeous ass of hers as if I were the man and she were about to be frisked.

I went to her and pressed my body to hers, gauging things, rubbing my cock back and forth against her pussy through the layers of fabric that separated us.

She was the perfect height in her boots to take me. I massaged her shoulders and she tensed even more until I murmured, "Relax, baby. It's gonna be all good, I promise. There's no bad here."

I grunted in appreciation and sucked in a breath past clenched teeth. "You are so goddamn sexy, " I whispered, and some more of the tension left her.

"Yeah?" she asked, stammering, her voice tripping over the word, her insecurities bubbling to the surface with the onset of her nervousness.

"Fuck yeah," I said and smacked her jeans-clad ass. She jumped slightly and moaned, thrusting herself back against me. I gripped her hips and pressed forward, meeting the backward jerk of her hips and the friction building between us was delicious.

"You like it dirty like this?" she asked, her voice husky.

"I'll take you any way I can get you," I answered. "But yeah, the filthier the better." I leaned over her and swept my hands to the front of her pants. She made to pull her hands off the top of the desk, to help me I think, and I admonished her with a sharp, "Ah!"

I paused in my attempts to get her pants undone and down, so I could fuck her first with my mouth then with my cock, until I was sure she was going to comply.

She didn't know it, but I'd already read her like a damn book. She was feisty, had the potential to be fiery, and it was a monumental turn-on to keep that fire tamed. The only way to do that was through firm consistency and so here we were. Her training started now.

"Keep those hands right where I can see them," I ordered coldly through a smile she couldn't see with the way she faced forward. She made to turn her head and I snapped, "Eyes front!"

She defied me, looking back and with a devilish grin, I made her pay for it, slapping her ass with a resounding crack of my hand. It only semi had the desired effect. She faced forward, but she also thrust her ass back against me and writhed so beautifully, I damn near bust a nut in my pants.

I worked her belt from its loops and asked her, "You trust me?"

"Yes and no," she said truthfully.

"You trust me not to hurt you?" I demanded.

"Physically?"

"We'll start there, yeah."

"Yes and no."

I paused.

"I will never hit you in any way that isn't erotic," I told her. "I will never hurt you without your prior consent. We clear on that?"

"Yes," she said softly.

"Do you believe me?"

She hesitated and I wondered who did what, exactly, to damage her ability to trust so thoroughly.

"Yes," she said finally, but it lacked the enthusiasm of her prior answer. I hesitated with what I wanted to do with that belt and decided fuck it – I knew I wouldn't hurt her, and I also knew the only way to earn her trust was to prove it. I slid the belt's tongue through the buckle and slipped the loop over her head, tightening it up, wrapping the length of faux leather around my fist, yoking her.

"Bad?" I asked, but I knew the answer by the way she shifted on her feet, her hips swaying sensually, rubbing herself against me.

"No," she answered, and I smiled with a savage glee.

"Pull your pants down, panties too and put your hands right back against that desk."

She did as I commanded and I smiled, uncoiling the tail end of her belt from around my fist as I took a step back, giving her some slack as I went to my knees behind her. I wanted her compliant, it was about control. I wasn't about to choke her out. That shit was for later and only if she consented.

"Thrust those hips back, baby," I murmured, intoxicated by the perfume of her arousal, her pussy slick with her desire – flesh glistening and begging for my kiss.

I licked along the seam of her sex and plunged my tongue inside of her and she cried out, legs quivering as she moved slightly away by leaning heavier onto her hands to support herself. I opened her up with my hands and went at her clit, teasing it with my tongue as she panted sharply.

God, that sound was music to my fucking ears.

I feasted on her pussy while she stood there, compliant, taking what I had to give her but oh, I had so very much to fuckin' give. I slid a finger inside her and worked her with my hand. She looked back at me, eyes glazed, pussy soaking wet, and that look was just as intoxicating as her taste and fragrance.

My cock throbbed behind my zipper and I stood up saying, "You stay right there, baby. I'm gonna fuck you so good. Mm."

I got myself out of my pants as she stood, hands on my desk, hips thrust back, pussy open and wanting as she shifted impatiently from foot to food and *goddamn*, it was a sight.

I fished a condom out of the pocket of my leather jacket, tearing it open with my teeth and rolling it on double time. She moaned slightly at the sound in anticipation and I about died with the deep ache of anticipation.

Grabbing her hips, I lined myself up with her opening and shoved into her hard in one stroke. She cried out, thrusting her hips back to meet me – her pussy tightening around the head of my cock in a way that made me grunt in deep satisfaction.

I had some girth, but thankfully I was just short enough in length that I could pound the shit out of a woman like I liked without being a total cervix buster and hot damn, Marisol could take a pounding.

She collapsed some over the desk, pressing her body against the calendar blotter and the scarred wood, thrusting her hips back, swaying slightly as I pressed into her balls fucking deep.

"Touch yourself, I want you to come all over my dick," I grated and she didn't hesitate, just reached a hand down her front to press her fingertips into her clit, her voice a breathy high whine of pleasure where it passed between her gorgeous, lush lips.

I hammered into her, felt her clench around my dick, her hot, soft walls pressing around my shaft, enveloping the head of my cock in rough sensuality, and I gritted my teeth. She was close, she was so fucking close. I couldn't let up; I wouldn't let up until –

The door crashed open behind us and Marisol jumped, straightening. I slipped out of her and put my arms around her reflexively, putting my back to the door, twisting her slightly as much as the desk would allow to shelter her with my body against whatever incoming threat might or might not be there. At the very least, I could try to preserve her modesty for her, even though I legit had none of my own, my ass hanging out in front of, it turned out, my best friend since childhood – Mallory. Dahlia to the rest of the guys around here. It was her burlesque stage name, Dahlia Darlin.'

"Oh, Jesus Christ, Mav!" Dahlia cried and the hard edge in her voice made me smirk at first, wondering who she was annoyed with this time. That smirk quickly fled when she said, "You, whore, *out!*"

Marisol stiffened and straightened turning her face as I locked my hands around her wrists and held her tight against my chest.

"Who you callin' a whore, *coño de mierda!*" Her nudity forgotten, she braced feet against the desk and kicked out, feisty.

I almost lost my hold on her and grinning savagely I yelled at

Dahlia, "Give us a minute, Flower!" Dahlia was in super bitch mode, and simply stepped to the inside of the room and leaned her back against the wall beside it, her willowy arms coming up to cross themselves under her tits.

She was dressed to the nines, as always. A white sleeveless silk blouse with a deep cut 'V' neckline, a gently breezy ruffle from her shoulders tapering elegantly in front of her breasts to point out her narrow waist which was ensconced in a tight, knee-length, black pencil skirt. Her black hose were perfect, the lines in the back straight as an arrow, the crimson heels she had on absolutely on point. Her hair was perfectly coiffed as well, the victory rolls in the 1940s style with no hair out of place and tucked behind her ear, into her raven locks, was a crimson dahlia flower, the match for those lofty heels she wore.

Her makeup was smoky and perfect, and she was beautiful, as always – she was also the equivalent of my little sister. My father's and her father's crime families closely intertwined and the way we grew up together? The way we played as children, and the secrets we both knew?

No, we kept each other in balance, in check, but there was nothing romantic about it. In fact, I'd told more than one motherfucker out there, *you make her cry, and I'm gonna make* you *cry.*

That was the way thing were, and they weren't changing.

Marisol, by comparison to Dahlia's cool, calm, and collected dagger staring, was an absolute wildcat at the perceived disrespect, ready to throw down with my bestie over her callin' her a whore. It was drama I didn't need, but a tinderbox that Dahlia was seemingly glad to throw a match to by the little smirk raising the corner of her equally crimson lips.

"Whoa there, *Zaychik*!" I cried and couldn't help the laughter. Dahlia didn't know it, but she'd be lucky to get out of here without getting her ass kicked. Just not by Marisol. I had a mind to set her a lesson myself on just where she fell in the actual hierarchy of this place because right now? She was damn sure above her station barging in here and starting a ruckus like this.

I eventually had to settle for shoving Marisol out the door to my office and across the hall into the chapel, sending her stumbling, sprawling into the chair at the foot of my table and calling sharply in after her, "Settle down!" and slightly less harshly, but no less sternly, "And pull yourself together."

I shut the door behind me, went back across the hall tucking myself into my pants and slammed the door to my office closed.

"Just what's the fucking problem, Dahl?" I growled out.

"You!" she hissed. "What's this I hear you're picking up *jailbait* out in fucking Yakima, Mav? That girl ain't a day over fifteen or sixteen." She sounded positively venomous, her Medusa out in full scale, but while I went to stone – it wasn't at her gaze. I was pissed.

"She's damn near *twenty years old,* what the fuck, Dahlia? Are you seriously standing there accusing me – *me!* Of being a goddamned *pedo?*"

"I saw *what I saw* just now, Maverick!" she hissed back.

"She's of *age,* Mallory!" I shot back coldly.

She scoffed, and just like always, didn't know when to fuckin' leave well enough alone, always having to get her digs in when she was fired up.

"I mean, the apple really never *does* fall far from the tree – your daddy—"

I confess. I felt like shit for what happened when those last two words fell from her crimson painted lips. My hand flashed out in a wicked back-handed strike and caught her right in the side of those lips. She knew, though. She'd been through it countless times before. When we were kids, for the most part, but still – that muscle memory never leaves.

She didn't stiffen up; it was always worse when you stiffened up. Instead, she let the blow snap her head to the side away from me, the report sharp and echoing off the walls in the small space. The snap of my fingers against her soft flesh making them sting, but the red-raised welts coming up on her chin and cheek, the smear of that red lipstick against her creamy flesh told me this lesson – albeit reflexive and unintentional – was damn sure gonna stick for a while.

We stared at each other, both of our chests heaving, the words we each had prepared to volley at one another sitting like boulders in our chests, piling like rockfall in our throats in the stunned silence between us.

Neither of us launched. Instead, we fixed eyes on each other and stood stalk still for several heaving and uncomfortable breaths.

"No women, no children, huh?" she asked mildly, and reached for the office door, jerking it open.

Her words cut to the quick and she knew it, but my heart wasn't sinking – it was already sunk. She looked back at me, pausing in the doorway but my words had all dried up and blown away.

I knew we would be alright, eventually, by the cruel little smirk she cast in my direction before walking out. Her heels clipping smartly up the hallway as she walked through the great room of the club, silence radiating – a palpable thing – as she passed. I stood outside my office and watched her go, her head held high, back straight, presence regal. She was a princess, after all. A mob princess of the highest order – one of the biggest crime family syndicates in the United States.

That family bled Merlot when you cut them. They were as Italian as you could get.

I shook my head at the shrouded and curious looks cast by the guys in my direction. All of them had the good sense not to fucking ask.

Fuck.

I finished putting myself together and just as I finished, the door to the chapel opened. Marisol was already flawlessly back in her clothes, her hair fixed, her belt back around her trim waist, the sparks still flying from her honeyed eyes which only deepened in their bronze hue with her rage.

"Get over here," I barked coldly at her and she flinched and though her feet complied, carrying her closer, her upper body leaned back away from me indicating her fear.

She had nothing to fear from me. Ever. And so, the mystery behind her motivations for coming here, to agreeing to the terms of our arrangement, deepened.

I frowned. Not at her, but at the puzzle she presented. I grabbed her by the back of the neck, thumb and forefinger pinching to either side and massaging at the base of her skull as I marched her back into my office and shut the door behind us.

"Sit," I demanded and she turned and only half complied, leaning her shapely ass against the edge of my desk, hands gripping it to either side of her fantastic hips until they were mottled in a white-knuckled grip.

It was the only sign of her outward discomfort. Her gaze remained locked and even with my own. I had to give her points for that.

"What?" she demanded. "You going to tell me I can't react to some *puta* disrespecting me like that?"

I smirked and shook my head.

"In some ways. I'm telling you that in this life, you never take any disrespect, but if you're disrespected – there are better ways of going about it than what you just did – more effective ways."

She eyed me warily and didn't say anything, so I took it as an invitation that she was listening and wanted to know more. Her thirst for more knowledge made me hard all over again.

CHAPTER TEN

*M*arisol…

"What's on your mind, *Zaychik?*"

I startled slightly, cuddled tight against his side, head on his shoulder in the close and intimate dark of his bedroom. He traced fingers lightly through my hair, sweeping it behind my ear, trailing the tip of a finger lightly along my jaw as I looked up at him, his face indistinct in the dark.

I stared at him silently. The truth was something I didn't want to share. I didn't trust him; not yet… but his words from earlier in the week were swirling around in my thoughts, a drop of ink in a glass of water, diffusing through my being and altering me at a molecular level.

He was right. There *were* better ways of handling the disrespect and I wasn't talking about his *puta* of a best friend. I was thinking about my whole life – but right now, the only way I could see to get out and get my brother back was *on* my back and so I was here.

The toughest part of that? Mav was an excellent lover. Slow, attentive, gentle, all the things I imagined it could be, that it should be, but had never been.

It had me all messed up inside, and rather than fight it, I was so very tempted to just give into it and to pretend.

"It's okay. You don't have to tell me," he said and pressed a firm kiss against my hairline.

I sighed out and closed my eyes, swallowing past the lump in my throat.

"You think you're ready for this?" he asked, changing the subject, but I was in such an exhausted state of feel good, it took me a second to realize he meant the ride we were leaving on in the morning, not me getting the fuck away from my toxic damn family and taking my brother with me where he would be safe from all their bullshit.

"Yeah!" I said a little too quickly and he chuckled deeply, pressing another kiss, full of affection, to my forehead.

"It's alright to be nervous," he murmured. "We get a little wild in a big ol' pack – it's true and the Eversong run is the *biggest* run we do as National. It'll be alright, so long as you follow the rules and unless you're in the water you keep that vest on."

"I won't go in the water," I vowed. Mostly because I didn't know how to swim, but also because I didn't want there to be *any* mistakes. I tried not to shudder, but I think I failed.

Mav squeezed me a little tighter and whispered, "Easy, *Zaychik*. You're gonna be just fine. I got you."

I wish I could believe that, I thought earnestly, because as much as I wanted to paint Maverick as just another villain in my story, as much as I wanted to consider him just a means to an end, over the last several days… he had treated me better than anyone had my whole life. He was kind, but firm. Sweet, but *definitely* alpha, and it left me feeling confused and vulnerable in his embrace. I didn't like that last part at all, but what could I do? The bargain had been struck, and I was his for the month and after that?

I didn't know, but I had to come up with *something* fast.

I fell into an uneasy sleep, light, and restless. I kept waking up. Finally, with the light starting to turn and the birds chirping loudly outside the window, I gave up on all pretense of getting some rest and got up for the day. I stood quietly in the early dawn's light, the air in the room cool against my skin and watched Maverick sleep for a moment or two.

He was just as attractive asleep as he was when he was awake, only when he slept, it was like the sharp edges smoothed out. His face somehow more open and vulnerable than when he was awake. He seemed… more human.

I sighed and lifted his robe from the hook on the back of his bedroom door, slipping the cool navy-blue satin over my arms and shrugging into it, belting it at my waist with a secure bow as I slipped from the room and down the unfinished hallway. I'd made some progress on cleaning and sorting his little hodge-podge house into some semblance of uniformity. There was, of course, only so much that I could do given the state of some rooms' finish.

I padded barefoot across the kitchen to the coffee maker and got started preparing a fresh brew. As I was filling the carafe with water at the kitchen sink to fill the machine, his hands fell on my hips in a light touch and he stepped up to my back, his warmth enveloping me.

"Couldn't sleep?" he asked, his voice an octave low, rough with waking up himself.

"Mm-mm, no," I murmured and shut off the tap. He swept my hair to one side, over my shoulder, and as I poured the fresh cool water into the reservoir of the coffeemaker, he kissed the side of my neck. He had this way of breathing me in deeply, intentionally, that always made me weak in the knees. I felt desired and wanted in a way that left me feeling confused and uneasy. A confusion and uneasiness that always melted away when he drew me, back against his chest, arms circling me protectively.

I barely slid the carafe home on its base, flipped the lid to the reservoir down, and flipped the switch to get the coffee brewing before he cuddled me so tightly I couldn't. I couldn't help the light chuckle that escaped me as he wrapped his teeth lightly in his lips and bit gently along the side of my neck, mock growling against my skin.

"Come back to bed," he urged, and I sighed, surprised at how much I wanted to.

"Shouldn't we get ready to leave?" I asked.

"Hmm, yeah, but I want you."

"You *always* want me," I teased.

"That's because you're always beautiful, always wild, and I get hard just looking at you." His stark admission held no hint of falsehood and I closed my eyes, soaking in the praise. I wanted to believe he meant more than just my looks… but I knew better.

"Thank you," I whispered and pulled gently away. He let me go.

I turned around and leaned my back against the edge of the counter and looked up at him, unable to help my blush. I was never able to contain it when he walked around his house nude like he did. It was unheard of back home. Then again, we were stacked like cordwood, one on top of the other, back home.

His blue eyes captured mine, and he grasped the point of my chin lightly between the pad of his thumb and the side of his index finger. The touch light, gentle, and I didn't move.

"When you going to trust me, *Zaychik,* hm? When are you going to let me in?" he asked. His voice was low, a living thing of its own that brushed sable soft fur along my spine, predatory like some great, sleek, black cat.

I suppressed a shiver and answered softly, "I trust you."

His lips quirked into a sad sort of smile and he let me go, taking a step back, "Now we both know that's a damn lie," he said. "You can get away with a lot of shit with me, Marisol… but lying isn't one of them. I'll give you some more time to come clean, to tell me your secrets all on your own." He paused, and it was for dramatic effect. "Don't make me come digging. You don't want me in the middle of it turning over rocks on my own."

Shit.

I most certainly did not.

He backed away, keeping me fixed with his deep blue eyes which had darkened to midnight skies.

"I'm takin' a shower. Bring me a cup of that when it's finished, yeah?"

I licked suddenly dry lips and found enough breath to say, "Yeah," and he turned and walked away. It was like his departure changed the very pressure in the atmosphere. Like a thunderstorm, roiling and loaded with energy had suddenly dissipated.

I was learning that Maverick was like that. Intense. Always intense, but you didn't always *feel it* like you did now. Still, it was there, always there, right below the surface.

No. I didn't trust him, and his words echoing in my head did nothing to improve that situation.

I made his coffee to his liking and took it to him – an offering of sorts. *Caffeine be with you;* I thought and suppressed a giggle. He took a drink, smiling behind the rim of his cup and pulled me laughing to him, kissing me, getting me soaked in his robe under the shower's spray. I laughed and kissed him back, the rich dark Colombian roast tingeing our kisses with extra zing and I thought… *and also with you, apparently.*

He had his way. He always did. He fucked me in his shower and made me come around his invading cock twice.

It left me shattered, weak in the knees, and it also made us both late.

The ride from the fruit grower's village to his home had nothing on the ride we took over the next several *days* to get to where we were going. The first day was a long, hard, four-hour slog, an hour's stop for lunch with another solid four hours on the other side. We made minimal stops for bathroom breaks and by the time we were through, it was dark. I didn't care. I just wanted sleep. I was exhausted, and we were doing it all over again the next day.

You can pretty much rinse and repeat for the next two or three days the same experience.

To his credit, Mav backed off when it came to fucking me those nights. I couldn't tell if it was because he felt sorry for me, or if it was that he was just as exhausted as I was and couldn't get it up if he tried.

I somehow doubted it was the latter. The man was, seemingly, always ready to go.

The one thing I wasn't spared in the evenings was conversation as we fell asleep. I would lie beside him in the dark, his strong arms around me, the warmth of him radiating through my back pleasantly, and he would ask questions. Simple ones, but that was merely a ploy. I was onto him by the second night.

He would ask innocuous things to start. Small talk about things we had seen along the way before transitioning to talk of my past or my homelife. I was careful there, not to give him too much information… It's not like I would have been believed anyway. That, and if *Abuela* knew I'd told any of the family business or secrets to an outsider? She was a vengeful, vindictive bitch and I couldn't be certain she wouldn't do something to Mateo in her rage.

I didn't care what happened to me. I cared a lot about what happened to my brother. He was an innocent in all of this and deserved a chance to stay that way… unlike me. I would never be able to go back or pretend.

"Don't much like it when you get all quiet like that, baby. Makes me think I said something to hurt you."

His fingertips roamed over my skin in a light caress, following the natural curve of my ribs as they dipped into the hollow my profile made at the waist. He kept his hand traveling and I closed my eyes, the sensation of his skin on mine, moving to follow the flare of my hip, almost hypnotic in a way.

"No," I denied his concern. "I was just thinking about Mateo. Wondering what he's doing right now…"

"Mm," he pressed a kiss to the cap of my shoulder, his arm up over me, hand pressed against my body, high up on my stomach, lightly holding me back against his body. I eased my tense posture and he smiled against my skin, lips curving against my shoulder. Pleased, but I didn't know why.

"Why are you so smug?" I challenged lightly in a bid to change the subject.

"Not smug," he whispered in my ear in a way that made me shudder. "Pleased."

Pleased? What did I do?

His hand tightened on my hip, drawing me back even as his warmth along my spine dissipated as he edged further behind us both onto the bed to turn me on my back. It was becoming a familiar move of his, indicating his arousal, his want to fuck me – but by the same token, his touch while insistent, *eager*, wasn't demanding.

The choice was always mine. If I said no, he would relinquish his hold on me. How did I know?

I'd begged off sex one night just to see if I had a choice or if, like so many things, it was an illusion. He'd quickly relented and had held me, but had otherwise let me be.

Now, I was curious. While I was exhausted, and we had one more day of riding to get to our destination, I was finding that I was starting to miss the delicious soreness he wrought between my thighs after a night of his absolutely mind-blowing brand of sex.

He lay over the top of me, the warmth of his body welcome, his mouth finding mine in the dark, air-conditioned hush of the roadside motel room.

I gasped as he deviated from my mouth, his lips and teeth lightly grazing and nipping that spot on the side of my neck that drove me wild.

"Mm," he half groaned, half growled in appreciation when I arched my back, body bowing closer to him. "I love it when you arch for me like that, baby."

"Yeah?" I asked softly.

"Mm-hmm," he muttered against my skin, kissing his way down my body in that way that told me he was about to absolutely rock my world.

I loved it when Maverick went down on me. He had a real love for eating pussy and the way he went after mine, it was like it was some world-class catnip or some shit.

He glided down my body, hands sliding along my skin, lips planting these beautiful little butterfly kisses at regular intervals as I grew wetter by the second, my anticipation growing and quickly outpacing my loathing for myself. I shouldn't enjoy this, but I couldn't help it. He made me feel just so damn good.

His mouth, hot and soft, made contact with my body and I writhed, closing my eyes, concentrating on the sensation of him – of his hands on my skin, above my hips, of his arms cradling me gently as he worked his mouth, velvet slick against my pussy – his tongue alternatively darting against and lavishing my clit with attention.

I arched again, voice escaping me in a deep *ugh* of surprise, although it should hardly be surprising by now. The things he was doing to me were only made better when he slipped a finger inside of me, gliding through my wetness, probing gently around looking for that *spot*.

I sucked in a strangled breath and my hips tried to lift unbidden from the bed when he found it, sparkling energy swirling out from that sensitive place deep inside me. His mouth worked magic on me from the outside very nearly overloading me with sensations that were so strong, fierce, and at once the gentlest storm I think I had ever had to weather.

He hummed appreciatively against my body and I jolted, the cascade of overlapping sensations overtaking me. The feeling of being overfull, falling, and tumbling even though my body was safely grounded in his arms, anchored in the too-hard hotel room bed – all of it was a distant memory as the pleasure swept through me, intense, overwhelming. I tapped on his arm, vaguely aware that I did it.

Too much, too many sensations, too many feelings, stop, stop, stop, stop, stop!

But he never did. He always took me through, carried me through to the other side where I found myself lying, groaning, hands pressed to my mouth, legs twitching of their own accord as he climbed my body the same way he'd descended, with light butterfly kisses. Wiping his mouth with his hand, a smug smirk on his lips; a sparkle of mischievous light in his deep indigo eyes as he kneeled between my legs and produced a condom seemingly out of thin air.

I lay panting, helpless in the aftermath of such a devastating orgasm, watching him make himself ready to take me, low-key eager to have him inside me. The orgasm he'd given me was suddenly just an appetizer, and I now found myself ravenous for him, wanting him, needing him inside me, desperate for that deeper touch of his cock as it filled me.

He gave me a crooked smile and murmured, "There's my dirty girl. I love it when you look at me like that."

I swallowed hard and pulled him down over the top of me, twining my legs around his lean hips as he smoothly penetrated me, filling me slowly – agonizingly slow, while I writhed against him in a desperate bid to take him in further.

"Slow it down, Marisol," he ordered. "I don't know about you, but I've got all night."

Oh. It was like *that*.

I lay back and let him sink into me, balls deep, on his own time and I would be lying if I said I didn't love it.

I loved everything about it from the warmth of his body against mine, the sensation of him inside me, to the way he gazed down at me, careful calculation and consideration in his deep blue eyes. I found myself reaching up, and he came to me, sinking lower so that my hands could reach him. I pulled his face to mine and kissed him deeply, a thank you for his patience and understanding… even if he couldn't understand the why of my reluctance.

CHAPTER ELEVEN

*M*averick...

"Well this is a right fuckin' mess," Dragon harrumphed and leaned back, ashing his cigarette off to the side before leaning back in, his forearms on the edge of the picnic table he was holding court at. I was in the uncomfortable position of delivering the bad news about the Eastern Washington chapter. Even though it wasn't *my* chapter, I felt like I was the one in the hot seat with Dragon and the mother chapter. That was the *last* place anyone wanted to fuckin' be.

"And what about you three fuckin' knuckleheads?" Dragon's obsidian eyes tracked to my left and behind me, fixing on Skeeter, Derry, and Goner. "How the fuck did you not know what the rest of your crew was up to?"

I stepped back and to the right where the rest of my crew had my back and gave the floor of crunchy fallen leaves to what was left of the Eastern Washington chapter.

Dragon efficiently eviscerated their stories. All except for Derry, who legit had a reason to not know what was up between spending some time in jail on a drunk and disorderly when the shit started to go sideways only to follow up with having to take care of his ailing mother, who later passed around the same time shit got real.

By the time all was said and done, Goner was on probation with the club and likely to be stripped of his patch and put out bad if he so much as stepped a toe out of line. Skeeter was stripped of his position as VP and wouldn't be allowed to hold an officer's position again for five years with any chapter. Derry had barely skirted any consequences, but that was because he was just as disgusted with the rest of his crew as anybody else here and had asked, practically on bended knee, to join mine for a fresh start away from the bullshit.

Me and mine were happy to take him, but the rest of the Eastern Washington Chapter was as good as dissolved. Every man in jail was proclaimed out bad for the murder of that family and truthfully? Jail or prison was as safe a place as they could be. Outside our reach – for the most part. There were a couple of Eastern Washington guys that were locked up during the whole damn mess that were still right with the club for not knowing anything.

Those two, in conjunction with a pack of nomads that were white knighting, riding to the rescue in from parts unknown, were going to rebuild the Eastern Washington chapter from the dusty ground on up.

It wasn't an overnight fix by any means, but my crew was prepared to pick up the slack and help the new crew coming in learn the ropes. Idaho was stepping up in a big way to help from the other side to help the new group of guys get settled.

We spent way too long banging out the details under the shade of those trees by the lake. The shade was good, the random puffs of breeze from the water refreshing when they came, but it was still hot as fuck out there and by the end, I was ready for a cold beer, some dinner, and some time by the fire.

Mostly, I wanted to see how my little *zaychik* was doing. I hadn't seen her since we'd gotten here. Of course, we'd arrived, had just enough time to put our stuff down in our respective rooms and whatnot before we'd hustled to get shit squared away with the big boss out back in the clearing by the head honcho's cabin.

I went up the path, Fenris on my right and Glass Jaw on my left and scratched an itch below my bottom lip with a thumbnail, still digesting everything that'd gone down.

"Glass, you put in a call back home as quick as you can and fill in D.T. on the immediate adjustments that need to be made."

"Copy that." Glass shot me a quick salute and surged up the pathway ahead of us.

"You believe that shit with Skeeter and Goner?" Fen growled low.

"Yes and no," I said. "Goner I believe it, but Skeeter? I think he was telling the truth. He didn't know shit – but he knew something wasn't right. He just didn't want to know."

"Right."

"What I can't believe," I continued, "was that they actually thought they wouldn't get caught out. Still, the new crew coming in is going to need some guidance and Skeeter has a real chance at redemption there. I don't envision Goner's gonna make it with the new leadership."

"Not sure what this is gonna look like," Fen said, the misgivings clear in his dispassionate tone. I told him the truth.

"Me either, brother. We'll just have to see when the FNG's show up how we mesh and how they want to handle things."

Someone just behind us laughed, and I looked back over my shoulder. Reaver, the mother chapter's enforcer, winked one bright blue eye at me and I just barely managed to keep the frown off my face.

"Don't let none of the nomads hear you callin' 'em Fucking New Guys," he said. "Definitely not the right way to kick things off with a new chapter."

"True," Fen muttered. "Also true that in the Pacific Northwest, they *are* the FNG's. We got a system."

Reaver's blue eyes went wintery, and I took in a deep slow breath when a growl like some mongrel dog trickled out of Fenris' chest in answer to the look. He took shit like that as a personal challenge.

I put a hand to my man's chest to stop him stepping out of turn.

"Reaver's right," I said succinctly. "No disrespect meant," I followed up in Reaver's direction. "Any of the boys from parts unknown come around, we'll be more than reasonable and accommodating but Fen is right too, and by that token – shit in our territory runs pretty good the way we have it. So long as it ain't some young buck lookin' to change a bunch of shit, everybody should be all good."

"Duly noted," Reaver said, but he was eying Fenris with a creepy smile on his face. "Fancy a go in the circle tonight?" he asked my boy. Fenris scowled.

"What'd you have in mind?"

Reaver's smile was slow to spread into an infectious grin.

"Knife fight, first blood wins."

Fenris had an answering grin take over the lower half of his face and I just stuffed my hands in my pockets and shook my head.

"See you boys tonight," I said and didn't bother to disguise the eye roll in the tone of my voice. "I'm going to go find Marisol."

I jerked my head at Glass Jaw who gave me a curt nod and continued up the path with me, leaving Fen behind to negotiate with Reaver.

"Not worried those two psychos gonna kill each other?" Glass asked me.

I sniffed. "Nah. Fen's doing better at keeping himself in check these days."

"I think that's less Fen and a whole lotta D.T., don't you?"

I looked back over my shoulder at Fen and Reaver who had their heads together and were working out the rules of their impending engagement.

"Guess we'll find out," I said dryly.

He switched subjects on me and asked, "Who you think Dragon is gonna send our way?"

I shook my head and said truthfully, "Your guess is as good as mine, bro. Your guess is as good as mine."

We went and grabbed some grub and I kept an eye out for Marisol. She was out on the lake in this giant yellow raft with some of the ol' ladies from the other chapters. One I recognized from Oregon, the rest were unknowns – wait, except a petite auburn-haired beauty. She was with the mother chapter's SAA.

I tell you what. I got the chemistry between those two, but I was still sorely lost on the physics involved. That dude was a big bastard. Not as big as Dump Truck, but who the fuck was? Still, he was a big dude and she was a freaking *tiny* little thing.

I watched my girl for a little bit from behind my black aviators and noted that she was guarded. She was *always* guarded, that one. Her posture was stiff, leaning back a little too far into the raft. It was hard to read her expression from here, but if I had to guess, it was a mix of her usual resting bitch face – which I found adorable – and her cautious guardedness.

The girl was this concrete maze. Walls high, and just as you turned the corner with a bit of self-satisfaction at *thinking* you had her figured out and the path would be clear? Nope. Another wall, as if the whole labyrinth had shifted on you when you weren't looking. I don't think I'd ever met a woman so closed off, guarded, and standoffish, yet so pliable and eager to please me in my life.

Truth be told, it bothered me; not knowing what she was hiding. It bothered me a lot, but there wasn't anything I could do about it. My focus had to be elsewhere. I could and would start digging when we got back home, though. I had only a short amount of time to do it in. A scant week, maybe a week and a half, depending on how far out I could push the run to buy myself some time with her.

Of course, I could tell she didn't want to go back. Her light quips about being indispensable to me, about how much I would miss her when she was gone, weren't lost on me at all.

She was right. I would miss her, for a variety of reasons.

She'd been a steady hand, having meals ready, anticipating what I'd need before I even knew I needed it quite often – food, a drink, hell even a joint. She always happened to come up with it when I needed it. A quiet support, a shadow – I was sure one that had probably heard too much by now but if she had, the girl was world-class at keeping it to herself. She knew just when to keep her mouth shut and just when I wanted that same lush mouth wrapped around my cock.

Fuck, I was getting hard just looking at her, leaned back, sipping from her red Solo cup. Long toned legs stretched out in front of her, flat stomach glistening along her honey-golden skin with whatever sunscreen or baby oil she'd slathered on herself. She looked damn inviting. Laying out like some offering on that raft under the sun in her little black bikini.

I think I exhausted her last night, but I was set to do it all over again tonight.

"Mav, come have a beer with me." I roused myself out of my self-indulgent musings and looked over at who had spoken.

"Sure thing, absolutely," I said. The mother chapter's VP practically never smiled unless it was at his lady or his kids. Even now, his mouth set in a grim line, wraparound sunglasses holding his long hair up, he simply gave me a nod and turned to the coolers lined up against the lodge walls.

"Something you need outta me?" I asked him, taking the bottle he passed me.

"Just trying to get a feel about how you *really* feel about what's going on in your region," he answered and took a pull off his beer. I echoed the motion and searched his face. He was good at giving nothing away by his expression. It was a talent I'd cultivated as well.

This was going to be an interesting chat.

"I'm good with it, brother," I said, and I meant it.

"Yeah? What about the rest of your crew?" he asked, and I figured Reaver must have caught up to him and spilled about Fen's misgivings.

"My crew trusts me implicitly, man. They'll be on board."

Dray nodded and said, "Come take a walk with me, my pops wants me to introduce you to a couple of guys."

I gave a nod and we strolled down toward the water's edge.

"You know many of the nomad fellas?" he asked me as we came to a stop with a view of the dock and the blob across the lake. It looked like Cipher was on it and a guy from another chapter was about to launch his ass into the ether.

I grinned at the sight and said, "A few. Lone Wolf comes through on the regular."

"Wolf, huh? He's a good dude."

"Very. He's helped us out in the past. If he would be willing to settle down, I'd love to have him on the other side of the Cascades. He'd be amazing."

Dray turned down the corners of his mouth and nodded. I think it was supposed to be noncommittal on his part but to me it just looked like he was trying to suppress a smile. I hid mine with a pull off my beer. Lone Wolf was at the top of my shortlist to be my chapter's neighbor and it looked like he was on Dragon's radar for the job, too.

Good fuckin' deal.

"Lemme ask you something; no bullshit."

"No bullshit," Dray agreed. "Shoot."

"Who you thinkin'?" I asked.

He nodded slowly and sighed. "You're a smart dude Maverick so I'll cut the shit so long as you can keep it on the down low."

I nodded. "You know I can, and I will, brother. I want this shit to work and I get it, the optics could be bad, you lettin' me have a hand in the deciding."

"That's why I'm standing here and not my pops. Not that the optics are much better," he muttered.

"Straight up, brother, I would avoid bringing in anyone from the east coast," I said. "They're good dudes out that way, but the P.N.W. isn't their speed. We're mellower out my way. East coast dudes tend to be wound tighter than a goddamn Timex and are liable to spring when shit doesn't go their way. You feel me?"

"I do know what you mean," Dray said nodding. "We weren't even considering him if it makes you feel better."

"You have no idea," I said dryly.

We were talking about a guy out of Boston, Southie. Dude was seriously rough, and he'd caused a bit of a dustup down in California a while back. I didn't want him anywhere near our operation.

"Any other hard 'nos'?" he asked. I listed off a couple more names and he nodded. "Now tell Santa what you want for Christmas," he said, and I chuckled.

"You get Lone Wolf to agree and you've already given me all I want for Christmas, my man."

"One man does not make a chapter," he said, and I nodded.

"No, he does not, but there's only one head that wears the crown and Lone Wolf is the right kind of man if you know what I'm sayin'."

"I do, and Dragon'll get him, don't you worry about that."

"Ryder would make a good second," I said.

"Ryder? Really?" Dray looked surprised by that and then thoughtful. He nodded along slowly the more he thought about it and shot off a text with his burner.

"Where Ryder goes, Dane follows," I said.

"I know, that's right," Dray mumbled, dark dragon-glass eyes skirting over the screen as something came back. "What about Riot?" he asked and looked up and over at me.

I grunted. "Never heard of him."

Dray grinned and we carried on negotiating and talking over who might be a good fit for the territory. I was keenly aware that even though Idaho and Eastern Oregon had reps from their respective clubs, including higher leadership – I was the only one he spoke to. Either that, or the others were being spoken to on their own, outside my presence. Why I couldn't fathom but Dragon had his methods, same as I had mine.

It took longer than I would have liked. My little *zaychik* had come out of the water at one point, had stalked toward me with that sexy sway of her hips she was wholly unaware of and I swear, it killed a part of me to subtly put up a hand and wave her off with the look that meant *club business*. She lifted her chin half defiantly, half in acknowledgement before changing her trajectory up the path through the garden beds back here leading up to the lodge's back side and the coolers under the deck.

"Zaychik!" I called after her and she looked back over her shoulder, her long dark hair swept over the opposite giving me a perfect view of her sexy back. I had the sudden urge to pull that bikini top off her with my teeth. Instead, I held up my beer with one hand and two fingers on my opposite hand to indicate what I wanted.

She nodded once, and it took some real effort to tear my eyes away from her. Dray chuckled beside me.

"I thought you were too white to like it spicy," he said.

"She's not what she seems," I said and sighed.

"By the looks of her, she's a little Habanero." He finished off his beer.

"She's sweeter than that," I said. "More like my little cinnamon girl."

"*Canela* girl, nice. What did you call her just now?"

"*Zaychik.*"

"What the fuck is that?"

"Loosely translated to English it means little rabbit or bunny."

"Nah." Dray grinned and shook his head. "*Canela* for sure."

"To be fair, you don't know her like I do." I polished off the last dregs of my beer and Dray nodded.

"This is true, this is true. Where'd you pick her up?"

"Yakima. Fruit grower's family."

"Yeah?" He arched an eyebrow.

"Not sure what's up, but she wanted out of there *so bad*. I worked out a deal with them, and her, but I couldn't tell you what's going on there. It's been a little low on my list of priorities."

Dray grunted as we watched her come toward us with three glass bottles. Two beers and a Coke.

"Time to get that off the back burner, my friend. She's a little hottie."

"She's a keeper, alright," I agreed just before she got back into earshot. The only problem I was having was the 'how' of it. Keeping her, I mean.

"Hey," she said softly as she came up to us. She held out the beers to us. Dray and I each took one.

He took my empty from me and said, "Just a sec," before walking up through one of the flower beds to one of the big recycling cans set out around the property to collect the dead soldiers.

"You doin' alright?" I asked Marisol.

She nodded, but didn't speak, choosing instead to take a draw off her Mexican Coke. She looked like she belonged in one of their damn commercials. She was beautiful enough. The only thing that wasn't commercial worthy about her was how tired she looked.

"Tired?" I asked and she nodded and sighed as Dray dropped back down beside us.

"I think I just need to eat something," she said, and I smiled, touching her shoulder lightly, her smooth, soft skin tantalizing. When she didn't flinch or shy away, I stepped in and curved my whole arm around her shoulders. She swayed slightly on her feet and leaned into me and I liked that. That she was comfortable with me today.

"Marisol, this is Dray. Dray, this is Marisol." I made the introductions.

"Hi," she murmured.

"Hey, Marisol." Dray winked at her and graced her with one of his rare smiles. Her timid one grew slightly in return.

"Anybody give you any flak?" I asked.

"No," she said, and for a second, I had to ask myself if it was a little too emphatic or if I was just reading into something that wasn't there.

"Did I hear something about food?" Dray asked. "You hungry?"

Marisol warmed to him a little bit more and nodded.

"Dinner's about to be up. Come on, let's go grab some grub." He jerked his head in the direction of the back deck and she smiled and nodded, and we turned that direction.

Dray gave me a meaningful look and I gave a nod. *To be continued* on that other thing we'd been talking about.

"Are you done for the day?" Marisol asked softly when she was sure Dray wouldn't hear as he greeted a couple of men up by the stairs leading up to the back deck.

"I think I can be if you need me to be," I said and arched a brow. I both was and wasn't surprised at how much I wanted to hear her say it... that she needed me to be.

I only half got what I wished for. She nodded silently, her look pensive and I couldn't resist. I leaned forward and lowered my lips to hers. She tipped her face toward mine and kissed me back, her lips soft against mine. The smell of coconut and rose petals drifted to my nose, a mix of her lotion and whatever sunscreen she'd used.

It was crazy how she took over every one of my senses. Soft, heady, sweet, and so fucking easy on the eyes, her soft little sigh of surrender as she yielded to my deepening the kiss was music to my ears. I loved it when she gave in like this. When it felt like she didn't hold anything in reserve.

Too soon, she caught herself and backed off.

"You good?" I asked her, voice pitched low and only for her ears.

"Yeah," she whispered gently, but pride swelled in my chest at her breathy, slightly stunned tone. Yeah. I took her breath away. I knew *exactly* the kind of effect I had on her and it was honestly all I ever wanted. To affect someone so deeply and honestly have them have the same effect on me.

I pulled her lithe body into the shelter of my own and held her for a minute, resting my chin on the top of her silky hair and breathing her in.

"It's gonna get cold out here when the sun goes down, you got a cover up or something?" I asked.

"No, but if it's okay, I would honestly just like to take a hot shower and crawl into bed after dinner. I'm tired."

I chuckled and asked, "You sure you don't want to watch the fights tonight? Reaver's going up against Fen."

She looked up at me with those wide, honey-brandy-soaked brown eyes of hers and blinked once, slowly as she tried to decide if she'd heard me right.

"Let me go get dressed."

"I'll fix you a plate while you do, how's that?" I asked and she blushed prettily.

"Aren't I supposed to be doing that?"

I stepped in and smacked her on the ass with a grin. "Go on, git. See you in a few."

She smiled at me and bit her bottom lip alluringly, casting a long look over her shoulder as she complied and went to get dressed. I got in line to fix her a plate; eyes fixed on her gorgeous ass as she walked away.

CHAPTER TWELVE

*M*arisol...

When I returned in a pair of shorts and my favorite peasant blouse over my bikini, Maverick was halfway down the long buffet set up, loaded with barbecue favorites. I went to him and touched his back and he turned, licking coleslaw dressing off his thumb as he gave me a sexy wink.

I smiled to myself, took the plate he handed me, and continued down the table with him, a little self-conscious and worried that someone was going to call me out or get pissed I was cutting in line. Nobody said anything, though.

We sat with some of the men from the Oregon and Idaho chapters at one of the picnic tables. I knew some of them from home.

There was a guy from Idaho, who wasn't huge but was *big* as in he was probably no more than five foot nine or so and he had to be four hundred and fifty pounds. He always smelled of a mixture of my father's cologne and engine grease, his big hands blackened with it in spotty patches that just never seemed to come completely clean.

He went by Baer, and one of the Eastern Oregon guys, an even *bigger* dude by the name of Buff, which apparently stood for Big Ugly Fat Fucker, was asking him about his first bike or something.

Baer laughed and said, "I still have it, it's in my garage back home."

"Oh, yeah?"

"Uh-huh, sweet 1990 FLHTC full dress Harley," Baer said.

"Nice," Maverick commented as we took seats down and across from Baer.

"Yah, skin a nice two-tone candy apple red with gold trim, soft lower fairing and highway pegs with heel rests. I upgraded her tranny from a four-speed to a five-speed for better power on the highway. I still ride her around town, but she just isn't reliable like she used to be for these long-haul rides anymore. I had to upgrade."

"Sounds like a sweet ride, brother."

"Better than any broad I've had lately, that's for sure," Buff commented. Baer grinned wide and exposed a missing eye tooth, the one next to it and further back missing too. Despite his graying beard and short ponytail, the gap-toothed grin made him somehow endearing. Baer was one of the most affable of the Idaho chapter by far and I always had a soft spot for him. Mostly because he would share his sugar-free butterscotch or strawberry hard candies with my little brother and he almost always had some on hand.

He winked at me and slid one of those strawberry candies wrapped in the shiny strawberry printed cellophanes down the table in my direction. I smiled back shyly and swept it toward me and shoved it into the pocket of my short shorts.

I listened to the men talk. Mostly about motorcycles and the mechanics, some about what parts Ironheart Salvage had to offer them for whatever repairs or varying projects they wanted to undertake regarding their bikes.

Maverick nodded, answered what he could and if he didn't have the answer? He would send the odd text or two back home to Dump Truck to get it.

That was Maverick, though. Always ahead, always ready to make another dime. He even made a few sales right then and there, texting orders to D.T. and the guys calling in payment to the yard over their phones. Some of them would even have their parts waiting for them by the time they got home.

For me, it was boring, but I wasn't there for the scintillating conversation. I was there to eat my dinner and to look pretty on Maverick's arm. Both, I managed to accomplish in silence for the most part, unless I was asked something directly.

I kept my answers short and to the point and tuned out anything I felt like I wasn't necessarily supposed to hear; pretending that I didn't see the furtive glances or notice the quick changes in the course of conversation when it strayed too close to 'club business.'

I was an old practiced hand at it after all, simply trading 'family business' for 'club business' when I'd stolen away on the back of Maverick's bike.

I turned my head and watched as several of the bikers from varying chapters started grooming a portion of the lakefront into a sort of impromptu fight ring, taking rakes to the sandy pebbled shore and staking out Tiki torches at regular intervals in a big circle. They dragged crude benches and stacking pallets to provide places to sit, stand, and stand higher still to provide views of the crude arena.

It sent both a thrill and a chill down my spine in equal measure.

"You sure you know what you're getting into?" Mav asked beside me, and I twisted on my seat and startled slightly. Fen was standing just the other side of Maverick, mammoth arms crossed over his big chest, staring over our heads at the ring taking shape just as I had been, except there was no chill in his blue eyes – just calculation and anticipation. The thrill etched into the hard planes and angles of his face, his smile nearly hidden by his blond beard, braided in places, and decorated with beads.

I couldn't see his woven and braided Mohawk. He had a hood up over his head, the sleeves cut off the thin sweater, his biker cut over it. It was an ominous and eerie look, as though he had stepped straight out of the past into modern day. His tattoos of whorls and ancient designs stood out beneath his pale skin. He was every inch the Viking warrior and I couldn't understand why Maverick sounded worried when I followed Fenris' gaze to his supposed adversary.

Fenris' gaze was locked on a wiry man, tall and slender yet absolutely shredded. His muscles stood out on his wiry frame like whipcord over bone, every motion as he stretched causing them to coil and lengthen like a work of art beneath his skin which was decorated with pale, slivery scars where it didn't hold ink.

Not that the man was heavily tattooed, quite the opposite in fact. He had only a few. Something sleek and long on the inside of each forearm, a spot of dark blue at the corner of one eye and where his cutoff cargo shorts rode low on his hips, some kind of loop tattooed at each hip descending below his waistband.

When he turned around, high on the back of his shoulder was the unmistakable art of the Sacred Hearts logo picked out in simple black and white.

I tried to understand why Maverick was concerned. I mean, the wiry man looked like no match for Fenris in a fist fight.

"I'm sure," Fenris said and his tone was deep, holding an almost oily quality of predation to it. It sent a shiver down my spine and Mav's arm automatically went around my shoulders.

"Cold?" he asked me, and I nodded mutely, staring out over the sand at the man that Fenris had apparently chosen to fight.

"That guy looks like he's gonna get creamed, is he crazy?" I asked. Maverick chuckled.

"If it were a fist fight, I wouldn't be worried," he said.

"It's not?" I asked.

"Nope."

"What kind of fight is it then?" I asked.

"Knife fight," Fenris intoned. He spit on the ground off to one side, grunted and plodded away, in the direction of the ring.

I felt my mouth drop open in a little 'o' of incredulity.

"He's serious, isn't he?" I asked.

"Dead serious," Maverick affirmed.

"That changes everything, doesn't it?"

I tore my eyes away from where Fen and the wiry guy were talking, their faces both neutral and very serious and looked up at Maverick who's deep, dark blue eyes were searching my face.

"Why do you think?" he asked.

"Fenris is big, *really big*, and powerful but he's not as fast as that guy. He can't be with all that bulk to him. Can he? A knife fight is about speed over power."

Maverick's lips quirked up at one corner and I could almost swear a shine of pride glimmered deep in his gaze which oddly suffused me with warmth that he would look at me like that.

"Fenris might surprise us," he said, "but you're spot on, *Zaychik*."

I turned my head to look back at Fenris and his opponent, a bare-footed club member from parts unknown behind them, grooming the ring they were about to fight in. Maverick pressed a kiss to my temple that I was barely aware of as I muttered, *"Los chicos blancos son tan estúpidos."*

A booming crack of laughter just behind and to my other side of me made me jump.

"I don't disagree with you there, Chica, *but I think it's just boys in general. White, brown, it makes no difference."* The man who spoke did so in flawless Spanish back to me and I swallowed hard. He was Mexican, like me, obsidian eyes full of laughter and mischief and could only be Dray's father. When I looked at him, it was as though looking into Dray's future. The only difference between the two of them was that Dray was taller.

"Dragon," Maverick intoned with a deference I had never heard from him. The respect of the men around us a palpable thing as they looked up to Dragon from our sitting position.

"Your boy got a death wish going up against Reaver in a knife fight?" Dragon asked. Mav smiled and shook his head.

"Reaver asked and Fen isn't one to back down from a challenge. He may surprise us," Maverick said.

Dragon gazed out over the sand at the two of them who locked hands around the other's forearm in a strange handshake.

Dragon grunted and said, "I doubt it. No offense."

"Truth be told, I think the only thing those two *do* match up in is they're both fuckin' crazy," Mav said.

Dragon chuckled and nodding, said, "I know that's right."

"Sun's gettin' real low," Buff said, and Dragon nodded.

"Let's get this show on the road," he said with a heavy sigh and he plodded forward, out toward the dock.

"What's happening?" I asked.

"Memorial," Maverick murmured.

"Oh."

He urged me up, and it seemed everyone was filtering down to the lakeside – and I do mean everyone – from club member to ol' lady, prospect to *prostituta del club*.

I stayed by Maverick's side and drifted along the sand with him to a place at the water's edge.

Paper lanterns were being passed through the crowd, the sun dipping low in the sky, darkness starting to rise from the water and filter out from the surrounding trees, creeping out from doorways and seeping from beneath the lodge's deck. Bics and Zippos alike clicked, flints hissing and spitting, flames passing among the tea light candles as Dragon gave his benediction from the dock.

It was beautiful. Even more beautiful still when Sunshine, one of the ol' ladies from the mother chapter that I'd met and hung with earlier in the day, began to sing as paper lanterns sailed softly out on the water, pinpoints of softly glimmering light to match the holes poked by God in the sky, letting his heavenly light shine through the dark.

I kissed my thumbnail and pressed my knuckle to forehead, heart, and each shoulder in the sign of the cross, murmuring my good wishes and prayers into the night.

The somber moment flitted along the breeze filling each of us in turn with deep emotion, the heaviness of the moment gradually lifting, dissipating slowly like thick and heavy mist under the onslaught of rising temperatures.

The rising temperatures in this case were more due to the free flow of alcohol and the excitement of the impending fights, though. Maverick had me go get him another beer while he chatted with some of the other guys. When I returned, one of them looked me over in a way that made my skin crawl. I didn't know him, had never seen him in Washington, anyway.

"So, she your ol' lady?" he asked, licking his bottom lip suggestively while staring at me a little too hard, a little too long.

God, he was old enough to be my father! Dirty, hair stringy around the red bandana that cut a wide swath across his forehead, his face had a scar that ran in a vertical seam under one eye in a straight line to disappear under his chin.

His dirty patched vest read 'Dumpster' and honestly it fit for a variety of reasons.

Maverick's smile never faltered as he tucked his arm over my shoulders and drew me into his side.

"She's with me," he said flatly, and Dumpster's eyebrows went up.

"Yeah, but is she your ol' lady?"

"Doesn't matter," Maverick declared and reiterated with emphasis, "*She's with me*, brother."

"Alright," Dumpster said with a laugh, holding up his hands in surrender. "Okay, no disrespect."

"None taken, no lines crossed," Maverick said but his look wasn't friendly or nearly as nonchalant as the motion of taking a swig from his beer.

"No lines crossed," Dumpster echoed, eyeing me one last time. I suddenly felt an extreme need to shower as we all shifted and started heading for the ring drawn in the sand.

The back of Dumpster's vest read 'New Mexico' and I was grateful that our paths would likely never meet again. Still, I tucked myself a little tighter into Maverick's side and made sure that if for some reason I couldn't stay close to him that I would remain close to one of the other guys who had ridden out here with us.

I felt better when Tic-Tac and Derry walked over and took up the space on the other side of me from Maverick. I felt even better when Mav muttered to them, "Keep an eye on him where Marisol is concerned," when Dumpster's retreating back was far enough out of earshot.

"You got it, Boss," Derry said, his expression thoughtful – blue eyes calculating in the torchlight.

Our attention was soon taken up by the animated club brother from parts unknown in the middle of the ring of torches. He was, apparently, the master of ceremonies and de facto fight announcer for the evening.

…let the games begin, I guess.

I had hoped that by eating something, my energy levels would come up some, but that hadn't been the case. I didn't think I was going to be good for many fights, but I really did want to see Fenris in action. I had been curious about the actual abilities of the men who rode through my little slice of life for a very long time. Though they exuded danger and cunning, I'd never had the occasion to see it for myself just how much of it was true versus just them fronting… if they ever were fronting.

I scraped my bottom lip between my teeth as two men from parts unknown entered the ring for, as the announcer had declared, was to be a good old-fashioned street fight.

There wasn't any telling where they were from as they'd removed their vests and stood, hands lightly wrapped for support, but otherwise bare from the waist up.

I'd seen some bare-knuckled boxing matches between some of the boys at home, but that didn't hold a candle to the savagery that unfolded in front of me now. These guys didn't *stop*. Not until one of them was unconscious in the dirt.

Cheers went up, fists rose into the dark, some of them with money clutched in them as bets were won and surrendered all around me.

My mouth was dry as Fenris stepped between two torches and into the circle of firelight. He held a big hunting knife in one of his big paws and his skin glistened with sweat as he jogged slightly in place and swung his big arms back, stretching and limbering up.

"He's lucky, he won't end up like me," an older guy on the other side of Mav said.

"Oh, yeah? How's that?" Maverick asked without looking at him. He held up a hand and flexed his fingers out, one of them refusing to extend.

"Y'see that? Cut my tendon clean in half in a knife fight like this. It ain't worked right since."

I bit my lips together and turned my attention back to Fen. I'd had faith that even though he might not *win*, that no permanent harm would befall him… up until now. Now, I was starting to doubt that very much.

The older guy with the messed-up finger laughed at the expression on my face as the crowd surged in a little tighter, bets being called, wagers set, and the two fighters, Fen and Reaver, who held a sharp looking little stiletto in one hand, squared off.

Heart in my throat, Reaver lunged, lightning quick, in Fen's direction. Fen leaped back and an awkward dance commenced between the two, neither one of them taking their eyes off the other, both of them a study in concentration.

The crowd cheered and jeered in equal measure but both fighters were locked inside their own heads, calculating, feinting; each trying to psych the other out and score a slick or a scratch against the other.

It was breathtaking to watch, a savage dance, a terrible beauty about it. Their athleticism undeniable, I suddenly understood the appeal of all those long-ago gladiator fights in Rome for the people's entertainment.

I held my breath, engrossed in the primal back and forth between the two men, gasping as each caught the other's wrist to hold the blades from them. Fen grinned savagely and head butted Reaver in the nose with a sickening crunch. Reaver's head snapped back, blood spurting from his nose and coating his teeth. His grinned a feral grin and I feared for them both. That neither would be able to contain whatever darkness that lived inside the other. That whoever won wouldn't be able to stop.

I found myself watching between my fingers, covering my eyes like with a horror movie yet unable to tear my eyes completely away.

The announcer shouted that it didn't count. That the first blood must be drawn by blade. The two competitors separated, and my heart edged into my throat when they circled again.

I caught myself praying for Fen. The other man, Reaver, was so *fast*. Moving in a blur, Fen was wearing down and then it happened. Fen leaped back, Reaver pressed on, and with a wide arcing slash he caught Fenris with the tip of his knife in a shallow but clean cut across Fen's stomach.

"Awww!" Fen straightened, his upper body going rigid, his head thrown back as his breath heaved. He dropped his chin to his chest and with a grin asked Reaver, "Best two out of three?"

I felt my heart plummet from my throat to my toes as the crowd went wild and Maverick laughed beside me. I let my breath out in a shuddering sigh.

I couldn't take anymore even if I wanted to. My hands shook, and I just wanted to be anywhere but here. I smiled up at Mav, hoping it wasn't too forced and said, "I'm really tired. Can I go to bed?"

"Sure thing, baby," he said, eyes a bit glassy with his buzz. He kissed me and I kissed him back.

"Cipher!" he called out and Cipher looked up from where he was a few men down from us. "Walk Marisol back to our room for me, would yah?"

"Sure, I gotta tap a kidney anyhow. C'mon, chick."

"Thanks." I smiled at Cipher and Maverick let me go.

"You good?" Cipher asked me when we'd drifted a ways from the crowd.

"Yeah," I said with a nod. "Just don't think my heart could take anymore."

"Aww!" He winked at me. "It's nice to know you care."

I was shocked a little to realize that I did… I really did.

When had that happened?

averick...

"She good?" I asked my secretary when he got back.

Cipher nodded, handed me a fresh beer and said, "Yeah, she's good. I think she was actually worried about our boy out there. Got to be a little too much for her."

Really now? I filed that away, but I'd be lying if I said it didn't put a smile on my face to hear it.

"What's that?" Fen asked, walking up. Tic-Tac handed him a towel and Cipher handed him a beer which he downed greedily while patting at the sweat and blood on his chest.

"Marisol was worried about you. Couldn't take anymore," I said. Fen grinned savagely and sniffed.

"She's a good girl," he said, and I smiled and nodded.

"That she is. Need stitches?" I asked.

"Nah, don't think so," he said.

"Better have the doc look at you anyway."

"I'm good."

I raised an eyebrow. "I'm sorry you took that as a suggestion instead of the order it was," I said dryly.

Fen laughed and said, "Alright, *Mom*."

I laughed back and said, "Fuck you." He went over to the mother chapter's damn doctor, who was set up at a table under a white easy up tent with a red cross painted on it, though.

"He held his own, your man," Dragon called over.

"That he did," I agreed and saluted the national pres with my beer.

"Come on over here, let's settle up," he said. I hadn't placed a wager, so I knew he meant to finish talking about Eastern Washington. Sounded like some decisions had been made and forewarned was indeed forearmed.

I went over and we drank while we talked.

The national president had a thing for tequila which wasn't always friendly when it came to me. Still, when the National P. told you to join him for a drink, you did just that. That shit fucked me up, though. Vodka was my usual go-to. I'd learned a long time ago tequila rhymed a little too close with *to kill yah* so I couldn't tell you if the result of those drinks was entirely my fault but it was about to shed a fuck of a lot of light into some dark corners.

By the time our talk concluded, I was pretty well wasted. Pleased at the result of said talks but *wasted,* it was time to take my ass to fuckin' bed.

Halfway back to the lodge I got an idea, lips curling into an evil grin as I dug the room key out of my front jeans pocket.

I slipped into the room I was sharing with Marisol and paused. She was asleep on her back, one hand resting on the pillow beside her head, the other by her hip and my cock was *instantly* hard.

I wanted to fuck her, and I mean down and *dirty*. I undid my belt and opened the front of my jeans, stroking myself as I looked down at her in the dim light through the window. I threw back the blankets and she was so out, she didn't even stir.

I didn't want her making a commotion, so I put my hand over her mouth. I mean, shit, she was safe. It was *me*. She inhaled sharply, those gorgeous eyes of hers flying wide as I climbed on top of her and slid into her. She was warm, wet, and waiting.

"Oh, yeah, baby," I groaned in her ear. "That's my good girl."

Did she dream of me? Was that why she was wet? Fuck, I wanted to know, but she felt so fucking good and I was enjoying the hell out of her.

I curse the fact that I was too fucking drunk to immediately realize that *she* wasn't enjoying herself – not one bit. I was several strokes in when I realized she was stiff as a fuckin' board and unresponsive beneath me. It took me even longer to realize the wet against my palm wasn't from her mouth, but from her tears.

I pushed up and took my hand off her mouth.

"Zaychik?"

She sobbed and I scrambled to my feet, my cock instantly shriveling.

"Marisol? Baby, what's wrong?"

She rolled off the opposite side of the bed, hands pressed over her mouth as she sobbed striding for the bathroom. I heard the spatter of her vomit hit the threshold before the scent assaulted my nose.

What the fuck?

"Marisol!" I went for her and damn my drunk fuckin' ass was too slow. I got to the bathroom just in time for her to shut it in my face, the lock clicking into place.

"Marisol?" I knocked and then I helplessly listened while she retched around uncontrollable sobs into the toilet on the other side of the locked door.

Shit.

I sobered up to the sound of her weeping as the shower ran. I couldn't do anything but wait her out, and I didn't want to make shit worse by pounding on the door and demanding fucking answers that I didn't have a fuckin' right to.

I'd stepped hip deep into one hell of a fucking hornet's nest, but *I didn't know.*

At any rate, it wasn't fucking about me right now. It was about her.

It was about getting the truth and if I had anything to say about it? It was about settling a fucking score.

The sobbing calmed to weeping, the weeping calmed to sniffles, and I waited calmly, ass planted on the floor, back to the wall beside the bathroom door, sobering up and patiently waiting her out.

The shower eventually cut, and I listened to the silence that echoed in its wake. A slight sniffle. Another. A shuffling movement. Another. The lock clicked and I bounded to my feet and waited. Several seconds went by, and my palm itched something fierce to put the fuckin' doorknob in it and twist, but I waited, and I waited some more, hands to my sides and finally the door opened.

Her sleek black hair hung limp and wet around her face. She wouldn't look at me. She just stood there looking small and afraid, *defeated*, wrapped from armpit to mid-thigh in one of the lodge's fluffy white towels.

"Come here," I whispered, and I held my arms open and waited.

She hesitated only briefly and practically fell into my arms, burying her face in the front of my tee beneath my cut as her pain welled fresh and hot from her beautiful eyes.

"I'm so sorry, baby. I am so sorry," I whispered against her hair and I held her tight against me while her emotions raged, swamping her, sweeping her under and drowning her in pain and sorrow.

"I've got you, baby. You're safe with me, I promise," I whispered, and she *was*. I hadn't known. I hadn't even *guessed,* and I felt like a fuckin' fool.

It took some time for the second squall to pass, but eventually it did, and I simply stood with her, waiting for her to make a move. By now, I was as sober as a fuckin' judge and in that place where I was so white hot angry, I was as calm and still on the inside as a winter's day – cold and ready to kill. I just needed a fuckin' target.

"Who did what, baby? You gotta talk to me, now. No more secrets."

She sniffed and pushed back from me and I let her, but I didn't let her go. Instead, I helped her to the bed and sat her down on the one side of it, taking a seat beside her.

She wouldn't look at me, and I didn't like it. I preferred her silent defiance and iron resolve much more, but I guess there wasn't any fronting now. The cat, as it were, was out of the bag. The genie out of its bottle and there wasn't any putting it back in.

I tipped her chin with gentle fingers and she met my gaze. The raw pain in her gaze turned my resolve to steel.

"Talk to me," I whispered, and I let the note of pleading in my voice ring clear. I was absolutely fucking *desperate* to make this better somehow.

"What does it matter?" she uttered dispassionately, and I raised my chin slightly, looking down at her ominously.

"It matters," I said. "Now *talk to me...*" I wasn't asking anymore, and she gasped at the look on my face. Fear flitted just behind her eyes and I couldn't say I was entirely sorry about it. I needed the whole story before I could make a play or set anything in motion.

"Who, what, when, where, why, and how," I said. "One at a time. Rack 'em up and knock 'em down, babe."

She took in a shuddering breath and searched my face and with a slight strangled noise I couldn't quite identify, started talking.

"My uncle," she said and closed her eyes. It was as if a visible burden had been set down, her face smoothing, losing some of the tightness around the edges. I stayed silent, knowing that it would wear on her. Knowing the need to fill it would overpower her. I wasn't wrong.

"I was twelve, the first time that it happened. He –" She swallowed hard, tears leaking out from beneath her closed eyelids. "He came into my room and put his hand over my mouth, climbed on top of me and–" Her shoulders rounded, and she hunched in on herself.

"I get the picture," I said softly. If I could spare her, I would, she'd been through enough by this point... *and it's all your fuckin' fault for not pressing the issue sooner*, I silently berated myself. I put a hand on her shoulder and gripped it firmly to support her, whispering, "Take your time."

She took several deep breaths and said, "I told *Abuela*."

"What did she do?" I prompted when she remained in miserable silence.

"She lost her shit. Called me a liar and beat me with a belt."

"Fuck."

"I tried telling a teacher, school counselors, none of it helped. CPS was called and *Abuela*, she always knew what to say. She convinced them I was a liar and a problem child. No one would listen to me, so I finally stopped trying… he moved when I was sixteen but, um, damage done I guess." She shrugged helplessly and I stayed silent.

She'd been betrayed by literally *everyone* who was supposed to protect her. My rage was churning in my gut, but she didn't need my rage. Not yet. Right now, she needed my empathy.

"I don't know why," she said.

"The why of it isn't on you, Marisol," I told her and swallowed hard myself. "The why of it is because he's a sick fuck."

She wouldn't look at me, fixing her eyes on an empty patch of carpet instead.

"What are you going to do?" she asked finally, her voice barely audible.

"Never you mind that, that's for me to figure out – later. Right now, I'm going to find you something to wear and tonight, I'm going to give you some room to breathe."

"You're leaving?" she asked and the note of alarm in her voice gave me pause.

"Not if you don't want," I said.

"What about our deal?" she asked sharply.

"Deal's changed, baby girl, and I'm not upset or sorry about it."

"But, Mateo!"

"Hush," I ordered. "Deal's *changed,* it's not *off.* You'll get out and I'll help you get your brother."

"Really?" She sounded so hopeful, and that note of hope in her voice was so heartbreakingly tenuous.

"Really."

"So… so, you believe me?" she whispered, and again she wouldn't look at me. She was hanging on by a thread, had been so strong, all by herself, for so long… *shit.*

"There's no faking that kind of reaction, girl. Of course, I believe you. I believe you and *I am so fucking sorry…*"

"Don't be," she said gently but sharply. "You didn't know."

"I should have guessed."

She snorted indelicately and looked at me then.

"Sorry your crystal ball was out of order," she said sarcastically, and I felt my lips twitch, barely resisting a smile. It was remarkable, watching her walls go back up in real time.

"Things are going to be different from here on out," I promised her and her expression – God, I've never seen anyone look so *tired,* so *weary*.

"Things will never change, Maverick," she said quietly. "I learned that a long time ago."

I pulled her against me, tucking her head under my chin, holding her tight.

"Things are gonna change, baby. Mark my words," I whispered savagely.

She didn't say anything, just slipped her arms around my waist and let me fucking hold her.

Trouble was that the damage was already done. There wasn't any protecting her from the big bad. It'd already been living inside her heart and head for years by now.

I tell you what, Karma was riding back to Washington and it was bringing hell with it. Some motherfuckers were fixin' to die. They just didn't know it yet.

I couldn't unilaterally make this type of decision, though. I needed to talk to my men. Get their take… so, I dressed Marisol in one of my clean tees and a spare clean pair of my boxers and laid down with her, holding her close, stroking her hair, waiting for her breathing to deepen and even out as I stared sightlessly into the dark, cogs and wheels going in my brain.

When she was finally out, it was too late to really do anything, but I wasn't going to get any sleep. So, I thought, planned, schemed, and generally just did what I did best. I Plotted like a motherfucker on how to get what I wanted and yet keep myself and my club off law enforcement's radar.

Of course, there was only so much I could plan for without knowing what the guys were going to think of this.

That in and of itself would be a delicate operation. I was sure Marisol wouldn't want them knowing her business, but that wasn't how club life worked. There were no secrets among the club.

I sighed and dropped into a light and uneasy sleep, but I was back awake before long, the birds chirping in the pre-dawn outside the lodge's windows.

CHAPTER FOURTEEN

*M*arisol...

He believed me. I'd seen it written all over his face by the dim light through the little room's window. He believed every word I'd said, and he was silently seething on my behalf.

It was more than a little mind-blowing to finally be believed after so long. I really didn't think it was possible. It was certainly vindicating to a degree, but by the same token, I didn't want to get my hopes up too high that it would change anything. I mean, what was to stop him from making the ride back to Washington and dropping me somewhere that was anywhere that just wasn't his problem anymore?

Still, it was hard *not* to get my hopes up when he held me like he did. Tight to his body, with this utter savagery to it, like he would straight murder anyone who dared come near me.

I couldn't help myself. I leaned into that embrace and pretended for the time being that that was precisely the intent with which he wrapped his arms around me.

We'd sat like that for a long time, with Maverick gently rocking me and stroking his hand over my hair. He didn't say anything. I don't honestly thing there was much of a need to. I mean, what was there to say?

He dressed me in one of his tees and a clean pair of his boxers and laid down with me, holding me gently, cuddling me, and I soaked it up shamelessly.

Comfort wasn't something I was used to being shown and it honestly meant the world to me… even if I didn't think it would last, I would take what I could get.

By morning, the spell was broken, though. I woke alone. The light in the room told me it was still morning, but I didn't know by how much and I wouldn't until I looked at an actual clock.

I looked around, relieved that Mav's stuff was still in the corner where I'd stacked it neatly alongside mine. He was still here. I doubted he would have taken off without me but… well, let's just say I couldn't put anything past anyone anymore.

I sighed heavily and got up, going through a half-paced morning routine of brushing hair and teeth and finding an outfit to wear.

I went for more covered than not – one of my traditional light peasant blouses and a pair of shorts. The blouse was one of my favorites. A black linen-type material, brightly embroidered at the neckline, along the wide short sleeves and hem. I gave it a French tuck and slid my feet into a pair of simple dark leather sandals.

I was feeling raw and vulnerable, so I stopped and took my time to do my full makeup. I don't know. It helped. Made me feel like I had a mask to hide behind. Made me feel more composed.

I slipped a pair of sunglasses up on top of my head to hold back my hair and stuffing the spare room key into the shallow pocket of my denim shorts, I slipped out of the room and let out a breath. Ready or not, it was time to face the day and the rest of the bikers out there.

"Hey, have you seen Mav?" I asked Sunshine who was already up and helping some of the lodge staff put out a late breakfast. It was already past ten in the morning and a lot of people hadn't so much as stirred – which wasn't surprising in the least. These guys treated noon like it was the new nine am.

"Oh, yeah. He and the rest of your chapter are off in the picnic area over by the cabin. Take the fork in the path to the left through the trees but make sure they know you're coming."

"Okay, thanks." I smiled, and she smiled back, and I went in the direction she'd pointed to.

I stopped at the end of the trail, outside the trees and turned my face into the sun for a moment, letting it warm me... closing my eyes and soaking in the fiery red glow through my lids. I felt as though I was marching into the unknown and it wasn't a good feeling.

I didn't know what to expect, but I would be lying if I said I expected more kindness. That wasn't how life worked in my experience. I'd had knives buried in my back so deeply I couldn't reach them to pull them out. They were still there, the flesh grown around them, the lessons from them so deeply ingrained, I would never be rid of them, would never heal, and I would never make the same mistakes that put them there in the first place again.

With a sigh I moved forward, the trail neatly maintained, lined with rounded river rock on either side, my footsteps muffled on the hard-packed pea gravel by the accumulation of leaf litter pulverized over time and the native soil. Together they formed a soft loam that all but silenced my tread and I could see why Sunshine had warned me to make my presence known... Of course, I didn't heed her advice, not when I spotted them through the trees gathered under the little lakeside gazebo out over the water. Not when I heard them clearly talking about me.

"Jesus Christ, girl's had it rough."

I froze.

"I never would have guessed," Glass Jaw said, rubbing a hand over the scruff on his chin, his mouth disappearing behind it in his dismay.

I swallowed hard and stood rooted to the spot. I wasn't hiding, but I couldn't bring myself to speak. I stared at Maverick's back and felt a fresh hot knife of betrayal twist between my shoulder blades, the point buried so deep it protruded from my chest. The feeling of it so visceral, so *physical,* I put a hand to my chest, between my breasts to stem the outpouring of agony.

He'd told them... how could he?

"Why are you telling us this, Mav?" Dump Truck's voice rumbled out through the speaker on the phone Mav held in front of him, hidden from my view.

"You know why."

"Right." A big sigh sounding thin and reedy filtered through the sunshine and over the lake. "Discuss it more in depth when you get back here. Thanks for the heads-up."

"Might be coming in early and hot," Maverick said. "Let you know the decision on that when we finish up here."

"Copy that, fly low, fly fast and try not to win any awards."

"Later, brother."

The phone chirped in his hand and he sighed as tears slipped down my cheeks in scalding twin lines.

Jesus, did everybody *have to know?*

"So that brings us to our next order of business," Maverick declared.

"We need to decide if we're leaving now?" Fenris asked and he looked up from where he was crouched on one of the benches around the outer edge of the gazebo. He was straight across from the entrance in front of Mav, but he had the hood up on his sweater and his head bowed and hadn't seen me.

He looked up, his blue eyes piercing about to say something but whatever it had been, the words died on his lips before getting past when he spotted me.

"Shit," he grated, and all eyes turned in my direction.

I hugged myself, feeling like my guts were spilling out for all of them to see, to mock, to pity, to do with as they pleased.

The guys straightened, took a helpless step, stood from where they were sitting, but *no one* moved toward me.

Maverick looked back over his shoulder and stood off the edge of the central stone firepit built in the middle of the little building.

"Babe, how long you been standing there?"

"Long enough," I said dispassionately, and I couldn't help myself. I lit off in a string of the most colorful curses I'd ever heard in Spanish.

A few of the guys looked surprised, Tic-Tac looked amused, confirming my suspicions that he somehow knew a little of my first language and I suddenly hated them all; hated them all with a deep and fiery loathing that was only outmatched by the loathing for myself.

"Give us a minute, huh, guys?"

"Keep your eye on the prize, P. We leave today or what?" Tic-Tac demanded.

"In favor?" Glass Jaw asked and raised a hand. Hands shot up like mushrooms after a rain but Maverick never took his eyes off me.

"That does it," Fenris said. "Let's all go pack our shit." He lumbered in my direction and I stood my ground, refusing to quail as the men took the only way out of there that was available, passing me by as if they were water in a stream and I were a stone.

Their booted tread against the built-up berm of earth leading out to the structure were muted, but their footfalls heavier than mine.

I was suddenly torn between wanting them to leave and wishing they would stay so I wouldn't have to be alone with Maverick… the traitor.

We stood, the silence sweeping in, filling the space between us in the wake of the rest of the guys' exit.

"Why?" I demanded, voice hollow.

"Why did I tell them?" he asked.

"Why did you betray me?" I demanded. "I told you that in confidence and you just couldn't wait, could you?"

"No, Marisol, it's not like that –" He took a step forward and I took one back and he froze. "Baby, don't," he said, and his voice was sharp.

"Why, then?" I demanded again. "What is it like, Maverick? Make me understand because from where I'm standing you look like a real *maldito bastardo!*"

"I get that," he readily confessed, hands out in front of him, his dark hair flopping over his forehead in that way that I'd always found incredibly disarming and sexy, but his mouth was set in a grim line rather than that charming rakish grin that always disarmed me to the max and his indigo eyes glittered with some overwhelming yet undefinable emotion and I don't know why… but that look in his eyes, it both comforted me and scared me at the same time.

It was a look of a man who was *still here*. Who wasn't about to give up on me despite knowing my secret? The look wasn't what I was used to. It wasn't exploitative, it wasn't calculating… he radiated genuine concern and that honestly freaked me the hell out.

I hugged myself tighter, my nails digging into my own arms, palms sweating against my skin despite the still-cool temperatures that had yet to grow uncomfortable.

"I want to help you, but you have to understand how this works," he said softly and took a cautious step forward.

I didn't move and he didn't press.

"Talk," I barked, willing to hear him out – at least for now.

"Nothing goes down without my say-so," he said. "But by the same token, if I want to stay in charge, I can't just go off on a lark and do whatever I want, especially when what I *want* to do could negatively affect every man whose put any faith in me and my ability to lead. All we've got is trust and I can't go and break it. I can't go off and do what needs doing on my own here. I mean, I can, but I can't have my cake and eat it, too. The kind of thing I'm talking about, it doesn't get done without a conversation."

"What are you talking about?" I asked, and the danger in his eyes told me all I needed to know.

Still, he voiced it anyway for my benefit.

"Retribution."

"What if I don't want it?" I asked.

He shook his head slowly, his expression pitying and more than a little sad.

"It's out of your hands, my little *zaychik*."

"Why?" I demanded, straightening my back, squaring my shoulders.

A slow smile curled at the corners of his lips as he asked me, "You really going to stand there and go toe to toe with me over that piece of shit?"

"I don't care about him," I said savagely.

"Your little brother?" he asked.

"I don't know what *Abuela* would do," I confessed. "She's unpredictable."

Maverick nodded slowly and said, "You let me worry about that."

I let my hands drop to my sides and stared out over the lake.

"What are you going to do?" I asked softly.

"Not your concern, baby. All you need to know is he hurt what's mine and he's gotta pay for that."

I jerked my gaze back to Maverick's and raised an eyebrow, my arms going back around my middle defensively.

"Yours?" I asked.

"Mine," he affirmed and then committed this little expression of acknowledgement and amended, "If you'll let me keep you."

I felt my brow crush down into a frown.

"Why would you want to?" I demanded.

"Why wouldn't I?" he shot back and took another few slow steps, gauging if I would rabbit on him or not with each one. I stood my ground while he went on…

"You're beautiful, smart, and cunning. You make my life better in a shitload of small ways I didn't even realize existed. You take care of me better than anyone has before. You keep up with me sexually, you've never lied to me – and believe me, I would know if you had, and I would hope that you could recognize that I'm here for you and that I want to take care of you, too… I think we could make good partners, baby." He cupped my elbows gently with his hands and stepped lightly into my space, letting his hands fall to my hips and I couldn't help it. I let mine fall back to my sides, let him in.

What he was offering was all I'd ever wanted and was so very tempting… but I couldn't, for the life of me, decide if it was the right move to make and despite my best efforts, I couldn't see it. Couldn't look into the glass like a *bruja* and see the future and what it might look like for us.

I swallowed hard and whispered, "I don't know…"

His lips curved into a secret little smile and he pulled me into the shelter of his arms carefully, kissing the top of my head, his arms around me. The embrace radiated warmth and strength, two things I felt as though I had never really known, and I stood frozen in the circle of his arms and simply soaked it up, not knowing if I would ever have the opportunity again.

"Why do you want to help me?" I asked softly against the worn leather and dirty patches of his cut.

"Because without even realizing it, I think you've helped *me*," he said.

"I don't know how."

"And that's okay," he murmured and pressed another kiss to the top of my hair. He sighed and said, "We have to work on some things if this shit is gonna work, though."

"Like what?" I asked.

"Communication is a big one."

I nodded.

"No more keeping things from me," he said.

"What about you? You keep things from me all the time."

"It's for your own safety. Your own good," he answered.

I snorted and sighed, saying, "I'm so fucking sick and tired of 'do as I say and not as I do.'".

"Touché, I get that, but this world—"

"Is one I've lived in since birth," I said sharply. "You think I care for the American laws? The American dream is a nightmare for people like me."

He drew in a deep, slow breath and let it out equally as measured.

"Talking about your immigration status?" he asked to be clear.

"Not *mine* or my brother's. We were born here… not that it really matters."

"The outlaw life isn't exactly the same thing," he pointed out.

"What's more violence?" I asked him with a one-shouldered shrug. "The worst has already happened to me." My voice was soft, but the reality was a hard one. The worst *had* already happened to me. I'd already been raped; I'd already been beaten… what was death as compared to that? A release was how I looked at it. It didn't scare me anymore.

Maverick's expression was a mix of so many things then, but finally settled into a grim resignation, a deeply dark understanding. He smoothed his hands over me, and gripped my shoulders firmly, giving me a little bit of a shake.

"Nothing is ever going to happen to you ever again," he said with such a steely resolve I felt my eyes widen, but not in disbelief. Everything about him made me believe every word coming out of his mouth. My own mouth going dry just when I felt the need to work up enough spit to swallow.

I managed, but just barely.

"Go pack our things," he said firmly, letting me go. "I need to have a talk with Dragon." He raised his chin and looked down at me imperiously when I drew breath to argue, talking right over me before I had the chance. "I won't tell him any of the gory details if I don't have to. Just go pack our things. We're leaving today."

I nodded and turned and missed it keenly when the typical playful smack didn't land against my denim-clad ass.

CHAPTER FIFTEEN

Maverick…

I gave her space as much as I could as we headed back to Washington. The absolute highlight of those days was having her pressed against my back, the evenings were a little rougher. I wanted her, but I was afraid to instigate any touching that was more sex and less comfort. I held her at night, but I let her wear some of my clothes as pajamas and I kept myself covered, too.

She would lie silent beside me, fingertips plucking at my tee over my collarbone, and I desperately wanted to know what she was thinking… but I never asked. I just thought it was better to give her time, let her call the shots on what she did and didn't want to share.

I simply lay in the dark beneath her and let my own thoughts wander, usually to what all needed to be done when we got back home.

I had leverage, but I needed the rest of the men of the club on board before I went there.

There were also a lot of questions that needed to be answered, like where was her uncle now? How did we go about tracking him down? All things I wanted answers to but had to hurry up and wait until other hurdles were cleared first.

I had to take this in a certain order of operations when I desperately just wanted to make that motherfucker *bleed*.

Marisol sighed restlessly and I eased off on the hold I had on her. I hadn't even realized I'd had tensed, tightening my arms around her, until she made the sound.

"Do I gross you out, now?"

Her question was like a bucket of ice water.

"What? No!"

"Then why haven't you made a move since… you know… I told you."

She looked up at me as I looked down at her and her gaze was a second shock to my system – haunted, aching, the raw hurt in her eyes went to my heart and slashed it with a razor. I cupped her cheek in my hand and smoothed a thumb over her so-soft skin.

"I honestly don't know what to do with that part of things, *Zaychik*. I know that I don't want to make you uncomfortable. I know that I don't want to cause you more pain…" I trailed off, a little helpless. I hated that, but it was the truth. I didn't know what to do. I didn't know how to fix it and there was no *fixing it*. There wasn't an ounce of retribution I could wring out of her putrid fuck of an uncle that would even come close to making up for what she'd endured.

Impotent rage swept through me and I just barely kept it from seeping into my eyes which were still locked with hers. I didn't want her thinking I was angry with her. I could *never* be angry with her over this. I was sure, in time, I would be pissed with her – but not over something like this.

"Can I kiss you?" she asked, her voice muted, strained with her longing.

"You never have to ask me that," I whispered.

"You don't have to ask me either," she said quickly, and I put my thumb to her lips, silencing her.

"Just the opposite," I said. "I feel like I should *always* ask."

She gave me a small smile and sat up murmuring, "You can ask, but you don't *have* to ask."

"Yeah?" I asked, my heart in my throat as I watched her lips, transfixed by them as they drew nearer, ever so slowly.

"Yeah," she whispered, breath warm against my lips, an electric thrill traveling through me as the silken softness of her mouth barely touched mine in a timid little kiss.

I groaned, capturing her face between my hands, and deepening the kiss. I was a starving man desperate for the nourishment only her touch could provide.

She was in it to win it, her hands slipping under the blankets, one reaching into the front of my boxers, gripping my cock firmly but carefully, massaging the already hard length of my shaft with this little magic twist of her wrist that sent me groaning all over again.

The little whimper of desire that escaped her lips was like candy – sweet, sensual, sumptuous on my tongue and stoking the fires of my desire for her even higher.

I rolled her onto her back in the bed we shared, nudging her knees apart with mine, shoving the tee she wore out of my way so I could kiss my way down her body, spending a length of time at each of her pert breasts, lavishing the nipples with attention. Her fingers caressed through my hair, her ragged breathing encouraging me, her slight whimpering moans begging me for more and I was going to give her my all – just on my own time.

"Maverick," she gasped when I started to work my way down her flat, toned stomach, her voice breathy, begging, and I loved the sound of my name on her lips.

I hooked fingers into the waistband of the pair of my boxers she wore and swept them down her long, shapely legs to get them out of my way. I wanted my mouth on her sweet cunt. I could never get enough of her taste; like summer sunshine on my tongue, and I wasted no time in feasting on her. I wanted to rock her world, so I slid a finger up inside her, teasing around for the right spot – *there*, right there. I knew because her hips bucked, her voice flying from her mouth in surprise.

I dipped another finger up into her wetness and hooked them in a come-hither motion, riding the pads over that rough, plump, patch of her anatomy guaranteed to drive her wild.

Her reaction did not disappoint, one hand knotting into the sheets at her hip, the other pressed to her mouth, trying to muffle her cries as I worked her inside with my fingers and her clit with my tongue. My free arm I had to use as a bar across her hips, restraining her to the bed as I worked my magic on her.

She was dripping wet, hot, and slick against my hand, and I wanted to push her over the edge so damn bad. I wanted her to come screaming, wanted her to come so hard all she could do was lie there and take my cock whichever way I chose to give it to her.

I would not be denied, not unless she told me to stop, and by the heavily lidded and passionate look she gave me between the valley of her breasts, down the length of her perfect body where it met mine, she had no desire whatsoever to be done with this.

She tangled one of her hands in my hair and pulled my mouth tightly against her body where I brought it to life with my tongue.

Game on, my little rabbit... I thought to myself, and *really* teased her g-spot to life.

"Oh, *God...*" she gave a strangled cry and fell back against the hard plane of mattress beneath us as I wound her up to watch her go.

She came beautifully for me. I loved that about her. So expressive, she used her whole body freely when she felt this good. When she could get out of her own head which is right where I wanted her to be, away from the past, fully present, with me.

She arched off the bed, tits thrust artfully to the water-stained ceiling tiles of the cheap-ass motel room, her legs snapping closed around my head as she sat up, trying to get away from me – but I wouldn't have it. I kept at her clit with my tongue, kept at her G-spot with my fingertips and dragged her gasping and crying out through the storm of her orgasm and through to the other side.

She collapsed back onto the bed and I rose above her to take her in, lying beneath me, eyes glazed, pupils dilated in the soft lamplight. Her perfect breasts rising and falling as she tried to catch her breath, golden skin lightly dewy with a shimmer of sweat.

She looked fresh, beautiful, sated, and I smiled at that. I wasn't done. Not by a longshot, and she wasn't either. She just didn't know it yet.

Her eyes had closed as I massaged the tops of her thighs, watching her, letting her come back to herself some before I got ready to enter her. She looked up at me as I shifted, eyes widening in surprise, inhaling a sharp intake of breath as I slipped inside her so easily. She was so incredibly wet, so ready to have my cock inside her, eager for me – I could tell by the way she squeezed down on me, her pelvic floor muscles tightening against my shaft, drawing me in, even as she reached her arms up to me.

I came down to her and she grabbed my face between her hands and dragged my mouth to hers, her long legs winding around my hips, heels pressing against my ass, drawing me in close with her entire body.

I loved it when she was like this. It felt as though I disappeared into her being more than skin on skin. This was deeper than that. Transcending just fucking.

This was the purest form of *love me* I had ever encountered with a woman and I did. Moving slowly, I set a pace that would leave us both gasping and shaking. I set a pace that would make us both feel good and keep us right on that edge for as long as she didn't beg me to come or to make her come again.

I loved this, being like this with her. It was mind-blowing, the trust she put in me right now, after what had happened back at the lake. It was as though she forgave me with her entire body. As though she forgave me soul deep… and I felt both grateful and wholly undeserving at the same time.

I should have known. I should have pried a lot sooner. I shouldn't have taken her at face value, and I felt like a real fucking dick that I'd exploited an obvious weakness in search of my own good time for as long as I had.

It was the first time I felt even a little bit guilty about my loyalty to the club and I didn't quite understand this *power* she had over me.

"Maverick," she gasped, her voice light but strained. She was ready to come again. I knew that desperate little note in her voice, knew when she clung to me like she did that she was getting close, and God, its ramped shit up for me.

Making love to Marisol gave me a feeling of possessing god-like powers and I had to admit, that was a high worth chasing. A high that I hoped would never go away.

I bowed over her protectively, my balls tightening, threatening a release that I so desperately wanted, *needed*, and I couldn't help myself. Her orgasm hit, her pussy rippling around the head of my cock and that did it.

I ripped myself from her and thrust hard, slicking my cock between her wet pussy lips, coming in a hot wash over her hip, both of us a hot sticky mess of our love gluing us together.

It was hot. Hot beyond measure for me. Hotter still when she pulled our mouths together and wouldn't hear of quitting the kiss we shared until our breathing returned to semi-normal and the fluids binding our pelvises began to cool uncomfortably.

"God that was hot," she whispered against my mouth and I smiled.

"Stay right there, baby. I'll get us cleaned up," I murmured.

"Mm, good thing I keep up on my birth control. You know the pull-out method is bullshit," she said, and her voice held a note of reproach.

"Fuck, yeah, I'm sorry. I got carried away."

"Mm," she stretched as I stood up, admittedly shaky, beside the bed. "If I hadn't wanted it, if I had fought you... would you have stopped?" she asked quietly.

I met her gaze and said, "You ain't ever have to test me on that. You ain't even gotta ask. Absolutely, yes, I would stop."

She looked uncomfortable for a moment, like at any second, she would start to squirm under the weight of my gaze, and I didn't let up. There was something there and I wasn't about to let anything slide anymore. Not when she carried the kinds of secrets that she did.

"No more secrets, *Zaychik*. Say what's on your mind," I ordered gently.

She drew a breath to speak, stopped, thought better of it, and closed her mouth. I raised eyebrows at her and stood there, waiting her out.

"Is it fucked up that I think it's hot?" she asked.

"That what is hot?" I needed more than that.

"When you hold me down. When you take without asking... I like it."

I sank to the edge of the bed and put a hand on her knee, searching her face.

"There's nothing wrong with liking what you like," I told her.

"Having you fuck me against your desk with your belt around my neck was the hottest thing... like the freest I've ever felt," she confessed and she swallowed hard, looking a little ill at having said it out loud.

"Technically it was *your* belt, and I have no problem doing anything like that with you again if it's what *you* want."

"Right," she whispered and then said, "Sometimes I want to say no but no isn't what I mean, you know?"

She put her hands over her face and sighed out, a frustrated sound.

"I get that, actually. Like when you're a kid being tickled and you're having so much fun and you yell 'no, no, no' but you don't really want it to stop."

"Right," she said nodding, her expression slightly haunted, slightly worried, more than slightly scared, and I felt the weight of this moment keenly.

She was opening up to me. Trusting me with her secrets and I wanted to give her no reason to doubt that I was here for it. I wanted all of her. I wanted to please her. I wanted her to want to please me, and I wanted it with a fierce throbbing ache that I hadn't felt in a really long time about *anything*.

"So, you need a safe word," I murmured.

"A what?" she asked, and I smiled. Sometimes I forgot how sheltered she was in some ways. How *young* she really was.

"A safe word. A word that is sort of out there that means 'no' for real so you can say 'no' all you want, and I know you really mean 'yes' or that you're okay."

"What, like if I scream 'bananas' at the top of my lungs mid-thrust that's it? Everything stops?"

"I would pick something other than bananas," I said with a slight laugh, stroking a hand up and down the smooth skin of her shin from the top of her foot up to her knee and back down, just loving the feel of her skin beneath my palm.

"Okay," she said. "Then you pick for me."

I laughed and shook my head.

"Not how that works. It's supposed to be *your* word." I patted her knee and stood back up feeling stronger. I went to the bathroom and ran the tap all the way to 'hot' to get it warmed up, rinsing a washcloth under the stream of water until it steamed.

I cleaned myself up and rinsed the cloth good, making sure it was hot and not just warm so when I brought it to her, it would be just right. I turned around to see her leaning up against the headboard, her expression deeply thoughtful.

I went and sat back down beside her, batting her hands away when she reached for the washcloth and she smiled with a light little giggle that turned into a lighter, sighing moan, as I cleaned her up carefully.

That sound made me instantly start to grow hard and I hoped she was ready to go again because goddamn, I needed her tonight. Desperately.

I leaned forward and kissed her, delighted when her hands came up to cradle my face, when her thumbs smoothed along my jaw, when she *let me in* when she had absolutely no real reason to that I could see.

"Meatloaf," she whispered, and I drew back and laughed.

"What?"

"My safe word. Meatloaf."

"*Meatloaf?*" I repeated incredulously.

"Yeah, because I would do anything for love, but I won't do *that*."

I couldn't help myself. I laughed. I laughed long and hard and kissed her between bouts of laughter and chuckling.

Meatloaf.

She was something else.

CHAPTER SIXTEEN

Marisol…

I don't know why, precisely, I had done it, but I had let go with Maverick. Had let him in like I'd never let anyone in in my life and it was absolutely exhilarating and totally exhausting all at the same time. I slept so hard, so well that night, yet woke ill-rested. As though I hadn't slept a wink.

It made for a rough day of riding the next day and I collapsed into bed that evening, forgoing dinner in favor of sleep. Maverick, to his credit, didn't wake me. He simply put my food aside in the mini-fridge and let me rest. When I did wake, it was in the wee hours of the morning. I was nude, I was warm, and I was safe in the circle of his arms, his chest pressed to my back, his deep and even breathing a comforting thing in the dark.

I lay there in peace, eyes closed and dared to dream for a moment of what this could be like if it were to last… but I didn't dare hope that it would.

"What's on your mind, baby?" he murmured, warm breath stirring my hair at the side of my neck.

"I don't know if I should say," I murmured with hesitance.

"Of course, you should," he said, arms tightening around me as he nuzzled my shoulder.

"I know I *could,* but I don't know if I *should,*" I hedged.

"Mm," he grunted lightly in acknowledgement. "You can tell me anything," he said, and I fought not to roll my eyes at the cliché, but then he tacked on, "Likewise, you ain't gotta tell me shit. Just whatever it is, I'm here for it."

I'd never had anyone take that approach with me.

"You're really fine with me keeping it to myself?" I whispered.

He kissed the back of my shoulder, once, twice, a third time and sighed in what sounded like contentment.

"Do I want to know all your secrets?" he asked rhetorically. "Yes. But I want to know them on your time. I think you've been pushed around enough, *Zaychik,* and those aren't the buttons I want to push with you. I want you to trust me. That doesn't happen on my time. It happens on yours."

I let his words sink in, food for thought and finally after swallowing hard asked, "You really mean that, don't you?"

"Damn straight, I do," he said gruffly, kissing the side of my neck and holding me tight.

I closed my eyes and sank into the feeling, confessing out loud, "I love it when you hold me like this."

"Yeah? Why's that?" he asked gently.

"Feels safe and good," I murmured. "Like you won't let anyone hurt me."

He went very still and with his lips against my skin swore, "I won't. Those days are over for you."

I closed my eyes and breathed in slowly. I wanted to believe him. I *desperately* wanted to believe him, but it was honestly outside his control, what other people did.

"Don't make promises you can't keep," I whispered softly, after a long time.

I thought he had drifted back off to sleep, but he kissed the back of my shoulder one more time and said, "I never do, baby. I never do."

It was even more food for thought, and something I chewed on until the sun came up outside.

It was our final day of travel back to Seattle, and I wasn't looking forward to it. I ached, and there was no getting comfortable. Though I loved to ride, especially with Maverick, I was quickly reaching the point I never cared if I got on the back of a bike again… which I was equally sure that feeling would only last around twenty-four hours or until the aches dissipated before I was dying to get back on again.

"Lookin' forward to today's wind therapy," Tic-Tac muttered as he strapped his pack to the passenger backrest of his bike, sitting the squat canvas pack on the passenger seat and winding a bungee cord around it like six times.

"Ready to be home, brother?" Glass Jaw asked.

"Like nobody's business."

Fenris slipped out of one of the rooms and grimaced at the sun, flipping his shades off the top of his head and over his eyes.

"You look rough," Maverick declared, looking the big Viking over.

"Hurt like a bitch," he complained and put a hand to himself, over his gray tee and the slash across his middle that rested underneath.

Nine laughed. "I thought it was just a scratch."

"Yeah, well, that scratch took nineteen stitches in areas," Cipher said, and Mav scowled.

"Say what now?"

"I was there with the bottle of whiskey watching each one go down. Fen, you're a fuckin' badass."

I stared at Fen who wouldn't make eye contact with any of us. He simply grunted and sat his own duffel on the back of his bike and started to strap it down.

Cipher wandered over and batted his hands away ignoring Fen's exasperation and finished the work for him.

"Right, let's get you home where you can rest," Maverick declared.

"I'm fine, you buncha fuckin' mother hens, you all acting like I'm some kinda pussy is gonna get old real damn quick."

"Don't go thinkin' I give a shit that Reaver tagged your dumb ass," Maverick said. "I told you it was a bad idea. No, my motives are purely selfish in nature, my man. I'm gonna need you healed up and in your prime – you feel me?"

The pointed look Maverick gave Fen and the slight head jerk he gave in my direction sent butterflies reeling in my stomach.

When he turned and made eye contact with me, those nerves fizzled out into nothing, though. The look Maverick gave me was a hard one, but not at me – *for me*. As though he owned me body, heart, and soul and would fiercely protect everything about me to the ends of the earth.

When his indigo eyes met mine? I felt all of that from my hair to my toes. The look telegraphed two things. One, that vengeance was riding back to Washington, and two, nothing and no one would touch me like that ever again.

I desperately wanted everything that went along with that look, but by the same token that very same look chilled me to the bone.

I pressed my lips together, biting them on the inside with my teeth to keep my mouth shut until Maverick and I were alone and could potentially discuss things further. He identified the misgivings on my face and gave me a slight chin lift.

We would talk later and that both was, and wasn't, reassuring.

The ride helped, and I turned the phrase that had been uttered over in my head – *wind therapy*.

It was an accurate descriptor. The summertime wind was hot, washing over us, carrying tension and heartache, worries and concerns off us and blowing it back down the highway where it could lay forgotten for the time being.

I relaxed into the rhythm of the bike that carried us and held onto the man who piloted us expertly down the cracked asphalt towards the Cascades, the jagged peaks jutting toward an endless blue sky that was unfathomably deep. I closed my eyes and dreamed of stars and being among them, far from the complications here on earth that I faced.

The turmoil churning in my gut over my secret being out was something awful. I honestly felt so drained, like all I wanted to do was sleep for a thousand years. God, I wasn't even certain *that* would do the trick to curb the deep tiredness living in the center of my soul.

I didn't know if this was a tiredness that could even be cured by sleep.

I held on as we approached the foothills, the bike rising and falling as we crested each one, and I held to Maverick tightly and imagined we rode along the spine of some great, sleeping dragon. That each rise and fall was a breath the great beast took, inhaling as we rose, the slight peak as we crested the hill, and the rush as the great beast exhaled.

It was a story I would tell my little brother. Later. When I could see him again.

Mateo loved my stories… I loved them too. They took me far away from myself and the pain. Gave me an escape when I needed to go somewhere without any actual money or ability to *go*.

If it was one hard lesson I had learned on this trip, it was that it didn't matter how far you rode, or how much you wanted to leave certain things behind… you couldn't. Not when they lived inside your head.

It was a tough and heartbreaking reality and one, which it was time, to face.

I hated riding through Eastern Washington. Just traveling through made me huddle against Maverick's back even more. He took his hand from the handlebars at least once to place it over mine where they rested over his stomach, giving them a squeeze as if to communicate, *I know, it's almost over.*

I didn't honestly feel like I could breathe again until we started to climb. Until the undulating brown hills started to give way to the unforgiving gray rock of the mountain and the withered grass shot up into deep green conifers.

It was high summer, but up high in the pass, it was much cooler than it had been on the sun-scorched eastern side. The cooler temperatures continued as we made our descent, the gray rock stark against the true-blue sky, bits of white still frosting the tops of the barren peaks around us. The trees provided us a lovely amount of shade and a reprieve from the punishing sun as we descended from Snoqualmie into Issaquah.

There was just something *lighter* about the western side of the Cascades. Brighter, so full of life with the deep blue waters of Lake Washington reflecting the true-blue skies above. Everything ringed in green and living things – even the buildings just seemed livelier over here.

I felt like I could breathe again, and I had to smile as we crossed the I-90 floating bridge. The wind off the water was refreshingly cool and the boats were out on the lake's glittering surface. I had to smile when we'd arrived at Lake Eversong. I had said I thought we were going to a lake. Tic-Tac had said we were, and the lake was right there. He hadn't caught on, but Maverick had and was already laughing when I'd said Eversong wasn't a lake, it was a mud puddle. It *was* a mud puddle when you compared it to the likes of Lake Washington.

Too soon, we left the lake behind and climbed the bridge into the tunnels beneath the houses on the ridge. We swept through those tunnels at a good clip, the roar of the motorcycles reverberating off the exhaust-stained walls back at us overbearing. The sound was like being grabbed by the shoulders and physically shaken; jarring and unpleasant. At least to me it was, but to look around at the guys' faces it made the unpleasantness I was experiencing worth it.

You could just see their wide, little boy glee-filled smiles stretching their faces. Even under the wraps and bandanas covering their mouths and noses from the bugs and grit of the road.

We were almost home… and that was another thing I felt as though I was falling over. Maverick's house had really started to feel like home over the last few weeks. I was actually *excited* to get back there. To the much cleaner little house I'd left behind. I'd put some work into it, and I was beginning to love it like it was my own – which I knew was a bad idea but still…

Someday, if I were ever lucky enough to own a house of my own for me and Mateo, I would want it to be like Maverick's. Big enough that we had our own space and we weren't tripping over each other all the time – just the two of us.

Except things were rapidly changing, were rapidly becoming different. Instead of the thought of it just being me and Mateo giving me the wings it usually did, this time it made me hold on to Maverick a little tighter.

I didn't want to let him go, but I would if I had to.

There was a big difference between want and need and I had learned that difference long ago.

Did I want Maverick?

Yes.

Did I need him?

Once, I would have said 'no' but now? I… I didn't know. Not anymore.

CHAPTER SEVENTEEN

*M*averick…

I just wanted a hot shower and my own fuckin' bed. Instead, I took a hard left at I-5, waved at the boys to fall in and bypassed the West Seattle Bridge exit which would have taken my ass toward home in favor of hitting up the Corson Ave/Michigan St. exit to go to the club. It was a short jaunt down Michigan, up over the 1st Ave S. drawbridge, the grating over the water setting my damn teeth on edge, then the Myers Way/White Center exit.

There were one of two routes to take from there. The fastest was up the absolute fucking *beast* of a hill that was Roxbury, the other was straight and a little longer and more convoluted up Myers Way and through some smaller back streets up through the Top Hat neighborhood which was riddled with weed shops cropping up every which way now that the shit was legal.

In the interest of expediency, I took Roxbury, powering up the hill and hitting every green light thankfully. I swung left on 15th SW and slowed as I approached the club on the right and the boneyard on the left.

Marisol obediently hopped off the back of the bike without being asked so I could back it in. The guys followed suit as she stood by wearily and worked the chin strap free of its D rings.

I shut off the bike and as the last engine cut, I asked her, "You alright?"

"Tired as *fuck*," she complained. "I thought we were going home."

"Soon," I promised. "Gotta debrief."

"Is everybody here already?" she asked.

"No, but they should be here PDQ."

"PDQ?"

I smiled, sometimes it was easy to forget she was so young.

"Pretty Damn Quick," I explained.

She didn't look thrilled, but she didn't complain, either. She simply nodded tiredly and kept her mouth shut and I appreciated that she didn't give me any shit so I got up, hooked a hand behind her head tenderly, and pressed a kiss to her forehead.

She sighed out in such a way I couldn't identify the meaning behind it, but I could tell you that I liked it. The way the tension drained from her sexy form, the way she swayed gently on her feet, and especially the way she tucked herself beneath my arm as I led her across the street to the back door of the club where Little Bird stood, reaching out, grasping with her hands, practically bouncing on the balls of her feet excitedly.

"You're home early!" she cried as we approached the back step.

"Something came up," I said, giving her a one-armed hug as I went by, digging the feel of having two beautiful women, one in each arm, for the fleeting moment I had them both there.

"Hey, Kestrel," I murmured. "Good to be home."

She left my embrace and went to hug my little *zaychik* enthusiastically. Marisol smiled and it was a genuine one, not forced in the slightest. I could read my girl like a book for the most part now. The barriers had all come toppling down with her confession. I was determined now, to build her a strong foundation but to do it, I would need help.

"How *are* you?" Little Bird asked her, and my girl smiled tiredly, her bandana around her neck.

"Tired," Marisol murmured.

"Let me get her comfortable," I said with a chuckle. "It was a long ride."

"Of course! You want me to order some food? Are you guys hungry?"

"Oh, man! I'm fuckin' starving!" Nine called out on the approach.

"Somebody say food?" Cipher asked, perking up.

"In a minute, it's gotta be ordered," I called back.

"Fuck," Tic-Tac griped.

"Fen, what's wrong with you?" Little Bird asked alarmed. I looked back at my enforcer who looked like he was hurting. He held an arm stiff across his middle and chuckled.

"Just played a little too hard, babes. It's all good…"

I went in the back door of my club, past my office, and took Marisol to the front, and the ring of leather couches and love seats around the thick glass and iron coffee table. I eased her down on the couch and kneeled in front of her, putting a booted foot atop my thigh, covered by my chaps, to work at the laces.

"What are you doing?" she asked with a tired laugh.

"Taking care of my lady. Making sure she's comfortable," I murmured.

Deacon came in the front door and looked down at me with a raised eyebrow. I ignored the look and went back to tugging on Marisol's laces telling our chaplain, "Go dig out a bottle of antibiotics from our stores and make sure Fen takes 'em. Check and see if we got any painkillers, but he's allowed to be a stubborn asshole about those."

"He get hurt?" Deac asked and I shook my head some.

"Slash across the belly. Some stitches. Way he's holding himself and how much pain he's in leads me to believe he might have scored an infection. Check him out for me."

"You got it, man."

Deacon moved past me and into the club, disappearing into my office to hit up the cache well hidden from any LEO's that could come lookin' while I tended to my girl.

"Thirsty?" I asked her.

"Yeah," she said softly.

"Yo, Little Bird?"

"Yeah?" My SAA's woman looked up from under Fen's arm as she helped him into a seat nearby.

"Could you get my woman a drink?" I asked.

"Sure! What you want?" she asked.

Marisol smiled and said, "A Coke, if you've got it."

"Sure do."

I slid her boot off and worked on the other one, cursing at the knots she put in her laces.

"Damn, girl."

"I can do it, if you'd like," she said with a mischievous smile.

"Naw, I got it," I said, and I did, pulling the laces loose and easing the other boot off her, setting the footwear aside.

"Thank you," she murmured, and I smiled up at her, massaging the tops of her thighs through her layers of chaps and jeans.

"Curl up, get comfortable, food'll be on the way soon. You just relax and let me take care of some business and we'll be home before you know it."

"Okay." Her smile grew and I leaned up and kissed her. When we parted, Little Bird held down a sparkling bar glass of Coke to my girl who took it and smiled up at the other woman.

"Thanks."

I stood up and let them catch up, Little Bird bursting with questions about the trip. Dump Truck was on his phone by the bar and I raised an eyebrow. He lifted his chin and flashed the screen at me, putting in an order for food at the bomb-ass mom-and-pop Italian place across 16th in front of the club.

"Thanks, man. Round everybody up, bring food into the chapel, we got a lotta ground to cover."

"What you want?" he asked me. I shook my head. I was hungry, but I was also tapped out on decision-making.

"Just surprise me," I said.

He nodded gravely and shot back, "I got you."

"Thanks."

I went into the chapel and dropped wearily into the seat at the head of the table, leaning back heavily and closing my eyes for a minute.

"Hey, Mav." I looked up and Deacon leaned in the doorway, holding up a beer.

"You're saving my life, brother," I said, and he came in, setting down a coaster and the pint glass atop it in front of me.

"Soul seems heavy," he commented slyly. "You alright?"

"Naw, man. I'm not. I'm really not," I said. "But in the interest of not repeating myself, I'd rather wait until everyone is here."

"I got you," he said and gripped my shoulder as he stood up. "Whatever it is, we'll deal with it."

I nodded and drank some of my beer, washing some of the lingering road dust out of my mouth and down my throat. God, there was nothing better than a cold beer after a long, hot ride. *So fucking good.*

I rested a while, waiting for the stragglers to arrive and for the food to get here. Little Bird brought me a fresh beer and some dinner, and I raised an eyebrow.

"She's out cold. Once you guys get started, I'll wake her up and make sure she eats."

I nodded and said, "Thanks, beautiful."

Her lips quirked and she leaned a hip against the table, crossing her arms lightly over her stomach.

"What happened out there, Mav?"

"That's something for her to tell," I said with a reluctant sigh, knowing that my *zaychik* wouldn't say shit.

"What can you tell me?" she asked.

"Nothing," I said finally and looked up. "Can I ask you something? A favor…"

"After all you and the club have done for me?" she countered. "You can ask me anything."

"Just look out for her. I want her to stay but she needs some… encouragement."

"You mean try to get Dahlia to soften up toward her?" she asked me and gave me a knowing look.

I nodded slowly and said, "If you can."

Kestrel rolled her eyes and threw up her hands, bringing them down with a light slap against her denim-clad thighs.

"You aren't asking much with that one, are you?" she asked wryly. When I didn't answer, she sighed. "The only person Dahlia even comes close to listening to is *you*, but I'll do what I can."

"Thanks."

"Have *you* tried talking to Dahlia?" she asked.

I swore softly. "It's been kind of low on my priority list," I confessed. I needed to, though. I mean, I *really* needed to.

"And that can't change anytime soon?" Her voice was gentle, no accusation to it but I felt accused all the same and rightfully so. Dahlia was my best friend and even though we were both stubborn mules, the silence of the last couple weeks was long, even for us.

"You made your point, Little Bird," I said with a fond smile. Her smile was small but sweet in return. She swept her hair over her shoulder and pushed off the table.

She had one seriously fine ass, and I helped myself to the view as she walked out like I had a million times before, only this time… I felt a tad guilty for it when my thoughts drifted back to Marisol.

That was new. I'd never had the occasion to feel guilty just for *looking* before.

I puzzled it out as I unwrapped my sandwich and waited for the guys to start filtering in with theirs.

Pretty soon, we were all seated except for Derry, who was waiting out in the bar for us to pull him in.

"Right, to order." I popped the gavel once and let it fall to the table with a clatter, to go for my sandwich. Before I took another bite, I got into the first order of business.

"Derry's been given the blessing from National to pull a lateral move into our ranks. Let's get that settled first. All in favor of accepting Derry into our ranks?"

Every hand went up and I nodded.

"So ordered, go on and get him in here."

Major popped up out of his seat and stuck his head out, looking up the hall.

"Hey Derry, leave your phone out there and come on in, okay?"

"Ho, yup!"

We listened to Derry heave himself up and the clatter of his phone hitting the bar.

"Watch this," Glass Jaw whispered loudly and snickered. I laughed lightly and we all schooled our faces into neutral expressions for the gag.

Derry came in and froze inside the door as we all looked at him.

"Why do I suddenly feel like a fuckin' prospect?" he demanded, and we all started losing our shit before Glass could even say whatever it was, he was going to say.

"Fuck, man. You ruined the gag," Glass said, wiping tears.

"Yeah, we voted. You're good, bro. Take a seat."

Derry laughed and shook his head. "Man, you almost had me," he said.

"Right, I don't know about you all, but I'm tired as fuck so let's get on with it…"

I went over the decisions regarding Eastern Washington and the plan. Everyone listened intently and there were nods. A few of those nods were accompanied by grim looks.

"We know who, yet?" Dump Truck asked.

"Some," I said. "The rest remain yet to be seen."

I went over who I knew would be moving in to take care of things next door and who I knew they were thinking about but had yet to confirm.

"Sounds like the bottom line is we're gonna be picking up the slack for *a while*," Deacon said.

I nodded.

"That is true."

"This can't be the reason you're back so damn early, though," Dump Truck said sagely.

I shook my head.

"Now *that* is personal," I declared, and everyone stopped every-thing. I mean, some of the fellas stopped mid-chew.

"Ain't nothing ever personal with you," Major said, tucking some of his dreads back.

"This time, it is…" Glass Jaw looked grim.

"What's going on?" Deacon asked, leaning back in his seat and I felt like shit, I really did, but I sat there and chose club over my woman once again and betrayed her all over. I told them her story.

CHAPTER EIGHTEEN

*M*arisol…

"Hey, you hungry?" Little Bird shook my shoulder and I startled awake. She held out a paper wrapped something that smelled divine. I had been about to wave her off and tell her 'no' until the smell hit me. I quickly changed my mind and pushed myself up into a sitting position.

"Mm, thank you."

"No problem."

Inside was the most amazing Italian sub sandwich I had ever put in my face. I looked up at Kestrel, eyes wide and cocked my head.

"Where did this come from?" I asked around my mouthful of food.

She laughed and pointed at the front door saying, "White Center Pizza and Spaghetti House. It's right out the front door, across the parking lot on the other side of 16th. Best Italian food I've ever had, and I don't think we've ever actually gotten the pizza from there. We always get the lasagna or the grinders."

"What's a grinder?" I asked, swallowing the bite of my sub.

She laughed and said, "You're eating one."

"Why do they call them that?" I wondered.

"Beats me. I said the same thing. It's a toasted sub."

I stopped and asked quietly, "How long have they been in there?"

"Awhile," she said and searched my face. "Derry went back almost an hour ago. You were *out* and I didn't want to wake you, but I promised Mav I would make sure you got something to eat."

"Thanks," I murmured and sighed heavily.

"I remember that feeling," she said.

"What feeling?"

"The weight of knowing they're in there talking about you. Not knowing what's going to happen, not knowing what they're saying…"

I barked a bitter laugh and shook my head, my appetite fleeing.

"I know what they're saying," I told her. "I don't know what's going to happen, though."

"Whatever it is," she said putting her hand over mine, "it's going to be okay."

"How do you know?" I asked.

She hesitated and I smiled, knowing it was brittle with jagged edges, but Lord knows, I had *never* been able to deliver my face from evil. Just about everything I thought was broadcast there, *especially* when I was this tired.

"No, it's not like that!" she cried.

"Like what?"

"It's not *you*… it's me."

I laughed slightly but the alarmed look on her face wiped the smile right off mine. We sat in silence searching each other's faces with caution and I said, "You're going to have to go first…"

Holy *shit* did she have a story. One that could get her and her man in a whole lot of trouble!

"Why are you trusting me with this?" I asked quietly.

"Because I really can't express hard enough how trustworthy these guys are otherwise," she said.

I set my sandwich aside on the glass coffee table's top and scrubbed my face with my hands.

"You know what they do?" I asked.

She wouldn't look at me right away and finally said, "I have a really good idea, but I know better than to talk about it. It's as much for their safety as for mine. Not that I think they would hurt me. They've done so much *for* me."

I chewed my bottom lip, my thoughts racing and said finally, "I don't know what to do or what to think. The only reason I'm here, the only reason I do *anything* is for Mateo. He's the only family I have left as far as I'm concerned."

Her brow wrinkled and I took a deep breath.

She would know anyway. I would rather she hears it from me than from her man like some fucked-up high school gossip game.

I was about to confess my shame when the door to the chapel opened and the men started filing out, all with grim expressions on their faces that made my heart sink.

Little Bird looked stricken and I simply felt defeated.

Even the universe wanted to keep things a secret, so it seemed.

I raised my eyes and met Maverick's past leather-clad bodies across the great expanse of floor, and he met my look with a somber one of his own.

Just what had they decided in there?

"You ready to go home, baby?" he called out to me and I nodded, perhaps a little too rapidly as I caught their furtive looks of pity around me.

I felt as though I was falling, spiraling, and I'd completely lost control and I hated it. Hated every moment of it.

All I wanted was to get out from under their somber looks mixed with fury. All I wanted was for the shame burning my cheeks to go away.

Anger bubbled up to take its place and I took a deep breath, breathing carefully around it. I didn't want to make a scene. I didn't want to be seen at all… all I wanted was to become invisible and to sleep.

I got my boots on and picked up the sandwich, wrapping it up. It was too good not to finish later.

"Night, Marisol," Major said as I walked by and I swallowed hard giving him a curt "Night," back.

I swept past Maverick to the back door of the club and heard him sigh and say, "Night fellas," as I took the steps off the little back porch to the cracked sidewalk below.

"Marisol," Maverick called gently, and I looked up. "Slow down, baby. Ain't going anywhere without me."

I lashed out; I couldn't help it. I was so helpless! I had no place to channel the absolute rage.

"I don't really know if I'm going anywhere *with* you, either, to be honest..." I said and I walked briskly across the street to his waiting bike.

He stood silent, staring, and I couldn't read his expression. He took his time stepping down and crossing the road. He stopped in front of me and cupped my cheek, but his expression was frosty at best. The chill radiated from him and I almost shivered despite the summer heat.

He stroked a thumb across my lips, and I jerked back. He smirked and there was nothing playful about it.

"I'm going to give you a pass right now. We're going to go home and we're going to sort this out," he said evenly, his voice pleasant but for its menacing undertone. "Don't ever make the mistake of disrespecting me in front of the boys," he said, and his voice lost all pretense of pleasantry at all. "I mean it, babe. I'll drop your ass like a bad habit."

I stared up at him, mouth dry, and tears sprang to my eyes at the thought. His expression softened, though his jaw tightened at the glassy sheen that blurred my vision.

"I'm beginning to love you," he said, and the confession was a stark one. I sniffed and didn't say anything because I didn't know *what* to say.

"I'm so angry," I said, shaking with it. "I don't know what to do or how to feel. I just want to punch something." The confession felt both good and terrifying at the same time. I stared up at him, trembling, too afraid to say the rest... *I don't want to lose you. You're the only thing holding me together.* Which is exactly what it felt like.

I wasn't sure what to do, how to feel, or how to act. Everything I had ever done had been judged and found wanting and all I knew was that whatever I did? It was always wrong, wrong, wrong, wrong; *wrong!*

"We're going to go home," he said succinctly. "Then we're going to do whatever you need to do to feel better for the time being. If that means I end up scratched and bloody, then so be it."

I felt my mouth drop open in surprise and he caressed my face gently, leaning down to put his lips to mine. I closed my eyes, twin scalding lines slipping down my cheeks, the sensation in perfect counterpoint to the softness of his lips.

I reached out and seized him, hauling myself close into the shelter of his body, tongue plunging past his lips and into his mouth, punishing, demanding, *desperate.*

I was so sorry, for everything – for pushing him away when I needed him the most, for being so desperately *afraid* of *everything,* for being so scared of more mental and emotional anguish I would do anything and everything to avoid it up to and including causing so much more I would drown us *both* in it.

I was so ungodly *confused,* and I needed help. I knew that now. I desperately needed help getting through this chaos and discord between my heart and my head, between my past and my present to have any chance at a future but damned if I was too proud to *ask.* I didn't know *how* to ask!

For so long, this self-reliance, basic survival shit was all I had ever known and now I was this Gordian knot of pain and there just was no absolution to be found except… except when Maverick touched me. Except when he held me close and let me breathe and took the burden of all the decision-making from my shoulders and just let me be me, like right now.

He tore his mouth from mine and ordered me gruffly but gently, "Get on the bike, *Zaychik.* I want to finish this at home."

We went home. The weather had cooled significantly with the setting of the sun as it was wanting to do on the western side of the mountains. The breeze coming in off the sound, and beyond that, the

Pacific, made it so everything was cooler on this side of things. I was slightly shivering by the time we pulled up behind Mav's house and I was honestly grateful to be back here.

"Leave it," he said when I went to bring things in from the bike.

I scowled at him and argued, "I don't want to leave it. It just means more work later."

"Leave. It." He would brook no argument, but I ignored him and hefted one of the packs strapped behind my seat anyway. He cursed, something in a language I didn't know, and marched back in my direction.

"I'm going to rail that ass against my kitchen counter," he declared, and I raised an eyebrow.

"Better use lube," I said defiantly.

Still, I got my way. He helped me bring the rest of the shit in and dropped it in front of the closet that held the washer and dryer.

That was honestly all I'd wanted.

Well, that, and what he did next. He grabbed me by my belt loops, my back to his front and steered me around, fetching me up against his kitchen counter as promised, pinning me with his body as he swept my wind-tangled hair over my shoulder so he could lay his lips against the side of my neck, just behind my ear.

"You want it this way?" he asked, his voice low, rough, and filled with need. "You want me to pull down these pants and fucking shove my cock in your waiting cunt balls deep?"

I lost my breath completely, my pussy giving a dull, aching, throb of *yes please!*

"Answer me," he demanded, and I sighed out.

"Yes, that's what I want."

"You know what to say to make it stop," he reminded me and then, with a savagery he'd never displayed before, his hands fell to undressing me in a flurry.

I went to aide him in disrobing and he gripped my wrists, planting my hands flat against the cool countertop, pressing them there for a heartbeat until I got the picture. That's where he wanted them. That's where they should stay.

"You know how hot it makes me when you defy me?" he demanded.

"No." I answered him honestly as he ran his hands over my jeans-clad ass, leaning back to check me out.

"Oh, baby. It makes me so hot. It makes me want to do all sorts of bad things with you."

I pressed my ass back into his crotch and rubbed it back and forth over the hot bulge in his jeans.

"You're trying to distract me," I said softly, and his hand came down on my ass with a sharp crack. I yelped and pushed back further into him.

"Is it working?" he asked as I rubbed myself against him with a sensual twist of my hips.

"Maybe," I said, breathy, not wanting to give him an inch, but he knew he had me taking that liquid slide into arousal. Into that place I went where it didn't matter what he pulled, what he did to me, as long as he kept the orgasms coming.

Never had I been with anyone where the sex was so dirty, but it made my soul feel so *clean*, but that was exactly as it was with Maverick.

I couldn't exactly explain how that worked. All I knew was that I couldn't get enough of the sensation and I wanted him inside of me so fucking bad right now.

I wanted him to drive into me so hard my hip bones cracked against the counter. I wanted bruises of his fingerprints in my hips as a lasting reminder of our passion and I couldn't tell you if it was right or wrong, couldn't tell you if it was healthy or not, all I could say was that I wanted it. I wanted it *badly* and it was probably a lot healthier to engage in rough and passionate sex that I wanted rather than to burn my whole fucking world down around me and to push the only person who was trying to help me away.

Of course, I'd started down that road back at the club, but Maverick had called me on my shit. Course corrected us here, where he was sliding my pants and chaps over my ass. Where he was kneeling on the floor behind me, where he was simultaneously pressing me against the counter – trapping me like a butterfly in a killing jar even as he ripped my panties away and thrust his tongue inside me.

God, *yes*; that felt good. I swear by all things that are holy that my soul left my fucking body with the first orgasm he dragged out of me at a record pace.

He left me sprawled over the countertop, chest heaving, his hand sliding up my back as he hummed satisfied.

"Beautiful," he murmured. "Beautiful and mine." He smacked his lips and smacked my ass, causing me to jump and writhe but I couldn't stand up. He had his hand tangled in the back of my hair, now; his arm braced against my back, flattening me to the countertop as he thrust two fingers inside me, pressing on *that spot*, jerking his arm in that way that sent me from zero to sixty and had me writhing against his hold but unable to stop what was coming.

I don't know why I resisted, other than resisting was fun and this was a game I actually wanted to lose, but I tried like hell to push up, to squirm out of his grasp, but it wasn't happening. That feeling of being full, of impending release, that vague sensation of *oh, shit! I'm going to piss myself,* built and I bit my bottom lip, my cries ragged and uneven as I rose onto my toes and finally with a gush and wet splatter down my legs, I came.

Holy shit, that was intense. Like nothing I had ever felt before – and God, did I want *more*.

I lay limp and gasping against the countertop, unable to move, basking in the erotic glow, legs too weak, shaking like a newborn foal as Maverick braced me with a light touch at my back as he worked his pants open to fuck me.

He pressed against my opening and groaned as he sank inside of me, filling me up and out, pressing against my walls that still tingled faintly from the intensity with which he'd made me come.

I was a happy girl, melting across the countertop as he slid in and out of me at a lazy, almost sedate pace, taking his time, enjoying my body and the pleasure it gave him like a fine wine.

The only thing better than the feel of him inside of me, gliding along my wetness, pressing out against my walls all hot velvet and steel length, were the sounds he made. The appreciative moans, the sighing little groans, the whispered compliments. I lived for them, and felt so special, so cherished in this moment, I was desperate for it to never fucking end.

CHAPTER NINETEEN

$\mathcal{M}$averick…

"Mm, yeah baby. So good…" I praised. After the second orgasm had left her devastated, had drained the fight and the anger right out of her, I'd flipped the script. I quit fucking her, which was nice – don't get me wrong, but I wanted in. I wanted past those shifting concrete maze-like walls and I wanted to touch her soul deep. Feed her, nourish her spirit. So, I both took what I wanted and gave her my all making love to her for the first time, I think, ever for her.

She lay limp and languid across the kitchen island in front of me and I took my time, stroking in and out of her, holding her firmly, but gently, kneading her with my hands through the leather of her jacket. I stroked deep and sure, listening to her lilting moans, her panting breath, and I don't think I'd ever felt so virile. I don't think I'd ever felt like more of a man than when I made her like this where she forgot her past, lost herself in the sensation of me, and let her burdens go.

When we were like this, she let me handle things and that made everything alright in my book, at least for the time being. I had big shoulders. I could be her Atlas. I *wanted* to be her Atlas. It was time someone else carried the world on their shoulders for her. I would be happy to be that man, she just had to trust me; had to let me in.

I took my time with her, let myself relax and enjoy this, but all good things must come to an end and what a spectacular end it was. I came in this weird dichotomy of gentle, but also so hard I saw stars. Grunting, barely pulling out in time – which was bullshit, and I knew it. I needed to take much more care than I was – but fuck she felt so damn good skin on skin.

I don't care what anybody said. The feel of her body wrapped tight around mine just wasn't the same through the barrier, however thin, that was a condom.

I slipped out of her, coming in a hot wash all over her ass, and *fuck* that was hot. I didn't care about the mess. She'd already squirted all over me, herself, and the floor and fuck if that hadn't been hotter than hell, too.

I curved my arms beneath her and bowed over her back, pressing myself against her, sandwiching her between me and the cool stone of the countertop. I lay atop her body and closed my eyes, willing my breath to still, feeling my heartbeat sync up with hers.

It was an intimacy I wasn't prone to allow myself with anyone but her.

"You okay?" I asked gently when we'd been there a time, breaths returned, quiet and still.

"Mm-hmm," she murmured in a satisfied purr.

I smiled, smugly satisfied and stood, bringing her with me saying softly, "Up you go. Let's get cleaned up and make our way to the bedroom."

I wanted us nude, cleaned up, and comfortably reclined in my bed. I made short work of getting us both undressed right there in the kitchen. Sliding open the slatted doors concealing the washer and dryer and leaving things in a pile in front of the machines to sort and get washed in the morning.

Fuck the bags. More than half the shit in them needed sorted and washed too, and they could wait.

I guided her from behind, arms around her waist, my chest pressed to her back in an awkward gait through the house to the bathroom and drew us a bath. Shower would have been faster, sure, but I wanted to soak some of the aches from the long trip spent too long in the same position.

When we were settled, her in front of me, music playing lightly, her body lax against mine, I felt a contentment I didn't even know could exist.

It was magical. The world fallen away until she and I were the only two people to exist. Too fuckin' good to be true, so of course I had to scrape some of the shine off the moment with some reality.

"You know how I can find your uncle?"

She stiffened in the water before me and asked, a thread of alarm in her voice, "Why would you want to do that?"

"You know why," I said calmly.

She hugged my arms around her a little tighter and was silent for a time.

"If you do anything to him, you'll alienate the only family I have left," she said finally, almost so quietly, I didn't hear her. I did hear the deep melancholy in her voice, the utter despair and I shook my head slowly.

"Those people may be blood, but they're not your family, baby." *We're your family now...* I thought to myself, but I didn't want to over-burden her, tax her poor heart and mind any more than they already were.

"What if I don't want you to do anything?" she asked, but there was a note in her voice, a quality that said she was just asking that. In all reality, she didn't know what she wanted, and that was okay.

"I think we're past that now, darlin.' There comes a point a man has to answer for what he's done."

"Isn't that the job for the system?" she asked.

"System had its chance and failed you," I reminded her. "I won't."

She sighed and shifted uncomfortably saying, "Can we please just not talk about it now?" and the pleading in her voice made me wish to give her anything, anything she asked for... so I could curb it tonight but this wasn't going to go away – not any time soon.

This discussion would be over when her perv of a kiddie-diddling uncle was in the ground.

I wish I could say I let it go completely then, but I couldn't. I got us out of the bath and Marisol wrapped in a large towel from the warmer. I got us both tucked into bed, my woman lying draped artfully over my body, a warm and comforting weight against my chest, her leg draped over mine, my arm around her and my free hand caressing up and down the silky skin of her outer thigh as I stared into the dark in thought until I was too exhausted to think.

I wanted my retribution to be swift, but this was delicate. I didn't want to cause a rift with my woman, and she *was* mine. I just needed to wait until she caught up to that fact. She was behind on the curve and was it any wonder?

I slept, and it was a deep sleep, waking up the next morning to muffled sounds coming from the kitchen, the hiss and spray of the washer running, and the click and clack of various things being moved around.

I got up and went out to her, leaning a shoulder against the arch-way, watching her move for a second as she pulled things from bags and sorted clothes into piles. Whites, darks, coloreds… the darks pile quite a bit larger than the rest.

"Oh! *Dios mío!* You scared the *shit* out of me!" She'd jumped, snapping her knees together beneath my one white button-down shirt I kept for court appearances, the sleeves rolled back over her slender wrists, the tails dragging tantalizingly across her long golden legs just above mid-thigh, perky tits pressing out against the thin material, her nipples a slightly darker shade against the fabric, hinting at the possibilities of my mouth suckling them through the cloth.

I stretched, languidly, arms above my head, cock jutting out in front of me bobbing in the cooler air of my kitchen and her gaze went from startled to hungry as she slowly let her eyes wander the length of my body in an appreciative slow roam.

"Want some sausage for breakfast?" I asked, grabbing myself and giving my dick a shake, once up, once down.

She rolled her eyes and her hand dropped from where she'd pressed it between her breasts.

"Want me to fry it up?" she asked, and my smile grew. There she was my sassy girl.

"I'm good," I declared, switching my grip on my junk to a protective one and she smirked.

She went back to what she was doing, emptying packs, sorting clothes, and tossing odd bits of things into the washer's barrel before finally closing the lid as it stopped spewing water and started to agitate.

"Got any big plans for today?" she asked with a gusty sigh that edged on satisfaction for whatever accomplishments she'd made before I got out here to bug her.

"Just one," I said carefully, and she swept around the kitchen island to the dishwasher to unload it.

"What's that?" she asked, semi-distractedly opening the machine and rolling out the top rack.

"Finishing our conversation from last night," I said, leaning back up against the wall and crossing my arms, cock wilting, all arousal fled under the knowledge of how unpleasant this was about to get for her.

She stiffened and a pair of glasses rattled rudely, a little sharply, as she handled them, the sound ringing loud in the space between us. I stiffened slightly, ready to dodge if she decided to launch one in my direction because I was going to have to be a dog with a bone here, and when you were actively hurting someone – even if it was 'just' emotionally, their behavior tended to lean toward unpredictable. I know I'd had my moments where I would have acted out, said, or done anything, just to get the pain to stop.

I'd outgrown that shit a long time ago, but Marisol? She'd never really been given that sort of room to grow – so I balanced myself to move if I had to.

She gave me a baleful look from across the kitchen and I looked back. I wouldn't be swayed, and I telegraphed that with my own look that I shot back in her direction. It was a silent battle of wills that I won.

"What about it?" she demanded curtly.

"I need to know how to find him, babe," I said softly and she turned away from me, rolling out the bottom rack of the dishwasher and plucking out the little bin meant for the silverware, turning, back still to me and pulling open the drawer.

The clatter of the flatware as she tossed each piece in the drawer in the slot where it belonged was loud.

"Can't you just let it go?" she demanded, and I sighed.

"No, baby. I can't, and I won't. This shit's gone on long enough."

She stopped, shoulders hunching with her pain, hands gripping the edge of the counter as she fought down a sob. The strangled noise she made, heartbreaking.

I stood still, didn't move a muscle. Her tears were angry, and I was afraid if I touched her now, she could become volatile and I didn't need her to suffer more guilt, more pain, when the storm passed.

So, I waited her out some more, and I wasn't disappointed.

"All I ever wanted was for someone to *do something*," she said turning around. "All I wanted was for someone, *anyone*, to make it stop."

"And no one did," I said simply.

"And no one did," she echoed dully.

"I'm sorry I showed up late to the party," I said gently, and she shook her head, wiping her face beneath her eyes and sniffing hard.

"It's not that…" she said trailing off and fixed me with her honey-toned gaze. "It's just… what's the point?" she asked miserably.

"Never too late for some street justice, baby. Especially since regular justice just chose to look the other way on you."

She bit her lips together and stared at me, mutely, for a real long time. All I could do was wait her out. Let her think it through for herself.

"It's just not that easy," she said. "You know?"

"For me it is," I told her. "For you? Not so much."

"I don't want anybody to get hurt," she whispered.

"I don't get why you care," I said honestly, shrugging the shoulder that wasn't pressed to the wall. "None of these people gave a shit about you, so why are you trying so hard to protect them?"

She turned her face, staring vacantly out the kitchen window out over the back, her gaze distant, her expression pinched with indecision as she tried to puzzle it out even for herself.

"I stopped caring what happens to me a long time ago," she murmured hollowly. "It doesn't matter anyway… but Mateo. I'm always afraid of what they might do to him if—"

"They ain't gonna do shit," I said and pushed off the wall. She jumped at the stormy darkness in my tone and jerked her head around in my direction, hugging herself. "I'm the Hades to your Persephone, babe. You just point and I'll unleash hell."

She stared at me long and hard, the wheels whirring and clicking behind her beautiful eyes and I knew I had her. She was smart. It was only a matter of time before she came to the right conclusion – that she would make the right decision and *trust me*.

I wasn't going to leave it alone until she did, and yeah – I knew what kind of monster that made me. Still, some motherfuckers were going to pay. I just wanted my queen at my side, on my knee, as we watched it go down. I didn't want to drive her further away, I wanted to bring her closer.

She closed her eyes, and I held my breath. When she opened her mouth it was to say, "My cousin, my uncle's son, works at an auto mechanic's shop somewhere on this side of the mountains. I honestly *don't* know where my uncle is, but my cousin? He might."

I felt a nasty little smile curve my lips.

"Happen to know where the shop is?" I asked.

She shook her head but said, "Let me make a call. I could maybe find out."

I nodded slowly.

"You do that."

I didn't like arguing with her. It didn't feel good, but this? Working *with* her, having her on board? This felt much better. She and I stared at each other over the expanse of kitchen that separated us and, in some ways, it remained mere feet, in other ways it might as well have been a chasm.

She eventually closed the gap, coming around the island and folding herself into my arms, pressing herself tightly into my front.

"They're still my family," she whispered dully, and I knew what it was that tortured her then. I shook my head and kissed the top of hers, clutching her tightly.

"They may be blood, my little *zaychik*, but they're not family." I sighed and closed my eyes. "We're your family now."

CHAPTER TWENTY

*M*arisol…

He dropped it for the time being but not before dropping a thermonuclear bomb in the middle of my heart first.

We're your family now… echoed over and over inside my head. His voice, those words, so very strong in their effect, grew fainter as the day wore on. Still, they resonated; picking up strength every time I looked at him and he looked at me.

I cleaned, took care of the laundry, and generally moved around the house in a bit of a daze. I kept telling myself that this was nothing, that once again this was all talk and no action and that everything would be fine. I couldn't convince myself of it, though. I knew, deep down, that the juggernaut was in motion and that fundamentally, things had shifted and changed. It was uncomfortable, but then again, change – *true* deep-seated change – always was.

It was closer to noon, after I had showered and gotten dressed to complete my chores and to tackle a new project in the house that was getting the spare room sorted, when I realized just how serious he was about everything.

I opened the bathroom door and he was there, dressed and holding the cellphone he'd bought me in one hand. He held it out to me mutely, his indigo eyes weighted with the gravity of the situation, with a devastating seriousness in them that usually chilled me to the bone but this time, somehow, it did the opposite. It warmed me, and an excitement fizzed through me.

Apparently, I was more on board with this idea of revenge than I even realized.

I took the phone and he gave me a single nod, once down, his chin coming back up slowly, his eyes never leaving mine, and he was just as abruptly gone as he'd appeared on the other side of the door.

I swallowed hard and leaned forward, peeking around the door frame at the dirty patches on the back of his vest, at the barbed wire wrapped sacred heart emblem on the back of it and I sighed.

I knew *exactly* how that felt. My own heart squeezing down painfully as I stared at the shiny black screen of the phone in my hand.

I swallowed hard and pressed the button, jumping when the thing lit up in my hand and closing my eyes for a second while I berated myself for being so dumb.

Except I wasn't dumb. He'd told me just to point and that he would unleash hell and I *believed him*. I knew in my heart of hearts that Maverick was far more dangerous than any physical weapon I had ever had the occasion to hold in my hand, because as long as *I* held it, I had control over it. Over the aim, over how it was used…

If I pulled Maverick's trigger, the outcome was wholly unpredictable. Unlike a gun where you pulled the trigger once and only one round fired, with Maverick it was more like opening a Pandora's Box and like Pandora's Box, whatever was let out wasn't going back in.

I opened my eyes and picked out the number I meant to call and let out a sigh, turning out the doorway to the bathroom and turning in the opposite direction of where Maverick had gone.

I shut myself in the bedroom and mouth as dry as a bone, I made the call…

"*Si,* who's this?" That was Lupe, straight and to the point.

"It's me, Marisol," I said, my accent naturally thickening any time I spoke English with one of my people from back home.

She gave a haughty laugh and asked, "You get tired of the gringos? Want to come home?"

"No, nothing like that," I said and tried to tamp down my irritation. Lupe and I weren't always friends – more like frenemies. Still, I was hoping she would help me out here. "I was hoping you knew the name of the shop Fernando works at out here, or where it's at."

"Fernando?" she asked incredulously, and I hissed.

"Don't pretend you don't talk to my cousin," I said harshly. "I know you two had a thing!"

She harrumphed and clicked her tongue on the other end of the line and demanded, "Why do you want to know?"

Shit.

"One of the gringo's has a car, it's acting up, I thought Fernando could use the work and maybe…" I trailed off hoping she would bite.

"Maybe what?" she demanded, the superiority back in her tone. Fucking *puta*.

"Okay," I said exasperated, making it sound like I was giving in. "I'm a little homesick and I thought it might be nice to see some family – even if they *do* hate me."

She laughed and it was a sharp, jagged sound.

"Mercutio's Used Tire, it's on some street called Aurora in the city. I can't wait to hear how this goes over." I could *hear* the eye roll in her voice, the sheer spite and malice abrasive through the line.

"*Gracias,*" I told her and sighed.

"You should have stayed here," she said.

"How is Mateo?" I asked and she scoffed.

"If you were here, you would know," she said as nasty as can be, and she hung up on me.

I was going to punch her the next time I saw her, but I got what I needed.

I sank down onto the edge of the bed and sighed.

I could stop this. I could lie and say that she wouldn't tell me – that I didn't know, but her malicious oily tone with which she spoke to me grated on my last good nerve. All of them… all of them were complicit. Some through fear, others like Lupe were just that big of a cunt, and you know what?

Fuck them. Fuck them all.

I got up, gathered my newfound power around me like a cape, and went out into the hall, my traditional skirt swishing around my legs. It looked awkward paired with the random tee shirt I had on, but the laundry wasn't finished, and I was comfortable as could be and not trying to impress anyone.

I paused at the edge of the living room, Maverick at his cluttered glass desk, pecking at the keys of his laptop. I froze and said nothing, simply waiting for him to notice me as my doubts began to niggle at the edges of my weak resolve.

This was no decision to be made for a petty sleight.

There is nothing petty about anything any of them have done to you... a voice in the back of my head reminded me.

"What's up?" he asked without looking up.

I drew in a deep slow breath. "His name is Fernando. He works at Mercutio's Used Tire on Aurora."

Maverick looked up then and fixed me with his gaze, his expression stone, yet still pride managed to shine lightly from his being.

"Okay," he said. "Get dressed, let's go."

"What?" I asked, alarmed.

"I said, get dressed and we'll go." He leaned back in his seat and fixed me with a calm, unreadable look, his gaze roving over me slowly.

"I…" I stopped before saying it. Before saying *I don't want to go*. I didn't, did I?

I blinked and he said evenly, "You don't have to go if you don't want to. I can do it on my own."

I swallowed hard and said, "No, I'll go, just let me get dressed, like you said…"

He nodded carefully and I turned and went back down the hall to our room, shutting the door firmly and leaning against it, feeling like I was caught up on this runaway train.

Something was being done… so why was I so resistant suddenly?

I didn't know. I was scared to analyze it too deeply. All I knew was that as awful as I was feeling, there was a part of me, deep down in the darkest pits, that was like *yessss.*

It was confusing, but I couldn't think about it. I needed to get dressed. We were going, and maybe if I was there, he wouldn't have to hurt Fernando who was angry with me. Who believed I was a liar and whose loyalty, understandably, remained with his father?

THE RIDE TOOK US NORTH, through the underground tunnel, which was big, well-lit, white, and still *so incredibly scary* for some reason. There was this old movie with Sylvester Stallone about some kind of disaster in a tunnel like this, where the lights went out and people were trapped in their cars in the dark.

I vaguely remember watching it with my papa when I was small, before Mateo. It had been a weekend and he had been drinking his *michelada* which was cerveza mixed with clamato. I thought it was disgusting, the smell was just blech… but I missed that smell now because it reminded me of him before my world was plunged into chaos and darkness.

I was relieved when we burst out from the big tunnel, back under the wide blue skies with its faint brush strokes of high wispy white cloud. The sun was bright and a little punishing but the wind washing over us helped some with cooling us.

The ride was beautiful, regardless of the close tunnel and the high and somewhat muggy heat. I mean, it was quite a bit more humid than I was used to here, but it wasn't an *oppressive* humidity. Rather, where the moisture hung in the air and the wind blew over the water, it was just a little bit cooler. Nice, and it got nicer still as we made the approach to the Aurora Bridge. Trees shaded the roadway from the worst of the sun, their broad green leaves rustling in the summer wind, making it several degrees cooler. The short reprieve from the punishing rays of the sun welcome and utterly refreshing until we hit the narrow lanes of the bridge and the world opened exponentially to either side.

The bridge took us over the Fremont Cut, a narrow body of water that was almost a roadway for boats and ships to come from the Puget Sound through the Ballard Locks to pass under the Aurora Bridge into Lake Union. I focused on our right, and the view through the suicide prevention bars of Lake Union, Gasworks Park was on the north end of the lake far down below with its rusting hulk of old machinery surrounded by manicured lawns. It looked particularly inviting and I wished we could go there, just me and Maverick, and sit on the big mound of grass built up there looking south across the lake at the Space Needle as the sun went down.

It seemed much preferable to where we were heading and what we were doing now.

In some ways, I hoped my cousin wasn't there and this trip ended up being all for naught. Then maybe I could suggest going to the park and pretend none of this was even happening.

Alas, it didn't pan out that way. Nothing ever really did in my favor, so why I thought this would be any different was beyond me.

We pulled into the left-hand turn lane in front of the used tire place somewhere past Green Lake but before 85th Street. The building was bright, obnoxiously, so. The main body of the building almost a traffic cone orange, the trim a blinding yellow around the windows, the door to the office and the single big garage bay door that was open on both ends, front and back, to have the ability to pull cars straight through.

The garage bay with its lift was empty and Maverick pulled right in, my heart sinking when Fernando stood up from a dirty red machine in the corner where he was putting a tire onto a rim.

Maverick cut the motor on the bike and leaned it, heeling down the kickstand while I jumped off.

"We don't got no motorcycle tires, mister. You should have called first," Fernando called out to us and I pulled the glasses off from over my eyes and the bandana down from over my face. My cousin's eyes went steely and he frowned.

"Oh, now what the fuck are *you* doing here?" he demanded.

"Her?" Maverick asked, groaning as he stood up. "She's just along for the ride," he said. "I'm the one who wants to talk to you."

"And what the fuck do *you* want?"

Maverick yanked his red bandana down and took off his helmet, setting it off to the side behind him on the seat of his bike, which he'd just vacated.

"I wanna have a talk with your daddy," Maverick said succinctly. "And you're gonna tell me how I can find him."

Fernando laughed in our faces and Maverick's friendly smile cooled by several thousand degrees.

"We can do this the easy way, or the hard way, Fernando. Our beef ain't with you."

"Yeah?" Fernando asked, reaching behind him for a sturdy wrench off the bench. "Fuck you."

"Marisol," Maverick said, and I stood frozen, like a deer in headlights out on the road. "Get the door for me."

I swallowed hard, mouth dry and Fernando crossed his arms over his dirty, grease-smudged white tee. He had on a pair of light blue, equally dirty, striped coveralls, the top part rolled down and bunched at his waist, the sleeves knotted there to hold them up.

He was strong, broad chested and chiseled. All muscle from hard labor and there was a reason why all the girls like Lupe fell all over themselves to get with him. The problem was, he was a raging *dick*. Had something like four kids already at twenty-seven and didn't see or keep up on his child support for any of them.

"*Now*," Maverick said, and I jumped slightly. I took the two steps over to the box with the three-square buttons on the wall and hit the bottom one marked *'down.'* The door rattled, the steel unfurling, as it slowly made its way down. The light diminished by a little, but it was late afternoon and was coming in the back door for the most part, now. There was no need to bring that door down, though. It just faced the back parking lot and a barren concrete wall. The houses perched high above on the artificial plateau of land created by said walls sat in such a way that the view from them would be of the roof of the ugly little shop, if they had a view down here at all.

"I'm not telling you shit," Fernando said dispassionately, spitting on the cement floor at Maverick's feet. "Now you can take that lying fucking *puta* out of here and never look back. You get me?"

Maverick looked completely unconcerned and unfazed by what came out of Fernando's mouth, but I knew different by the slight tick of the muscle in Mav's jaw.

"See, now what happens next is solely predicated on the decisions you're about to make," Maverick said calmly. So calmly, it rose the hair on the back of my neck.

"Fernando…" I said and his head whipped in my direction.

"Shut up!" he snarled.

"Fernando," Maverick said firmly, and my cousin's attention whipped back in Mav's direction.

"I'm going to ask one more time, nicely… How do I find your daddy?"

"Man, fuck you, and fuck this." Fernando advanced on Maverick with the wrench and I jumped but Maverick just stood his ground. Fernando swung at Mav and I yelped in fear, jumping, pressing my hands to my mouth but I needn't have worried – at least not for Maverick.

He smoothly side-stepped my cousin who swung again, Mav leaning back, arching just out of the way. Fernando growled and Mav struck so lightning quickly, I almost didn't see it.

He shoved Fernando and sent him sprawling, the wrench clattering and clanging against the stained concrete and skittering out of my cousin's reach.

"Last chance," Maverick declared in an almost singsong mocking voice. My cousin growled and got to his feet, raising his fists. He and Mav started circling and Maverick shook his head.

"Just remember," he said, my cousin straightening slightly and frowning harder, "you chose this."

Fernando roared like an angry bull and came for Mav, but Maverick was both smarter and faster. He let Fernando overbalance and swept my cousin past him. Mav's hand knotted in the back of my cousin's tee as he fetched him up hard, face first, into one of the legs of the auto lift.

My man pressed his body into my cousin's back almost lover-like and intimate, bringing his face close in, pressing the barrel of the gun that appeared like magic in his other hand into my cousin's cheek that wasn't pressed into the lift.

Fernando's eyes widened and he held up his hands in surrender.

"Now, I'm not asking nice anymore," Maverick declared coldly. "Where's your fucking daddy at?"

"Come on, man!" Fernando's voice was high and tight with panic and I stared at the scene in front of me. I stared at my cousin's wide and frightened eyes and wondered how many times he'd put that same look on my face. How many times he'd backed me into the side of one of the houses and put his nose practically to mine and threatened me into silence. How many times he'd told me if I didn't shut the fuck up about his father, how he would make sure I was raped for real. Or how he would hurt me so bad I would wish I were dead.

A moment of clarity overtook me in that moment, staring at him like that. So, scared he was about to piss himself, all his power stripped away.

My eyes tracked to Maverick, my lover, my man, and his words came back to me… *you just point, and I'll unleash hell.*

I'd pointed, and he was here, and if this wasn't hell, I didn't know what was but for once *I* wasn't the one expected to suffer. What's more? I hadn't done anything *wrong* unlike Fernando.

I mean, I couldn't say that Fernando had done anything wrong either; at least not initially. In one regard I did pity him… he had a child molester for a father and his only sin was that he didn't want to believe that. I could understand that. I could… and so watching what was happening now made my gut do an uncomfortable twist.

"Fernando," I pleaded. "Just tell him what he wants to know so we can go!"

Maverick pressed a little more insistently with the barrel of the gun and Fernando cried, "Okay, okay!" and babbled like a brook. Information flowed freely after that. The brook giving way to a torrent.

I breathed a silent sigh of relief and didn't understand why Maverick didn't back off when he'd gotten what he wanted.

"He ever lay a hand on you?" Maverick asked and it was only

when Fernando yipped out, "What? No!" that I realized that he was talking to me.

"Not sexually, no," I answered, because that time pinned against the side of my grandmother's house, his fingers digging into my face as he grabbed my chin was all too fresh in my memory.

"Not sexually, but he's hurt you?" Maverick demanded.

I nodded.

"Where you want him shot?" he asked me.

"I don't want you to shoot him," I said, and Mav bore into Fernando that much harder.

"You hear that, Junior? She doesn't want you shot. She doesn't want you hurt, but we don't always get what we want, now do we?"

He clubbed my cousin in the head with his gun. Blood spurted from Fernando's eyebrow and he planted on his ass on the cement beside the lift, a hand going to his head in a daze. Maverick leaned down and grabbed my cousin's chin in an eerie echo of how he'd grabbed mine, forcing Fernando to look up at him. Fernando gripped Mav's wrist and Maverick doubled down, forcing the barrel of the gun into Fernando's mouth.

"Mav, stop!" I cried, alarmed.

"You listen here," Maverick commanded, ignoring me. "That there had better leave a scar. I mean it. I want it to be a reminder, every time you look in the mirror, that that girl showed you mercy today. The mercy you never afforded her, you ignorant fucking fuck. Next time a woman tells you something, you better fuckin' believe her and I swear to God, you call the cops? You tell anyone about this at all, I'm gonna find you, and I'm gonna finish what I fucking started here. I'm all outta mercy. Now nod if you understand me."

Fernando nodded emphatically and I felt like I was going to throw up.

"Marisol, get on the bike."

I did what I was told, and Maverick let my cousin go. Straightening, he kneed him in the face, Fernando's nose crunched, and his hands flew to cover it and to catch the blood spilling down it.

"Glad I could make myself clear," Maverick said, tucking the gun into the back of his pants and coming over to me. I handed him his helmet and he got onto the front of his bike, starting her up.

I clung to him, giving one last look down on my cousin who looked up at me in terror through the mask of blood on his face and tears glossing his eyes and I felt my own expression close down.

I felt nothing, then. No pity, and certainly no satisfaction.

I didn't know what I felt, but the closest thing I could say was probably numb?

We pulled around the side of the building and up to the street.

"You hungry?" Maverick called over his shoulder as though he hadn't just terrorized a member of my family and half bashed his face in. The question caught me off guard and I realized that *yeah…* yeah, I was hungry.

"Yeah!" I called back to him and he smiled as though pleased.

"That's my girl!" he called out and turned us right out of the driveway and onto the street, back in the direction from which we came.

CHAPTER TWENTY-ONE

*M*averick…

I took us to the Salmon House on Northlake Way. She perked up a little when we passed Gasworks Park, and I made a mental note to ask her about it later.

I wasn't interested in going into the fine dining part of the restaurant with the killer views of the city from across the lake. No, the cool thing about the Salmon House was the fact that they had a more down-to-earth counter out front with some picnic tables. A sort of food truck vibe out of the building front.

I pulled up to the curb and Marisol got down off the bike, her hands automatically going to her chinstrap to take her helmet off. I held out my hand for it after I shut off my ride and slipped the strap over one of the handlebars, letting it dangle. She put her sunglasses up on top of her head and her eyes were sullen, almost sad but not angry, her expression otherwise unreadable.

"You doin' alright?" I asked her, and she looked me over, her eyes wandering over my face.

She frowned slightly, a small line appearing between her perfectly winged brows and she said, "I don't know yet."

"That's fair," I said with a nod and swung a leg over the bike, standing after hanging my helmet off the other handlebar, my mirrored sunglasses still in place. She held out her hand to me and I took it, giving it a couple of squeezes. "For what it's worth, you did good back there."

She shuddered slightly and sighed, saying, "I almost feel like we should be far away from here. I mean, I don't think he will but we can't be sure he won't..." she gave a furtive glance around us, at anyone who may or may not be listening and finished with a quiet, "You know."

"Yeah, I know," I said with a nod. "There'll be consequences if he does."

She nodded and I sighed. I'd gone own fucking program today and I knew it, but she didn't need to know. The guys would be pissed – I should have brought at least two of them with me, a typical wrecking crew. That, or I should have just sent Fen and D.T. to get the information – but in my own way, I'd needed to do this with her. Needed to know what she could handle and needed her to see firsthand that something was being done.

I put my trust in her today, and I was hoping to get a little of that back.

We went and got in line with the rest of the citizens and waited our turn.

"Thank you," she murmured, and I linked my fingers with hers.

We got up to the counter after a bit, ordering our fried fish and chips, me the salmon, her the halibut. We waited in silence for our number to be called and took a seat at a rickety, two-seater and metal mesh table set with two hard plastic lawn chairs.

We ate in yet more silence, and it was a comfortable one – at least for me. She seemed troubled, but also, judging by the expression on her face, thoughtful. She was still processing, and I let her. If she had questions, she would ask them, I was sure of it – and if she didn't, I would urge her to when we were alone or in a safe place to have that talk.

"Can we go to the park back there at the end of the lake?" she asked suddenly, and I looked up from my cardboard boat of fried food.

"Yeah," I said. "Got something on your mind?"

"A lot, but nothing I want to talk about here," she said, giving a furtive glance at a nearby table.

I nodded and we finished our meal.

We took a short ride back to Gasworks Park and I pulled up in a spot that wasn't exactly a designated parking spot, but the bike fit, and it was kept out of the way so… yeah, it was now. She linked her fingers with mine and we strolled along one of the wide pathways. There were people, but it was a lot less crowded than it had been back at the restaurant. I waited on her to be comfortable enough to speak.

"My dad brought me here once," she said abruptly. "A long time ago, before Mateo."

"Ah, yeah?" I asked and smiled.

She nodded and her expression was somber.

"We sat up on the hill."

"Want to go there now?" I asked.

"Yeah," she said, and we gently changed trajectory in that direction.

"What's going to happen now?" she asked when we were free and clear of any potential eavesdropping.

"Not for you to worry about, babe," I told her.

"But I do worry. Not about my cousin or my uncle… not anymore. I worry about *you*."

"*Me*?" I asked and I had to confess, my grin was cocky. I liked hearing it. No, I *loved* hearing that from her. Her words suffused me with a tingling warmth.

"Yes, you," she said, and her tone was an exasperated one. "You're right," her voice softly came this time, her hand tightening around mine. "They aren't my family. I've been alone for a very long time – I just didn't realize it."

I tugged her into my side and put the arm that had been holding her hand around her, taking her under my wing, so to speak.

"You don't have to be alone like that if you don't want to. Not anymore," I said, and she looked up at me, her face the most open I'd ever seen it. "I like having you around, *Zaychik*. I would love it if you thought about staying."

"Staying?" she asked, as though the thought hadn't occurred to her – and maybe it hadn't. Shit, she was used to everyone *not* wanting her around, except for maybe her little brother. It was an oversight I committed to avoid making again. She had a lot of lost love and acceptance that needed making up for and I really aimed to be the man to make up for all of it.

"Yeah," I said. "And not just to clean or act as some friggin' sex doll. I fucked up in the beginning thinking that's what you wanted. That you were just some kind of kinky, which I am all on board for, don't get me wrong, but that was my mistake. I thought that was what you really wanted – not that it was desperation driving you. I was too distracted by my own shit. I feel like I screwed the pooch and I'm sorry."

She shrugged her shoulders, lifting my arm that went across them slightly, but not shrugging me off. Without looking at me she said, "It's not your fault. I would have said or done *anything* to get you to take me with you, to get away from there. I just latched on to whatever you wanted to believe just to make that happen."

"You're a clever girl, *Zaychik*. I'll give you that," I said and smiled to myself wondering if I'd let myself be played for a fool on that front as much as she had casually just said I'd been, or if deep down, I'd let my sixth sense about these kinds of things take the handlebars. Either way, I wasn't upset. I'd known from the beginning something was odd, something was off about *Abuela* and the rest of that camp.

I came up in a crime family, myself. Lift a few rocks at the base of anybody's family tree and you'd be surprised at the vermin that came out. I was no exception to that rule. Neither was Marisol, but it was about time the vermin in her family, bloated with their ichor, felt what it was like to starve a little.

The rest of the family that'd been starving, like Marisol, well, it was their time to feast at the tables that turned.

"What do you want in all of this, baby?" I asked her when we reached a certain point up the big mound of grass off to one side of the old rusting coal gasification plant. That was how the park had gotten its name. The rusting hulk of machinery was fenced off and just interesting to look at, now. A lot of the locals used it as a backdrop for their steampunk pics for their cosplays. It was a cool old feature of Seattle's rapidly diminishing history in the face of modern invention. I couldn't tell you how many classical old buildings had fallen at the hands of whatever tech giant that'd demolished them for more office space.

It was a personal philosophy of mine that you needed to remember where the fuck you came from in order to avoid the mistakes of the past.

It was also a philosophy to ponder a different time as Marisol dipped out from under my arm to sit in the dry grass on the hillside. I joined her, planting my ass beside hers, the dry grass prickling me through the seat of my jeans left exposed by the added protection of my chaps.

She looked over at me and scooted closer and I smiled and pulled her in. She cuddled into my chest and I laid us back, staring up at the true-blue sky as she answered my question.

"I don't know what I want. It's like I am shattered into a million pieces and each part of me wants something different," she said.

"Make a list," I suggested.

"I want Mateo with me," she said. "I don't want *Abuela* to turn on him because I'm not there."

"Okay, what else?"

"I don't know what to do about *Abuela*," she said, and she sounded so hopeless, so lost. "She is so confusing. She rules everyone with this surface kindness until you dare disagree with her and then suddenly, it's like the snakes come out of her head and she turns into this big monster. Everyone is afraid of her and that's why no one will cross her. Everyone is just too afraid to step a toe out of line..." She hugged herself to me closer and shuddered.

Sounded to me like she'd taken a real damn big risk coming with me. I mean, what if things had gone differently? What if she'd managed to keep her secret, or I hadn't known or found out about things and I'd gone and handed her back in a week or two?

I asked her, and she wouldn't speak on it. The resounding silence telling me everything I needed to know.

"Sounds to me like *Abuela* needs to be taken down a few pegs."

"I honestly think things could be so much better for the people if she were but by the same token… what if it's better the devil you know?"

I nodded slowly, the wheels turning in my head.

Far be it from me to tell another man how to live his life. That wasn't exactly what this life was about… but maybe there was a way in all of this to have our cake and eat it too. Make life just a little better for those that needed it and bring a little street justice to those that deserved it.

We talked, me and my girl. The afternoon sun lazing on its downhill slide toward the horizon.

It was one of those magic times where time slowed significantly and it was just her and I, the rest of the world a light and distant buzz of activity around us – simply white noise. Eventually, that white noise broke through in the form of some whooping and hollering down the way toward the water.

Marisol and I sat up, a troupe of hippie-looking street kids gathered down below setting up a big ol' speaker and unrolling tapestries full of charred equipment. Fans, swords, balls at the ends of chains, and I smiled.

"Looks like we came on the right day," I said.

"Who are they?" Marisol asked, shading her eyes with her hand despite the sunglasses perched atop her hair.

"Fire spinners," I answered. "Come on down, let's get closer."

"Okay."

And that's how we spent the rest of our evening, watching the local fire spinners and performers practice, the thrum of electronic and industrial dance music pulsing through our bodies as the sun set.

It was a good way to end the day and I felt closer than ever to my girl. Like she had finally let me in.

<hr>

CHAPTER TWENTY-TWO

<hr>

*M*arisol...

The next few days were quiet. Maverick didn't bring up my uncle or *Abuela*, but we did talk about Mateo. He told me to fix up the other room for my brother, gave me his credit card and told me to order what I needed to for my little brother.

I stood frozen to the spot, my heart filling to bursting for this rough and wild man in front of me.

Just like that, he held out the small rectangle of plastic to me and with it, everything my heart had ever desired. A home. My brother. A life away from the orchards of Eastern Washington and my corrupt grandmother. He held out everything I had ever wanted, and I took it, throwing my arms around him and kissing him soundly. My desire for him unmatched in that moment.

"Okay," he said, laughing between fierce kisses. "Okay, I've got to go. Use the laptop on my desk, I'll see you when I get home."

"Okay," I breathed and then, there I was standing in the room that would be my brother's trying to decide what to do with it. There were endless possibilities but a lot of work yet to be done before I could get to them.

When Mav came through the kitchen door, it was to find me somewhat frazzled and exhausted, primer freckling my face and the bandana I used to cover my hair as I stirred some fresh made *pico de gallo* in a bowl at the cutting board.

"Smells good," he said, shrugging out of his jacket and cut, hanging them on the back of one of the kitchen chairs at the counter. He slid up onto the same seat at the same time I slid some Juanita's chips and the fresh *pico* across the counter at him.

"It's gonna be a bit before the main course is ready," I told him, checking its progress in the oven. "Thought you might want a snack when you got in."

"Mm." He crunched through one of the tortilla chips loaded with fresh vegetables. "Mm-hm!" He nodded appreciatively.

"Trying something American," I said. "Figured you might be getting a little tired of Mexican every night."

He chuckled, chewing slowly, and swallowing his bite before asking, "What have you got going on in there?"

"Just a chicken," I said with a shrug. "Looked up a recipe online. Figured some baked chicken and a salad with some chips and salsa sounded light and healthy – well, all except maybe the chips part."

Mav laughed and nodded. "Sounds good, babe. Sounds really good."

"Awesome," I said with a smile. I set out a couple of plates and moved around the kitchen getting various things ready for the bird to come out of the oven. The salad was already made and waiting. I'd done that along with the salsa.

"So, how much progress you make?" he asked, and I smiled and answered, "Not enough. I have the primer on the walls and ceiling – still trying to decide what to do with the rest. I haven't spent any money yet."

"I ain't worried about it. You need help, you just holler."

"I was thinking about painting it in his favorite soccer team's colors. He loves *fútbol*, just like our dad."

"Nice." Maverick nodded.

"You seriously don't care what I do to your house?" I asked and stared at him across the kitchen island.

"Our house," he corrected with a shrug.

"You're serious…"

"Why wouldn't I be?"

I rolled my eyes.

"Uh, you barely know me?"

"I know enough about you," he said. "I know enough to know that you and me? We're a good fit."

I blushed at the intense look he gave me, the double entendre stark.

I cleared my throat and finished dinner without a word. Maverick kept checking his phone, but when I asked, wouldn't tell me why. I shrugged it off. It was probably club business and I didn't need to know.

"Leave them for later," he said when I started the dishes after we'd finished our meal and I frowned.

"*Abuela* would have my ass if I left a sink full of dirty dishes after a meal," I said with a dark laugh.

"Yeah, well, that bitch ain't here to tell you what to do, now is she?" he asked, and I smiled and shook my head.

"No, but just because she *is* a bitch doesn't mean all of her lessons were bad ones," I countered.

"True enough," he said with a nod and sighed.

"I'll leave them for now," I murmured, and he smiled at me, reaching out to cup my cheek, smoothing a thumb over my skin and the way he looked at me? It was as if I were a work of art.

I lived sometimes for the way he looked at me. Especially when it was like that.

"Let's get you cleaned up, huh?" he murmured gently, and I bit my bottom lip to contain my smile.

"You just want to get me naked," I said playfully, and he grinned.

"Fuck yeah, I do."

I left the damn dishes for later.

He took me into the bathroom, and we showered together. Long, the water hot, the foreplay steamy as we took care of each other, reverently washing the other's body while kissing slowly. I took his hard length in my hand, stroking him surely, his moan soft and sensual amid the rainfall from his showerhead.

I wouldn't be denied. I wanted to make him feel good, and so I went to my knees and took him into my mouth, looking up the lean muscled length of his torso into those deep blue indigo eyes of his while I made love to him with my mouth.

The velvet length of him was hot, like steel against my tongue which I tantalized him with so softly, sucking on him like a popsicle on a hot sunny day.

I loved the look in his eyes, the way his lips slightly parted, the way he threw back his head, his fists knotted at his sides to keep from grabbing my head. The way he held himself in check but just barely.

God, all of it – everything about him was super fucking hot and I wanted so badly for him to be mine and only mine. I just didn't know how that worked in his world…

"God, baby, get up here," he demanded gasping, and I let his dick fall from my lips with an audible pop.

He reached down and hauled me to my feet, crushing his mouth over mine. I wrapped my arms around his shoulders and pressed my body tight to his as the gentle rainfall of his showerhead soaked us, and I couldn't think of anyplace I would rather be.

"Fuck, you're gorgeous," he growled, and I smiled, nipping the side of his neck lightly.

"Take me to bed," I ordered deviously, and he grinned.

"Thought you'd never ask."

"Cute how you think I'm asking," I said, gasping myself when he kissed the side of my neck.

He gave me a slap on my ass, and I yipped, laughing, and let him lead me into the bedroom.

The playfulness between us quickly gave way to a sudden and fierce ardor. Mouths clashed, hands gripped, arms pulling each other tightly into the curve and shelter of the other. Warm skin still damp from the shower, bodies pressing tight. It was different this time, mostly because I wholly gave myself over to it.

By now, I could trust that Maverick had nothing but the best of intentions where I was concerned and I wanted so desperately to know what it felt like to… to really be *loved*, that I was willing to lie to myself and believe that he did.

Eres estúpida, I thought savagely to myself. *Of course, he loves you! What man does what he is doing for you that doesn't love the woman he does these things for?*

He'd also as good as said he loved me, too… or rather he'd said *"I'm beginning to love you."* That was the same thing, though, right?

I didn't know, but what I *did* know was that I was feeling it too. This deep desire to always be near him and not just because of what he was doing for me. He treated me better than I had ever been treated before. He treated me like his *queen*, but not like a trophy girl on his arm.

He asked questions, wanted my opinion, in fact – he was asking me more frequently on my perspective on things I wasn't entirely sure I should know… things that should have been under the umbrella of 'club business.'

I didn't mind, though. In fact, I preferred not to be kept in the dark. I was a big girl, I could handle it, and I was determined to prove it every day if I had to by listening and by keeping my mouth shut.

Of course, with the way Maverick was laying me down in the center of his bed, and with how he kissed his way down my body, his gaze intense, his intentions clear, I wouldn't be keeping my mouth shut very much longer. Then again, I think he preferred it when I got loud in the bedroom.

His mouth was warm, wet, and soft, his tongue against my clit sending a pleasurable fission of energy throughout my body. I gripped his sable soft hair in my hands and pulled his mouth tight against my pussy, moaning loudly, that moan interrupted by a short cry as he introduced fingers inside of me.

He knew just the spot, how to play me like a fiddle. I arched for him, loosening my hold on his hair so I wouldn't hurt him as he moaned in satisfaction against my body, excited to be there. Like he'd found his ultimate happy place between my thighs.

I cannot impress what a pure, unadulterated, *joy* the sounds he made brought to me, both on an intellectual and a physical plane. The vibrations of his voice through his lips sent sparks of light flitting through me. The pads of his fingertips teasing inside me created a growing weight, a warmth in my pussy that almost, *almost* mimicked the sensation of a full bladder.

I'd learned, though, that if I just *relaxed* and let it happen, that he could do amazing things with my body and that growing warmth.

"Oh, yes!" I cried breathy. "Oh, yes! Yes, yes, yes, yes, *yes! Oh, God!*"

I jolted, body rocking against his mouth, fists relocating to grip the sheets to either side of my hips, holding on for dear life as the orgasm *rocked me* to my core. Gasping, screaming, body writhing with the pleasure as he leaned up and I felt a *gush* of wetness between my thighs, around his invading fingers.

"That's my girl," he said happily, a lazy, self-satisfied, and smug grin turning up the corners of his mouth.

"Don't stop, don't stop," I begged, bucking my hips against his hand.

"Shhh, relax, baby. Just relax, I ain't gonna quit. You just lie there and feel good."

He pulled me all the way thorough one orgasm, out the other side, then kept teasing me all through the resulting tremors to slowly start building me up again for more.

"I need you," I whispered, eyes heavy lidded with passion.

"You want my cock?" he asked, and I smiled.

"I need your cock," I countered, and his smile grew. He reached for a condom on the bedside table, pulling his fingers out of me, and I shivered. It was always so fucking hot watching him roll the rubber down his thick shaft, watching him make himself ready to claim me body first, then soul...

He walked up the bed on his knees and lifted one of my legs, pressing my calf to his shoulder, stroking his cock between us, pressing a reverent kiss to my leg, his lips warm and silky. The juxtaposition of his gentle touches and the savagery with which he shoved his cock inside my wet and waiting cunt left me arching off the bed and crying out in surprise.

He seated himself deep inside me, balls deep, body pressed tight to mine, hugging my leg with both of his arms, grinding against me, touching off a firestorm of sensations and emotions within me.

"That's it," he murmured encouragingly. "That's it."

I gasped, massaging my own breasts for his lustful gaze, and let the world, my troubles, and everything else that clung to me at every other time completely fall away.

The only other time I felt this free was when I rode with Maverick on his bike and this? Having him inside me, looking at me like that? It was far better than *any* wind therapy out there.

____

CHAPTER TWENTY-THREE

____

*M*averick...

My phone rang in the middle of the night, and it was Dahlia's ringtone. I frowned, stirring as the song played and Marisol wiggled her spectacular ass against my soft cock, quickly giving me a semi. I put a hand to her hip to stop her from moving and groped for my phone on the nightstand.

"Hey, what's wrong?" I asked in greeting. Dahlia and I hadn't spoken since our fight over Marisol at the club a couple of weeks before.

"Mav?" Dahlia's voice was weak, out of sorts. She sounded dazed and confused.

"Mallory," I said using her given name, "What's wrong?" I sat up and listened to her groan slightly on the other end of the line.

"Can you come get me?" she asked, and I threw the blankets off, Marisol sitting up sharply.

"Where you at, baby?"

I waved Marisol down when she sat up sharply scowling.

"Mav, can you come get me?" she repeated and said, "Something's wrong. I don't... I don't feel right."

"You just hang on, Mal, I'll be right there. Just hang on, for me. I'll track your phone." I handed the phone to Marisol who looked both alarmed and suddenly eager to help.

"Keep her talking," I said and she nodded putting the phone to her ear.

"Hello?" she said, then a pause. "He's getting dressed right now, he said to talk to you." Another pause and then, "That's fine, you don't have to talk to me, you just need to stay on the line. Do you know where you are?"

Marisol took it like a champ, talking to my best friend who was clearly being her bitchy self on the other end of the line while I put on clothes, scooped up my burner and put out a mass text to the guys.

Tic-Tac, Glass Jaw, and Dump Truck answered. I picked Tic-Tac and Dump Truck to get their asses up and meet up with me, texting them the coordinates my regular phone was spitting out as to where Mallory was at.

As my best friend, I knew what a pain in the ass she could be, and it frustrated me that we were at odds over Marisol, but there was a reason Mal was my platonic hetero life mate. Reasons I wish I could put into words, but there just weren't any.

Marisol, to her credit, helped me help my best friend without complaint, at least for right now.

"Tell her we're on our way and let me get hooked up," I said, and Marisol nodded.

"Yeah, honey. He's on his way, just a few more seconds and I'll give you back to him. Just hold on a minute. Yeah," she rolled her eyes, "I know I'm the last bitch you want to talk to but right now, I'm the bitch trying to help you out so spare me for the moment, yeah?"

I pressed the button on my Bluetooth, and it connected and suddenly my bestie was in my ear, "It's not that I don't like you, no… it's just that you're a fucking *child*."

"I'll let you tell her that the next time you see her and I'm not helping you out if she tries to kick your ass, now hang tight. I'm on my way."

Marisol handed me my phone and got up on her knees to press a quick kiss to my lips.

"Be careful," my woman, my queen, intoned, and I nodded.

"Mav, where are you?" Mallory asked and she sounded like she was slipping.

"Mal, baby, stay awake," I ordered and hauled ass to get to where she was.

I had no idea what the fuck was going on, but when I got to the coordinates, I was determined to find out. Tic-Tac and I had met up on the road, and when we pulled up, Dump Truck was already there – efficient bastard. That's one of the things I liked about him the most.

"Okay, we're here," I said into the phone. "We're here, baby, you just need to tell me where *you* are."

"Third floor, apartment 3B."

"3B!" I called for the benefit of the other two and pointed at a doorway that looked like it led to some stairs up. We were in Pioneer Square, and nobody but some seriously rich motherfuckers lived here. The building was not only a historic one, since the viaduct had come down, but they now possessed multi-million-dollar views as a result.

"What the fuck she got herself into?" Dump Truck growled and I knew he was only half-pissed at Dahlia, the rest of his ire stemming from the need to haul his big, half crippled ass up three floors worth of stairs.

"Dunno," Tic-Tac answered for me. "Whatever it is, fucker's gonna wish he'd never been born." To punctuate his statement, he threw down his fist, the steel collapsible baton he held in it telescoping out to its full length.

"Hold up," Dump Truck said, pointing. "Cameras."

"Boys, put your party dresses on," I said and we each shrugged out of our cuts, turning them inside out and shrugging back into them, wrapping our lower faces in bandanas and balaclavas to shield our identities.

"Gonna have to move fast," Dump Truck said. "Place like this is bound to be alarmed, closed circuit maybe, but any security is bad news for us bears."

"Stay down here," I told him, and he gave a nod.

"Me and stairs does not equal fast," he agreed.

"Tic-Tac, let's go."

We surged across the cracked and crumbling asphalt to the door to the stairs leading up into the rest of the building. It was wood and ancient, framing a large glass pane with the street number for the building gold leafed onto its front. It fit the building, looking all classy and historically accurate, but it didn't do shit about keeping us out.

"Mav, he's waking up," Dahlia said in my ear, the alarm clearly telegraphed through her voice.

"Man, *move*, we gotta *move*." I slipped through the portal left behind by the shattered glass first, double-timing it up the stairs as Mallory made a noise in my ear somewhere between frightened and desperate, the phone on her end clattering to the floor.

I reached the wooden door on the third floor marked '3B' with its shiny brass plate and lunged at it with my shoulder. The door shuddered in its frame and groaned under the onslaught. Close, one more ought to do it. I squared up and let fly with a booted foot and the door-frame cracked and splintered, the plank flying inward, swinging on its hinges to crack against the drywall behind it.

Tic-Tac followed my breech, sliding through into the apartment and I was right on his six.

He swept through a posh living room with views of the sound and through a doorway that must have been a bedroom. I was right behind him, just in time to see Tic-Tac tee off with his asp, cracking the motherfucker that was on top of Dahlia in the back of his skull, laying him out.

He pitched forward, his hands coming off Dahlia's throat. I went for her and let Tic-Tac deal with the fucker that'd been choking my best friend out.

"I got you, hold on, baby, I got you." I helped her up onto her feet and she choked and wobbled on her heels, trying to get air. She was in her underwear, her dress was gone, and I looked around the tousled bed covers for it somewhat frantically.

"You two move the fuck out of the way," Tic-Tac gritted between his clenched teeth. He was seething, breathing in and out, barely able to contain his rage.

"Don't kill him," Dahlia choked out. "You cripple that son of a bitch, though. Break every fucking limb!"

"You don't call these kinds of shots," I reminded her tersely. I looked to Tic-Tac who looked to me and I said, "No witnesses."

Savage glee sparked in his light blue eyes and he took his asp handle in two hands and beat that motherfucker to death. I mean, he just caved that rat bastard's skull in. I got me and Dahlia both out of the way of cast off from the weapon and shoved her out into the living room, helping her into the ruin of her dress.

"What happened?" I demanded.

"Picked me up after the show at the bar, came back here for some sexy times, he got rough – I wasn't having any of it. Mav, he stuck me with something, a needle. I barely got my taser out of my purse. Knocked him out cold. I called you."

"You can always call me," I reminded her.

"I know," she said, shaking.

"Now come on."

"Go!" Tic-Tac called. "I got the rest of her shit."

"You good to ride?" I asked.

"I don't know," she said, wobbling on her heels like a newborn gazelle. I supported her out the door and down the stairs.

"Just a few blocks, until we can get a cage to come get you."

"Okay," she said breathlessly, fighting the effects of whatever he'd given her and losing now that the adrenaline was starting to wear off.

"Goddamnit Dahlia – whatever happened to being *safe?*" I demanded.

"I was," she said feebly as we stepped awkwardly over the bottom part of the door.

"Get her a few blocks out," I commanded and passed her off to D.T.

He took her and said, "Triangle."

I nodded. He meant he would post up over near the old historic Triangle Pub near the end of the city's historical district near the football stadium.

Tic-Tac came down the stairs with a pillowcase full of shit. I nodded. Good man – make it look like a robbery.

"Let's go," he said and we got on our bikes. Dump Truck was already away.

"Triangle!" I called over the roar and with a nod, Tic-Tac fell in beside me. I pressed the button on my Bluetooth and got it to ask me who I wanted to call.

There was only one person I knew that could handle this shit, who would do what needed doing simply because I needed her to. Who wouldn't ask questions and who I could, without a doubt, rely on.

"*Zaychik*," I said into the receiver when she answered the line.

"Is she okay?" she asked first, and I knew I was making the right call.

"Yeah, but I need a favor from you."

"Anything," she said, and I knew she meant it.

"You know how to drive?"

"Do I know how? Yes. Can I? If I had a car. Do I have my license? No."

"Get dressed, in the kitchen by the back door there's a set of keys. Dump Truck is coming to get you. Ride with him to the Public Storage in Burien. The gate code is 9278, the storage locker is 98. He knows where it is and which key. I need you to follow him to where we are and drive Dahlia. Can you do all that for me?"

"I did say *anything*, Maverick. The question is, is she going to be cool with me or is she going to act like a dumb bitch?"

"I think she OD'ed on dumb bitch juice tonight. Tic-Tac and I will be with her. It'll be okay."

"On my way, sort of. I mean, I'll be ready when Dump Truck gets here."

"Thanks," I said, pulling into the lot across the street from the Triangle. Dump Truck was sitting astride his bike, Dahlia sagging back against his chest. Looks like the drugs won.

"What's the plan?" Dump Truck called as soon as I shut off my bike.

"Tic-Tac and I are staying here with Dahlia, you're heading to my place, pick up Marisol and take her to my storage unit. She'll drive the El Camino down; you just lead her here. We'll take care of the rest."

"You sure, P? I can always call up Little Bird."

"Marisol's used to violence," I said. "No offense, brother, but your Little Bird is a delicate thing."

"When you're right, you're right. Still, fuck the extra steps. I'll run Marisol to my place, and we'll grab my grocery getter. It'll be faster than messing with gates in the middle of the fucking night."

"Didn't want to impose," I said, lifting Dahlia and taking her off his hands.

Tic-Tac took her off mine, holding onto her tight, muttering to her. I knew he had a soft spot for her, even though I swore they should be oil and water, they somehow managed to jive. I'd even go as far as to say he was Dahlia's favorite out of the guys, which was saying something.

"No imposition, man. Dahlia's family."

He swung his leg back over, twisting in his seat so he wasn't sitting backward anymore, and he fired up his bike.

"Hurry up as soon as you get a chance."

"Say no more, I'm gone," he said and left us with a shivering and sick Dahlia who retched on Tic-Tac's boots.

"Fucking great," I muttered. I had no fucking idea what kind of shit that douchebag had given her.

CHAPTER TWENTY-FOUR

*M*arisol…

It was a harrowing trip in the middle of the night, but I rode with Dump Truck back to his place where he handed me a key to Little Bird's car. When he'd picked me up, he'd said there was a slight change of plans in favor of expediency and truthfully, I was relieved. I had no idea what kind of car Maverick kept in storage, but I was betting it was worth a hell of a lot. Driving Little Bird's automatic SUV thing would be a hell of a lot easier and a lot less nerve-racking.

I followed Dump Truck downtown and to this weird parking lot near the football stadium. Maverick and Tic-Tac were both near their bikes, holding Dahlia up between them and sweet Jesus, she looked *rough* – her lipstick smeared, her eyeliner and mascara in muddy tracks down her face.

"She's fuckin' freezin'," Tic-Tac declared as Dump Truck opened the back door. I turned the heat on in the cabin to blasting from the vents as they got her in the back seat.

"What happened to her?" I asked.

"Not for us to say," Tic-Tac said, and I nodded. He was one brother I didn't want to piss off. He seemed angry all the time, so pissing him off was a real short trip.

"Take her back to our place. You don't mind, we'll bring the cage back to the shop tomorrow like usual," Maverick said, and I could tell he was agitated. Unhappy.

"You do what you gotta do," Dump Truck said. "You need anything else?"

"Nah, bro. Take your ass home to your woman." Maverick laid his jacket over Dahlia and shrugged back into his cut.

"Don't have to tell me twice, holler if you need something else." Dump Truck waved, revved his bike once and pulled back out onto First Avenue back the way we'd come from.

"Follow me home," Maverick said and leaned across the seats to press a fast kiss to my lips.

"I'll follow you guys, pitch this shit off the West Seattle Bridge," Tic-Tac said.

"Sounds good," Maverick declared and shut the door, leaving me and Dahlia in the hushed dark of the SUV.

"Just fuckin' great," she slurred from the back seat. "I suppose you'll lord this over me forever."

"Depends," I said as Maverick started up his bike. "Stop being a bitch and I won't be tempted to."

Dahlia barked a bitter laugh and said, "Maybe I misjudged you."

"You did," I declared, and pulled around to follow Mav. The territory around here was still unfamiliar when it came to me getting around on my own.

"Maybe I did," she said, and her voice was strained.

"We can forget about it for now," I said. "Get through tonight and you can go back to hating me or whatever, but for right now? Let's get you taken care of…"

"Why?" she asked.

"Why what?" I countered.

"Why would you do that for me?"

I sighed and said, "Because that's what family does… at least that's what a *normal* family does."

She didn't say anything after that, and I didn't either. I followed Maverick home, pulled up to the back of the house, and helped him help Dahlia inside and to the couch. We'd lost Tic-Tac somewhere on the high point of the bridge, somewhere over the water, but he caught up quickly. I heard him pull up out back as we got Dahlia settled.

"How is she?" he demanded, coming in through the back door.

"Tired," I said, getting a cool glass of water at the sink. "Sick."

"What can I do?" he demanded and the look on his face… It was the same anguished look Maverick had given me when I'd stepped out of the bathroom back at the lodge at the Lake Run.

I softened and wondered for how long Tic-Tac had been in love with Dahlia.

"She's a mess, maybe get a washcloth from the bathroom? She could probably stand to brush her teeth, she said she threw up."

"Yeah, good idea. Thanks, *Zaychik*."

I snorted a laugh and he paused mid-step.

"What?"

"Just sounds funny when you say it," I said.

"Yeah, Russian ain't my first language," he shot over his shoulder and went for the bathroom.

I went in to where Maverick was crouched by the couch, talking softly with Dahlia, a little annoyed I didn't know what they were saying, and confused at the same time. What Mav was speaking was clearly one language but what Dahlia was speaking back was another.

"What is that?" I asked, holding down the glass. Maverick took it.

"Russian outta me, Italian out of her," he said.

"Oh, if you guys don't need anything else right now, I'm going to go back to bed," I said.

"Thank you, *Zaychik*."

"Of course." I gave his shoulder a light squeeze and smiled at Dahlia who was looking quite a bit more with it than she had earlier, the effects of whatever wearing off.

"Thank you," she said, and I gave a nod.

"Truce?"

She nodded, winced, and stopped the motion, echoing back, "Truce."

"Look at you go." I smiled at the gentle teasing in Maverick's tone as I went down the hall, nearly colliding with Tic-Tac as he came out of the bathroom, a dripping washcloth in one hand and a dry towel in the other.

"Goodnight," I murmured, and he gave me a nod.

"Night, and… um… thanks for doing that. I know you and Dahlia don't get along, so…"

"I think we might be getting over our differences," I said gently.

"I hope so," he said, and I smiled.

"Never a dull moment," I said lightly, and he chuckled.

"Welcome to the life."

We smiled at each other one last time and passed in the hall. The phrase *like ships in the night,* came to my mind, but that was just silly. Didn't passing like ships in the night mean we would have passed silently, neither knowing the other was there? I think that was what that meant.

I dressed for bed and as I was getting beneath the blankets, the bedroom door opened and Maverick stepped in. He shut the door tightly but quietly behind him and came over, dropping onto the side of the bed, the weight of the world on his shoulders and I cocked my head.

He hung his and looked at me sideways and I could see the fear and the pain radiate from him.

"Oh, baby," I murmured and got up onto my knees, putting my arms around him. He leaned heavily into me and sighed out, sagging into the curve of my arms and I just held him, kissing the top of his head, providing comfort where I could like he had for me countless times…

"What happened?" I asked and he looked up, searched my face, and spilled. He told me all of it, and I sat in silence just soaking it all in.

"Why did he do that? I mean, why would anyone do that?"

"Your guess is as good as mine, *Zaychik*. Why does anyone do anything?"

"She okay?" I asked.

He nodded and said, "Tic-Tac is staying out there with her tonight."

I nodded sagely and declared, "Well Dahlia's safe and it sounds like this guy got what he deserved. Are you sure you guys got away clean?"

"Only time will tell," he said.

"Well, then we'll worry about it only if and when the cops come knocking," I said.

He nodded slowly, considering me and I smiled gently.

"You're too good to me," he said finally.

"Only because you were good to me first," I whispered and we both just sort of naturally leaned forward and kissed gently. "Come to bed and let me hold you for a minute," I whispered, and he nodded gently.

"I'd like that."

THE NEXT MORNING WAS... interesting, to say the least.

I came out of the bedroom wrapped in a satin robe that Maverick had bought me off Amazon, so I would be more comfortable around the house. I just wasn't comfortable being nude all the time, even when it was just me and Mav. The way I was raised, you kept your clothes on.

I'd left Maverick sleeping and crept down the hall stopping short at the end of it when I caught sight of Tic-Tac and Dahlia.

They were locked in an embrace on the couch and it was beautiful, but also sort of sad.

Dahlia held Tic-Tac, not the other way around. His head rested on her chest, ear over her coffin tattoo piece, his face almost angelic, slack with sleep. Dahlia ran her fingernails along his scalp lightly, running her hands through his chin length blond curls, a soothing almost maternal gesture, a slight smile on her face and a gentleness to her I don't think I'd ever seen before. I mean, she was a hard lady.

Likewise, Tic-Tac, who always seemed angry, was the most at peace I had ever seen *him*. His eyes closed, drifting under Dahlia's light touch.

Clearly, I had stepped into something intimate and if I moved wrong, I would be caught standing here like a total creeper perving on that intimate moment. I carefully retreated into the hall out of sight and half coughed, half sneezed to alert them to my presence before stepping back out into the living room.

One set of blue and one set of dark eyes fixed on me from the couch as I stepped out this time.

"Morning," I murmured and they both just stared at me, not saying a word.

Great, I thought to myself.

"Coffee?" I asked and that seemed to engage them a little more.

"Yes, please, oh, my God!" Dahlia rolled her eyes at the suggestion like it was the most heavenly thing she devised could happen right this moment. Tic-Tac just grunted what sounded like assent but didn't look at all happy about it. I think that had more to do with me shattering the peace, though. I smiled and slipped around the corner, back through to the kitchen to get a pot brewing.

Dahlia wandered in a moment after I heard the bathroom door shut. She slid up onto one of the kitchen stools and sighed asking, "So, how old are you and when's your birthday?"

I rolled my eyes and said, "Strange way to make peace."

"I'm trying here, in my own way, now just answer the fucking question," she said and plastered on this award-winning smile. I had to laugh.

"I turn twenty the beginning of the month after next," I said, and she nodded slowly, looking me over as though reevaluating me. Like she was taking my measure with fresh eyes. I ignored that part and went about brewing a fresh, strong pot of coffee. We were all dragging ass today and it showed in the dark circles beneath our eyes and the tired lines etched around our mouths.

I gave Dahlia the first cup of coffee. Tic-Tac and I looked tired, sure, but Dahlia looked like absolute *death* had nearly claimed her and though I didn't know the full story, I got the impression that it very nearly had. Tic-Tac came in from the bathroom and I poured him the second cup, not even waiting for the carafe of the coffeemaker to fill all the way.

I had to wait for my cup, but that was okay. I'd gotten more sleep than anyone. Granted it was broken sleep, but I'd still gotten *more.*

"Feel like talking about it?" I asked when Dahlia's eyes had gone distant and she looked like she'd gotten a little lost in whatever had happened last night.

"No," she said, sucking in a deep breath. She again put on a smile, more genuine than the last in its tiredness. The regret it displayed was probably only the second fully genuine emotion I'd ever read on her face, aside from the pure anger she'd displayed when she'd crashed the party for two Mav and I were having in his office a couple of weeks back.

"You're sure?" I asked, giving her one last opportunity to get it off her chest.

"Ah, I think we're of two different schools of thought, you and I," she declared, wrapping her hands around her steaming mug and bringing it to her lips.

"Yeah? How's that?" I asked without looking, finally able to pour myself a cup.

"I'm not one of those new age, talk about your feelings types," she said, waving me off.

"I'm not either," I said frowning.

"You sure about that?" Tic-Tac asked, snorting a laugh into his coffee.

"Why, because I can talk to Mav?" I asked, stirring sugar into my drink.

"They're just being assholes, *Zaychik*," Maverick declared from the kitchen entryway.

I dropped what I was doing to pour him a cup of coffee and to fix it to his liking. He slid up onto the stool beside Dahlia's while Tic-Tac just sort of stood around behind them both.

"We're not being assholes," Dahlia said, waving him off with a gesture of her hand and a roll of her eyes.

"Bullshit," Mav said and his tone brooked no argument. "You're trying to imply she's soft and she's not," he said and I rolled my own eyes, setting his coffee down in front of him.

"She's also standing *right fucking here* and is getting sick of people talking like she isn't," I said with a fake plastic smile to rival one of Dahlia's.

"Point well made, baby. I apologize," Maverick said, blowing on his coffee.

Dahlia and Tic-Tac traded a look and I kept my smile hidden by the rim of my own mug.

"Anybody want some actual breakfast?" I asked after taking a swallow of my coffee.

"I'm good with just this," Tic-Tac said, his own tone a mix of subdued and mildly interested, certainly not about breakfast though. I think Maverick had somehow just drawn a line in the sand with them both where I was concerned, because Dahlia was openly staring at him and I couldn't even begin to describe the look on her face. I would be lying if I said it didn't bring a little savage glee to my heart to see it, though.

CHAPTER TWENTY-FIVE

---

*M*averick…

The message came in on a night where the rain was coming down and I'd forgone the club to spend some time, just me and my girl, at home.

We were lying on the couch, Marisol leaning back against me, a blanket thrown over us as we watched some movie or show on television. It had her laughing, but I wasn't entirely paying attention. I was expecting this message and the subsequent FaceTime that was about to go down.

It was a necessary evil in order for myself and my woman to move on.

Those three little words on the screen seemed innocuous, but I knew they meant a world of hurt – whose pain, precisely, remained yet to be seen.

We got him.

"Baby, pause that for a minute for me, k?"

"What? Oh, sure." She paused the television and rolled her head back on her elegant neck, moving those honey-kissed eyes up to mine.

"Everything okay?" she asked.

"Depends," I said and sighed. "Just a sec."

I put the video call through and Fenris picked up, his rugged mug filling the screen.

"Talk to me," I said and held the phone out far enough so Marisol could see too.

"Hey, baby doll," Fen said and Marisol shifted in my lap.

"Hey, what's going on?" she asked.

"Need you to make a decision for me," he said and she looked up to me. I shook my head.

"This is all you, *Zaychik*."

"Ooookaaay." She drew the word out long. "What's going on?" She turned back to Fen who sighed heavily and shifted the phone.

They were in a garage somewhere, an industrial sort, and a man hung from chains from the vehicle lift. Marisol sucked in a sharp breath as she recognized him, and I felt bile rise in the back of my throat.

The dude was Mexican, a laborer by the looks of it, his face cragged partially from being older and partially from too much time spent under the punishing sun. He had a paunch hanging over his belt, and his chest was sort of sunken. His hair was hanging in there, but sort of greasy, and his beard was a patchy, half-assed effort.

He wasn't too roughed up yet. Yet being the operative word. The phone tipped, the camera whizzing and going crazy for a second before it settled back on Fen's serious expression.

"What do you want us to do with him?" Fenris asked.

Marisol swallowed so hard it made an audible click and she looked up at me, a mixture of sadness and horror in her eyes etched into every curve and plane of her lovely face.

Again, I shook my head.

"This decision is all yours, baby. I can't make it for you."

"Where are they?" she asked me. "Can we go there?"

"You sure that's a good idea?" Fenris asked and I turned my attention back to my enforcer and said, "Let's hear her out."

"I don't know," she said visibly rattled. "I mean, all I know is it's not right that you all should have to deal with this without me actually *there*, right?" she asked.

"It's our pleasure," Dump Truck rumbled from somewhere nearby on the other end.

"Absolutely, our pleasure," I heard Glass Jaw say.

"You don't want to be here for this," Fenris said gently, his light blue eyes stormy. "You just need to say the word. Let him hear you say it, that's enough."

"Hold the phone up?" I asked and Fenris went over, closer to the gagged man hanging by his wrists. He held up the phone and the dude's eyes widened, nostril's flaring. Marisol took the phone from me and sat up.

Calmly she spoke in Spanish to the man, her uncle, her rapist and his eyes widened even more, tears leaking from them as he made muffled little 'mm-mm-mm' noises.

"Fenris, can you still hear me?" Marisol asked.

"Loud and clear, little lady," he called.

"Do whatever you want," she said judiciously. "I just never want to worry about seeing him again."

The phone turned and Fen stared into the screen, searching her face in the little rectangle.

"You got it," he said. "Never is the operative word, I *give you my word*."

Marisol bit her lips together, raising her chin imperiously and nodded.

"You heard the lady," Dump Truck declared and with a little salute past Marisol at me, Fen cut the line.

She sat stalk still for the longest time and I put my hand to the back of her shoulder.

"Don't!" she said sharply and jerked away.

"I want to help you," I said low and careful, trying to be soothing without coming off as placating or insincere.

"I don't know how you can help," she said and her whole body trembled like she was fighting off being sick – and who knew, maybe she was. We'd been down that road before once already.

"I'm gonna be sick," she declared and leaped to her feet. She raced for the bathroom while I struggled to sit up. My damn couch was comfortable, sure, but it had a bad habit of swallowing anyone who sat on it whole.

I got to my feet and went up the hall, relieved that she hadn't shut me out this time.

I didn't say anything. I mean, what the fuck could I say? So, instead, I slipped past where she kneeled in front of our toilet retching and grabbed a clean washcloth, wetting it at the sink with cold water from the tap, wringing it out and folding it into thirds.

I went to my little rabbit and warned her gently, "This is gonna be cold, but it'll help you feel better." She nodded, spitting into the porcelain bowl and I lifted her long hair aside, laying the cold cloth on the back of her neck where I pressed it against her firmly with my hand.

"Oh, thank you," she said, and I nodded.

"You just take your time," I told her when she shifted on her knees. She settled and I said, "I'm gonna get you your toothbrush, hang on a second and don't move."

"Kay," she said, her voice brittle.

"I'm also gonna draw you a bath," I said and cut off her protest with, "No arguing."

"Okay," she said a little stronger as I loaded her toothbrush with paste and ran it under some fresh cold water. I handed it down to her and she stuck it in her mouth.

"Don't get up until you feel for sure you're ready."

She mumbled something around the brush in her mouth and I asked, "What?"

She looked up at me and said, "I asked if you would flush the toilet."

"Oh, yeah. Sorry." I pulled the chain above her head, just out of her reach for her and sent the mess in the bowl swirling, getting it out of her face.

While she sat still on the floor and brushed her teeth, I set about getting her a bath ready which honestly didn't take much, just get the water going and throw in one of those compressed powder bomb things that fizzed like a motherfucker and left my tub looking like someone slaughtered a unicorn in it.

I didn't mind. She always cleaned up after herself with them. The glitter kind of got everywhere sometimes, which that could sometimes be a bitch. Still, I guess it really *was* love when I thought about it. Not minding when they got fuckin' glitter everywhere? How the hell else could you tell if you really loved a woman?

She groaned, getting to her feet, and went over to the sink; turning on the tap to spit the froth of toothpaste in her mouth down the drain. I stuck my hand out and she reached out and took it after dropping her brush in the glass that held them.

"Too hot?" I asked her, drawing her near. She sat down on the edge of the tub beside me and reached out to check the water's temperature.

"A little," she murmured.

"Can I touch you, or would you rather do it yourself?" I asked.

She jerked her head and looked slightly horrified.

"Of course, you can touch me!" she declared.

"Wasn't sure, babe. It was a different story back at the lake."

She looked embarrassed.

"That whole thing was out of the ordinary," she said. "I'm really sorry if I made you feel like—"

"Hey, no, hush that beautiful mouth of yours," I said. "I get it. Really, I do."

"Yeah?" she asked meekly.

"Yeah, absolutely. I do," I said, nodding gravely.

She sighed and said, "Thank you," her gratitude palpable and in its own way heartbreaking. I mean, for fuck's sake, any time anybody showed even a little bit of kindness or understanding to the woman, she was so *grateful*. It really put some shit into perspective on how much a lot of us took for granted.

She let me take the hem of her tee, lifting her arms over her head so I could sweep it up and off her body. I undressed her gently, hands careful, placing a light touch of my lips here and there as occasion and mood called for it.

I lived for each sharp intake of breath as my lips fell against her sun-kissed bronze skin, and even though I was hard, I ignored that part of me for the time being. This wasn't about me. This was about her and her comfort, about the ritual washing her past away to make way for a brighter future with us, with *me*… About getting the stain out of her soul left behind by that monster, who by night's end would be the dust of distant memory if my boys had anything to say about it.

The blood spilled tonight would be on us, and the purifying waters of this bath would keep any more taint off my girl than had already been applied.

There would be plenty more dirt in the future, I was sure. It was part of living this life, but for now, for tonight, I would do my damnedest to keep her clean.

"Aren't you getting in with me?" she asked when I went to help her over the tall lip of the tub.

I shook my head. "No. Tonight, this is about you."

I helped lower her into my tub which had been turned into a vat of iridescent white unicorn sparkles, the water swirling in subtle pinks, blues, and purples as the light caught the flecks of whatever in the water to make it glitter.

She lowered herself gingerly into the steaming bath and hugged her knees. I told her to stay put and went for a few things to set the mood for relaxation.

Candles, and a cool glass of white wine from the fridge. I moved around her carefully, quietly, and when I switched out the overhead light, I had to smile at my handiwork – the pure magic of it.

I went to her, brushing her hair, sweeping it up in my hands, twisting it lightly like I'd seen her do a thousand times before I clipped it up off her slender, beautiful shoulders, exposing the sweeping line of her gorgeous back. She sighed and closed her eyes, relishing the careful, caring touches I bestowed on her and I felt like I was on top of the world to be the man to bring even the simplest of pleasures to this beautiful and fabled woman. A goddess in her own right – she just didn't know it. Couldn't feel it… and I aimed to changed that one day, one moment at a time.

I sat on a low stool I kept as a step, and a place to set my beer when I was in the tub myself taking a long soak after a long hard ride so that I could tend to my lady.

I washed her back while she rested her cheek atop her knees as she hugged her shins, her eyes drifting shut, a light blush creeping across her nose and cheeks at the gentle attention. Either that, or I was reading too much into things, the blush could very well just have been a deep flush from a slightly too-hot bath.

Something about the peace on her face, the way her expression said she was soaking this up like parched earth soaked in a fresh rain told me I may have been a little too on the money with my first inclination.

We both remained silent, both saturating ourselves in the peace that the warmth, steam, and candlelight brought to us.

It was as near a perfect expression of my love and devotion as I could muster, as intimate as I could get without adding sex to the mix, but it wasn't about sex. Not tonight. It was about care. It was about giving her what she wanted and needed when no one else would or could.

It was about fulfilling deep and hidden desires that she had no name for but always, instinctively, knew that she needed.

It was about proving to her that men were sworn to protect their women, their families, and that how she'd been raised wasn't anything close to right or normal. It was about establishing a new normal for her, and to introducing her to the first day of the rest of her life.

Tonight, was about unshackling her from the millstone of shame that'd been dragging her down by the neck for years. A stone of shame that wasn't hers to bear and never had been.

It was about proving to my woman that she had so much more worth than she'd ever been taught she held.

"It's time I got off my ass and made you mine in every way that matters," I murmured.

"Oh?" she asked with a dry chuckle. "Strange way of proposing, if that's what that is. I mean, isn't there supposed to be a question mark in there somewhere?"

I shook my head, once left, and once right. "No. Making you my property has nothing to do with proposing or marriage, that part comes later. Making you mine, giving you my rag, means anyone even thinks about touching you, they can have their ass beat for it. It means if they ever *do* touch you, I'll fucking kill them for it."

She went very still in the bath, the water tinkling, a high, light, crystalline sound, pure and completely out of step with the shadows gathering in the corners with the newest topic of conversation.

"I don't understand, I don't think…"

"In our world, being a man's property isn't like one of us going out and buying a cage or a boat," I explained. "Those are just *things*. They burn, they fall apart, and you just go out and get another one."

"Okay." She drew a shaky breath. "So, *belonging* to you, being your property is what?"

"It's permanent, is what it is. At least with me."

She was quiet, the wheels turning in that beautiful, clever head of hers as she mulled the implications over.

"It means you would die for me?" she asked quietly, and I think she was getting emotional.

"It means I live for you, and only you. It means anyone hurts you, I hurt them. They make you cry; I make them cry. They lay a finger on you, and you don't take care of it yourself to our mutual satisfaction, I handle it."

"It means safety?" she asked, and I nodded.

"The likes I don't think you've ever felt," I said and reached up, cradling her cheek lightly in the palm of my hand, tracing her bottom lip with the pad of my thumb.

"I want that so much," she whispered. "But at what cost? Everything has its price."

"Stay with me. Agree to be mine and only mine. Either way, I pledge to protect you, but baby I don't want any other woman… I want to settle my ass down, figure out what it means to be a one-woman man. I want to go through it all. I want the days you drive me crazy and the days I know no peace until I fall into your arms."

She sniffed, her bottom lip pouting out beautifully as she kneeled up abruptly. She lunged over the edge of the tub, water sloshing and barely staying contained as she threw her arms around me and sobbed by my ear.

I put my arms around her, holding her as tightly as she clutched at me and laying a reverent kiss against her bare shoulder I asked, "Is that a yes?"

She didn't answer with words, simply drew back, placing her hand to my cheek, and her lips to mine in a kiss that tasted of hope and gratitude.

It was enough for me.

Our fate sealed with that kiss for all time.

Commitment never tasted so fucking good.

CHAPTER TWENTY-SIX

*M*arisol…

It was a strange sort of love Maverick offered me. A fierce love, an unwavering one, a love so deep it resonated in chambers of my heart I hadn't known existed before now.

I was fully immersed, fully indoctrinated with my commitment to him and it not only felt so *right* it felt so incredibly *good*.

He helped me out of the bath, drying me thoroughly with warmed towels, leading me to the bedroom, both of us settling atop the covers as he let down my hair and spent the better part of an hour brushing it for me, brushing it dry where it'd gotten wet before tucking us both in and laying us down to sleep.

We kissed, and though we had kissed probably a thousand times before, this was new, this was *different*. Because there was no denying it now.

I loved him.

I had lost my heart to his debonair smile and his careful hands and I didn't care to ever have it back. He could keep it. He had done so much to earn it, and as I fell asleep in his arms with him pressing the occasional reverent kiss to my forehead that night, I found broken bits of my spirit mended.

He had given me so much in the last week in recognizing my pain, in acknowledging my bravery and in trusting me with his secrets, his way of life. He had given me everything I could want, had handed me respect and worth, and his devotion as though it were nothing and I felt as though there was no debt here but I simultaneously felt forever indebted.

I looked forward to a lifetime of sensual give and take with this man, but first? First there was something I needed to do… for myself.

"*Zaychik.*" Maverick scowled at me, for the first time ever, darkly.

I swallowed hard, as every set of eyes around the chapel's table fixated on me as I shut the door tightly behind me.

"I want to go with you," I said and looks were exchanged.

"That's not how that works," Tic-Tac said dismissively, looking to Maverick to throw my ass out.

I swallowed hard and would not be deterred.

"Hear me out…" I plead and those eyes that'd been fixated on me exchanged looks.

"All in favor?" Mav intoned and he raised his hand. The majority of the table raised theirs, the few hands that didn't go up – Tic-Tac's, Derry's, and Major's simply raised eyebrows or shrugged accepting that they'd been clearly outvoted and not looking too terribly upset about it. Their curiosity likely getting the better of them just a little too late.

"Well, go on, say your piece, girl." Glass Jaw leaned back in his boardroom chair.

"I want to go with you on this run. Mateo won't go with you otherwise and *Abuela* will put up a fight… but if I go, I think I can mitigate the damage from the family drama which I'm so sorry I feel like I've dragged you all into."

"You have an idea," Maverick said, and I nodded. He knew my face so well and I didn't bother to hide it from him.

"I have an idea…" I said and nodded.

"Well, let's hear it," Derry said, and his smug look said he didn't think whatever was going to come out of my mouth was going to be worth it.

"I propose a coup," I murmured.

That got their attention.

"Do what now?" Major asked.

"Look, I know *Abuela*. She raised me. She's my grandmother – and I know that she would rather burn the whole world for her only remaining son than admit he did anything wrong. Believe me, I've lived it for years now." I swallowed hard and pressed on.

"She will hurt every single one of those people in my village, cut them off from their medicine, just to get back at me and think she's getting back at you somehow. Now, *I* know you can just turn around and sell it elsewhere, but a lot of the people under her thumb are just scared of her. It's easier to placate her crazy than stand up to her."

"You got someone in mind to take her place?" Maverick asked.

I nodded.

"Julio Sanchez," I said. "He's fair, he's got the leadership ability, the only thing that he has going against him is that he's young."

"How young?" Glass Jaw demanded.

"My age young," I said. "But between him and the doctor, the people will listen."

The men around the table all exchanged a look and Maverick met my gaze with a cool and appraising one of his own. I swallowed hard, but a subtle shift in his expression, the way his eyes flashed; I knew what came next wasn't how he felt. Not truly. I understood, though. It needed to be said…

"Right, now get the fuck out – and don't you *ever* barge in here like this again." Maverick gave me a pointed look and he meant every single one of the next words that fell from his lips. "You won't like the consequences if you do, and neither will I."

I nodded and went out, unfriendly gazes from various points around the table causing me to itch between my shoulder blades. Shutting the door firmly behind me, I slipped across the hall to Maverick's office to wait for him there.

It was a long wait, but not excruciating. I mean, I didn't think I was in trouble, per se… I didn't get that vibe from *him*, although by the looks on the rest of the guys' faces, I'd definitely overstepped.

The more the second hand clicked its way around the clockface, the more apprehensive I became. Finally, I heard the door across the hall open. I straightened, standing tall as I waited for him to open the door and step through. I listened to the low, grumbling voices, the creak of leather, and the shuffle of booted feet out in the hall as they moved down the hallway toward the barroom.

Finally, the door opened, and Maverick stepped through, shutting it tightly behind him. He turned to me and his expression softened from its stormy neutrality it'd held as he'd come through into something else entirely. Something that spoke of love and sorrow in equal measure.

"What?" I asked, barely breathing.

"What you just did." He shook his head slightly.

"I know," I murmured. "I'm sorry, it's just—"

"Just nothing," he said sharply, but not unkindly. Just a mark that it was his turn to speak and for me to listen.

"You have to answer for it, but it's not in me to hurt you."

"Hurt me?" I asked. "I thought you guys didn't do that."

"Not as a general rule, but, babe… what you just did…"

I pursed my lips and nodded and said softly, "I understand. You do what you have to. To keep their trust, right?"

He nodded slowly and smiled gently, "You know," he said. "You understand."

"Yeah. I'm sorry… I didn't know it was that bad."

"It's for your own good, *Zaychik*. It's for your own safety."

"I don't understand that," I said and threw up my hands, rolling my eyes. "I already say '*yes*' Maverick. I want to stay with you, I am *in this* with you… I don't understand why you all shut us out."

"Us?" he asked, stepping up to me, putting his hands on my hips, looking down into my eyes.

"Law enforcement?" he asked gently. "Bad enough one or more of us get locked up, but what could happen to you?" He shook his head. "We want you free. We need you to be able to come see us, to keep us going should it come to that."

"I see," I uttered and I did. He smoothed his hands around to my ass and pulled me into him. I put my arms around his waist and looked up into his eyes which were suddenly smiling, twinkling with mischief. "So, what happens now?" I asked.

"Now?" he whispered against my lips.

"Yeah?" I dared not breathe.

"Now I fuck you over that desk, make you scream, and make those fuckers believe I pulled you back into line."

"I don't see how that's a punishment," I murmured, the warmth of my own breath fanning back across my lips with his close proximity, his warm, kissable mouth a mere hairs breadth from mine, the ache of desire a deep and fractured one as I held out and waited... waited to see what he would do.

"I'm going to lay you across that desk," he whispered, "and fuck you rough." He pecked my lips, a quick light kiss. "Make you scream my name as you come around my cock," he whispered in my ear, capturing my earlobe lightly, sending a tingling wash of sensation down the side of my neck, his warm breath soft but loud in my ear as I shivered with anticipation.

"Still doesn't sound like a punishment," I whispered.

"That's the point," he whispered, his hands sliding up into the back of my hair. "It's not supposed to sound like a punishment... to *you*."

Ah. Clever man.

"Oh, I see..." I shuddered as he made a fist in the back of my hair, my scalp pulling tight while the rest of my body felt like it went loose, turning to JELL-O under his touch. I gasped as he attacked the side of my neck with his mouth, the stubble around his lips and along his cheek a rough contrast to the slick velvet of his tongue against my skin.

I gasped and he pulled me in tight against his body, and from the outside I imagined it would look like a vampire lover pulling his victim into an embrace – darkly beautiful, sensational, erotic, and sensual. He worked the erogenous zone at the side of my neck and I felt a warm, tingling rush between my thighs.

I stood on shaky legs, pressing my thighs together as he worked his mouth expertly across my collarbone, his hand still in my hair, tugging, his other hand smoothing around from my ass to the front of my body where he made quick work of my jeans.

Savagely, he stripped me, ordering me to do what he couldn't reach with his one hand, the other he left tangled in my long hair, refusing to let me get away, controlling my movements in such a way that just made me wetter and want him more.

He was as good as his word, laying me back across his desk, stepping between my thighs, shoving himself inside of me whether I was ready or not but *God,* he had me turned on and so, so wet. I was more than ready, wrapping my legs around him, begging him wordlessly with savage little pants and my pleading gaze for him to fuck me the way I liked, begging him to take me, make me his, and he smiled with this feral grin that should have scared me but didn't. He shoved into me all the way, balls deep, and I yowled with pleasure which to the ear of someone who wasn't in the room could be interpreted in many different ways.

His second hand joined the first in the back of my long tresses and he pulled my head all the way back, the stinging pain in my scalp a delicious and beautiful counterpoint to the pleasure mounting between my thighs as he used my hair for leverage to pull himself that much further inside of me.

He fucked me with a punishing rhythm and I *loved* it. Hot tears slicked down my temples in a beautiful catharsis, my eyes watering from the pain in my scalp even as the sensation lent to the building orgasm between us. My pussy throbbed and felt so full, the weight of him pressing me into the desk speaking to the frightened part of my soul that I was *his* and that he had me, that nothing and no one would get past him, that all I needed to do was *submit,* give myself over to the pain and the pleasure would follow and I did as he silently asked.

I arched my back as he drove into me, painting the walls of his office with the cries he wrought from me and gave into his deepest, darkest desires and I *reveled* in it.

I did precisely what he said I would earlier. I screamed his name as I came and wondered at how remarkably well our mutual darkness fit together, roiled and danced together, and how exquisite the sex became as a result.

Querido Dios, this man turned me the fuck on, and by the cheer that went up out in the barroom, I think we sold it.

"Good girl," Maverick whispered in my ear, kissing my jaw just beneath it. "That's my good girl."

Christ, he knew just what to say to make my heart melt.

CHAPTER TWENTY-SEVEN

---

*M*averick…

"What'd you do to him?" I asked and Fen spit on the ground.

"You really wanna know?" he asked.

"I really wanna know," I said firmly.

We stood outside the Smuggler's Inn smoking a joint, passing it back and forth between hits, talking with our breaths held like a couple of teenagers. It would be laughable if the subject matter weren't so damn serious.

"Beat him, fucked his shit up but good. Broke every one of his damn fingers he touched her with, stomped his nuts, cut him up – little things. Don't worry, he wasn't gonna bleed out or nothin'. No dying slow. Not for what he'd done."

"Then what?" I asked after taking a hit of my own, chest burning from the long inhale, from holding the smoke as tight muscles eased and the euphoric body high from the Indica strain swirled through my veins.

It was some good shit.

"Put his ass in a fifty-five-gallon drum, filled it about halfway with diesel, and sealed him in."

"Oof." I shook my head and didn't feel one iota sorry for the son of a bitch. "That'll leave you screaming," I said.

Fenris nodded. "Any luck, he'll die that way, yeah. Not about to go back and check if he has or not."

"It's been more than a few days; I reckon he's done."

"Sure as fuck's never gonna be *found*," Fenris said. I nodded and put a hand to my man's shoulder and gripped it.

"I owe you one," I said.

"You don't owe me shit. Just one more rapist piece of shit the world ain't gotta contend with anymore."

I nodded again.

"You sure this is a good idea, poking the bear?" he asked.

I snorted. "Bitch has no power anymore. Lie down with dogs, you come up with fleas and I ain't about it. It's time for a new world order out that way."

"You and Marisol? It the real deal?" he asked somewhat skeptically.

"Yeah." I nodded. "Yeah it is."

"Never thought I'd see that day," he said, shaking his head incredulously. "Definitely didn't see you ending up with the likes of her—"

"Mexican?" I asked, curious.

He snorted this time. "Nah, *young*. I always pictured you with someone your own age or even older."

"Yeah?"

"Yeah. I gotta give it to her, though. She's got big brass balls for being such a little lady."

"She's got big fuckin' balls period going through the shit she's been through and still being brave enough to get on the back of my bike like that," I said.

"She's smart," he said, nodding.

"She's clever, I'll give her that," I agreed. "But it wasn't smarts that put her with me, it was desperation."

"Yeah, but it's more than desperation that's kept her with you and a hell of a lot of smarts that's let her navigate the life like she's been."

"Some of that's been luck," I said.

He nodded. "Smirk on your face says you're being modest, you fucker."

I laughed and nodded, stubbing out the last of the fragrant joint and said, "Gonna be interesting tomorrow."

"Yes. It. Is," he agreed.

I was looking forward to it.

THE NEXT DAY brought me back to my girl. She met us in Monroe in Little Bird's rig. Little Bird had driven her and would be riding back with D.T. as our party split in two. I had her drive behind us, a sort of de facto crash truck.

We had to get the changes in place before the new guard for the Eastern Washington chapter showed up, so it was now or never to put her plan in action.

"You ready for this?" I asked and she nodded grimly.

I cupped her cheek and kissed her fiercely, pouring every ounce of pride I had into it, hoping she would feel it, because right now I highly doubt she'd believe anything complimentary. She had her moods when it came to that. Sometimes she was doing just fine, and others? Well, others the marks left by her upbringing showed like welts across her very soul. You could see it in her eyes.

Today, now, was one of those times but I had every faith that she'd pull herself up by the bootstraps for the task that lay ahead.

"Let's go get your brother," I murmured and that made her smile. She nodded softly and I held the door open to Little Bird's rig. She slipped into the seat and then her seatbelt, clicking it home as I shut the door.

"Let's roll out!" I called and everyone quit fucking around and mounted up.

It was good riding weather and a long-ass fucking ride. As always, the whole little fruit grower's village turned out to greet us, only this time there would be a change of plans.

We rolled up, shut off our motors and I looked up at *Abuela* who sat her fat ass on her lawn chair throne up on her sagging front porch in her imperious way. The woman had looked down her nose at people her whole life and now? Now it was time to take her down a few pegs.

"Doctor." I nodded to the clinic doc who stood nearby, smirking when greeting him first caused *Abuela's* nostrils to flare in indignation.

"You brought her back," *Abuela* said with disdain as Marisol came up beside me on foot. "We don't want her."

"Well, you can't have her," I said matter-of-factly, putting an arm around my girl's waist. "In fact, so long as you're running the show, I think we're done here."

Abuela scoffed and rolled her eyes.

"Disrespect my man again," Marisol growled at her, "see what happens."

"Seems to me you been running the show a bit too long around here," I called out. "That ends now."

Abuela looked apoplectic, her face growing crimson, a vein standing out on her forehead. She fired off in Spanish at Marisol and Marisol's grip tightened around my shoulders. I tightened my hand on my girl's hip to let her know I was with her.

"English, Grandma!" she shouted back. "The people of this village are used to you calling me a whore and these men are obviously disinterested in dealing with you anymore, so what do you care if they hear it? It's not like half of them don't speak Spanish anyway! You're not hiding anything. Not anymore!"

"Keep talking to my woman that way," I said, "I'll disappear you." I leveled a flat and unfriendly look in *Abuela's* direction.

"Go get your brother," I said to Marisol. "The rest of you get ready to roll out. Seems these good folks just want to spectate and aren't interested in these drugs. They'd rather kowtow to the wildebeest up there."

Marisol went forward and up the steps. *Abuela* grabbed her arm and Marisol was a champion of her own destiny. She whipped out the pistol I'd given her and pressed it under *Abuela's* chin. She gave her grandmother a scathing look and through gritted teeth declared, "No one is *ever* putting a hand on me that I don't want there *ever* again. You want to keep your brain in your skull, take it off of me – *now!*"

Abuela glared, stubborn as a mule for a second and took her hand away and Marisol said, "I'm taking my brother and if *any* of you want this little arrangement to continue, I suggest you step forward and start negotiating with my man before I get back out of this house!"

She muttered something to her grandmother and put the gun up, back under her jacket and went into the house.

Abuela went white as a sheet and collapsed into the lawn chair on her porch.

"I'm deadly serious now. Y'all stand together and she goes or we go and we take these meds with us."

"We need those pills, mister. We'll die without them." I looked over to where the doctor was standing but it wasn't him that had spoken. It was a young man, around Marisol's age.

"Well, alright then," I said. "What's your name, boy?"

"Julio. Julio Sanchez."

I nodded slowly and said, "Get on over here, Julio, and let's parlay."

"What?"

"Let's make a deal," I stated.

He nodded and jerked his head at the clinic doctor who nodded and ghosted up after him.

"Nothing has to change here," I said quietly, for their ears only. "Same usual rate…"

I listed off prices for each thing and the doctor and the boy frowned and looked at each other. I lowered the prices, just a bit from what we'd been charging before, just enough to make a noticeable difference and listened as Julio and the doctor had an exchange. By the dour look on the doctor's face, I think my hunch played out right. My play had been designed to make it look like *Abuela* had been skimming. If she had been aboveboard, it would have been a light skim, but if not? It looked like the fat old broad was as rotten to the core as I thought she might be, and these people now had a personal beef with her.

"Problem, boys?" I demanded when their rapid fire back and forth in Spanish had gone on for too long.

The doctor looked uncomfortable and Julio leaped in, a little inept and declared, "No, the usual rate is fine! Just fine!"

"I got no interest in raising prices on y'all, I just want her out of power."

Julio glanced up in *Abuela's* direction and his mouth thinned down into a grim line. He nodded and called up to *Abuela* in Spanish. She gripped her cane which she had planted between her feet and raised her chin, turning her face away, refusing to look at him. People in the crowd shifted and muttered uneasily.

"Might want to hand over the cash," I called and Julio marched right up to her and more Spanish was exchanged with her little toadies behind her who reluctantly handed over the envelope to Julio.

He opened it up and counted it, his expression hard and going harder just as Marisol came out the front door with her little brother, a suitcase in her hand and his thin shoulders dwarfed by an overstuffed backpack.

"*Abuela!*" he cried happily and he and his grandmother had a sweet moment. All hugs and a few tears out of the old woman, but to her credit, where none was really due, she let her grandson go. He took Marisol's hand and they descended the steps, the little boy oblivious to the drama playing out around him.

Julio stayed up on the porch, counting the money and raising an eyebrow. He murmured something to Marisol and she nodded and he slipped the cash back in and came down.

"It's short," he said, handing it over. "Only by a little."

I counted it out, and it was short alright – only by the amount I'd bumped it to make it look like the old broad was skimming. By the look on Julio's face, a combination of anger and worry, I'd say *Abuela* was gonna have a heart attack or something tonight at the hands of her own people.

"I think it's been a stressful enough time for all involved, don't you think?"

Julio looked at me and nodded.

"I'm not an unkind man, Julio. Let's just call this here the new normal, shall we? Not having to deal with her dank ass more than makes up the difference."

The doctor and Julio exchanged a look and both nodded.

"Fen! Squatch! Get these people the medicine they need," I called out.

The doctor went forward and so did a few of the villagers, eager to unload.

Julio looked back at Marisol who was helping her little brother into the back seat of the 4Runner. He gave her a nod and she gave him a grave look and a nod back. I raised an eyebrow at that. Seems I may have underestimated my girl. Maybe this had been a part of her end game all along. She and Julio maybe had some kind of a bargain of their own.

Whatever it was, it was a conversation for another time and by my estimation, it felt right. No harm was coming to these people. By all accounting, they'd be coming out better for this in the offing and I think we were all good with that.

I twisted around on the seat of my bike and asked my girl, "You set?" She stood behind the open driver's side door of the SUV, fire in her eyes, and simply gave me a silent, solitary nod in my direction.

"What about you, boys?" I asked as the doctor and another dude rolled their collapsible wagon of meds off in a direction to take full stock and put them away.

"All good," Squatch declared.

"Until next time," I said and gave Julio a respectful nod which he returned. I glanced up at *Abuela* who sat unperturbed on her throne, a few of the men and women from the village drifting up to her porch and I put my middle finger to my forehead and gave the bitch a literal one-fingered salute.

Her expression grew stormy, but she didn't do or say shit. She'd been as thoroughly shut down from the word go as she could have been and the bitch deserved it. If she caused problems again – which given the muttering and shifting among her own people, didn't seem likely – I would disappear her fat ass just like I disappeared her pedophile son.

I still harbored a bitter contempt for the rest of these fuckin' people who knew and did nothing, as long as they kept getting their own, Marisol had been an acceptable sacrifice and I fuckin' hated that. We rode out, and I was glad I wouldn't have to see any of their faces for another month. It might give me the chance to cool down some, although it was just a matter of time. I would get mine from them and then they'd be the new Eastern Washington chapter's problem.

I split off from the rest of the boys at their urging when we stopped for some food. Their insistence I escort my lady and her brother home one I was secretly grateful for. I still felt some guilt for it, though. I wasn't one to cut and run. I was the guy that always saw everything through to the bitter end. I guess, this time, priorities…

I certainly had a new set and that was a little awkward, at least for now, to begin with. Still, I was happy to make my little *zaychik* my new normal, and all that came along with that.

Her little brother was zany, funny, and exuberant. He put a smile on my girl's face and the same love that radiated from her honey-gold eyes in his direction was one I recognized. She looked at me the same way, and even though she hadn't had the occasion to say it yet, I knew, and that was honestly enough for me.

It was late when we got home. Past Mateo's bedtime but the kid was excited. His excitement only went up a notch when he got a load of his new bedroom. It wasn't much by my standards. Ikea furniture, cheap but well put together by Marisol herself. Well, she'd had a little help from me with the dresser. Still, it was all done up in his favorite soccer team's colors and Marisol had gotten posters of his favorite players on the pitch doing their thing from some Mexican grocery nearby and had framed them up nice.

He loved it, of course, but it took some time with his sister to calm his little ass down. She handled him like a pro, and I'd never really put a mind toward being a father before, but she had me rethinking the vasectomy I'd had. I guess, if she ever wanted, IVF was an option. I could get that shit extracted with a needle or something – not that the thought was all that appealing.

Still, she made me believe in myself that maybe the whole fatherhood thing could be possible for me. If anyone could keep me from being my father, I believed it could be her.

"Hey," she said softly from the bedroom doorway, shutting the door softly behind her. I turned from where I was getting ready for bed, toweling off my head from the shower I'd taken.

She came to me and wound her arms loosely around my waist. I tossed the towel into the laundry hamper in the corner, half making it. She looked up at me, those eyes of hers captivating in the low light from the bedside lamp.

"Kiss me," she murmured.

"You sure you wanna start this?" I asked, glancing meaningfully at the bedroom door.

"He sleeps like the dead and I'm not going to stop living my life simply because he's here," she said. "I can be quiet."

"Mm." I lowered my mouth to hers and kissed her softly. Her hands drifted from my hips to my face, cupping my stubbled cheeks gently as she kissed me, her body drawing closer to fit in the circle of my arms, her hands slipping around to the back of my head, nails scratching lightly against my scalp sending tingles down my spine.

I moaned softly into her luxurious mouth and felt her lips curl into a smile against my own.

God, she was such sweet perfection one minute and a guilty pleasure of my deepest, darkest fantasies the next. Tonight felt light and sweet, though, and I took my time undressing her, slipping her blouse over her head, cupping her perfect tits, kissing my way down her chest to suck lightly at her dusky nipples until she moaned all breathy, the sound of her being all hot and bothered like music to my ears.

"Oh, God, Mav…" her voice was breathy and throaty all at once as she tipped her head back, holding mine to her breast as I worked her tit with lips, teeth, and tongue, lavishing her beautiful breasts with attention.

I pulled back, letting her nipple pop from my mouth and queried, "Yes, my queen?"

"Mm, make love to me?" she asked, looking down into my eyes.

"Thought you'd never ask," I growled and picked her up. Her legs twined around my hips, too much material between my throbbing dick and her sweet sensual pussy.

I laid her down on the bed and went for the easiest clothing first, slipping my pajama pants down off my hips and freeing my erection. Her hot little hand wrapping around its length and stroking me, an erotic tease, a promise of pleasure, and I couldn't wait to be inside her, but she'd asked me to make love to her, and making love bespoke of something slower, gentler, and yet still deeply passionate.

I undid the button on her little denim shorts and lowered the little zipper, slipping the offending garment out of my way down her long legs and dropping them carelessly to my bedroom floor. The only thing remaining between us, her scrap of a white lace thong.

I kissed her then, my arms around her, hand pressed flat and splayed open against the warm, smooth skin of her back, drawing her up tight against my body as I dry humped between her legs, reveling in the sensation of rough lace, damp with her sweetness against the head of my cock.

The light fragrance of her desire perfumed the air, driving me wild and I had to hold myself in check. I wanted so badly to fist that scrap of material in my hand and jerk it from her body. I wanted to plunge inside of her in one sure, deep, even stroke and I wanted to pound that sweet ass into my mattress, but that's not what she'd asked for.

Instead, I did as she asked, dragging her to the end of the bed, slipping that final barrier off her body, and kneeling between her knees, I put my hand against her sweet cunt, massaging her, gazing up the golden length of her body into those deep brown eyes tinged with golden honey, watching the color shrink as her pupils grew larger with her want of me.

"Maverick, yes, *please*," she begged and I kneeled up, laying over the top of her lower body, kissing my way down in worship until I could almost taste her, my mouth watering in anticipation, my cock hard to the point of sweet pain.

God, I wanted her. I wanted her and no one else. This woman filled every one of my senses, put my mind on overload with feelings I'd only ever heard of but was quite sure I'd never felt them myself before and Jesus, *fuck,* did I want to. I wanted everything with her in this moment. My whole damn life flashed before my eyes as I laid my tongue against her clit and teased, and not my past but my future life, with her.

I could see it all. Wedding bells and wild rides, making love to her under the stars on the coast, attending Mateo's graduation, and family dinners with the club.

I could see it all, I wanted it all, and it all started right here.

CHAPTER TWENTY-EIGHT

*M*arisol...

The look in his deep blue eyes as he went down on me was unlike anything I had ever seen before. I'd asked him to make love to me, desperately wanted to know what that was even like, and I got my answer with that one look as he played his velvet tongue against my clit, in sharp contrast with the rough stubble around his lips.

"Oh, *God,*" I moaned as I closed my eyes and let my head fall back in surrender to this man who cradled me so gently in his hands.

He teased me so cruelly but lovingly, his mouth soft, his touch gentle, but also so, so, maddening. I needed him inside me. His cock, his fingers, it didn't matter. I felt so empty and so ravenous, all I wanted was that one touch inside that would touch off the firestorm of sensation that I so deeply craved.

He spent such a long time building me up that I thought I would die from the lack of that one, crucial touch, and I found myself gripping the sheets at my hips which writhed up and down of their own volition.

He played me expertly, like a virtuoso, slipping a finger or two inside of me – I couldn't honestly tell, I was so wet for him, so painfully aroused, it was exquisite. All of it good as he tortured me beautifully into a slow spiraling lift, riding the thermals of his love higher and higher until I could touch the very stars in the sky.

He brought me so close to the sun I thought I would burn, but I was ever safe, in his bed, wrapped in his arms, the starbursts of light clearing my vision from that first orgasm to him sitting up and wiping his mouth, the vision of him thick and hard, the length of him turgid and resting against his stomach, a pearly drop of precum at his crown setting me ablaze with desire all over again.

I struggled to scoot up on the bed to give him enough room to fully get on it and he did, crawling up after me, cock bobbing thickly between his thighs and oh, God, how I wanted him. My pussy gave a long, fractured ache, complaining that it wasn't fulfilled and I felt absolutely insatiable. I needed him on me, I needed him inside of me, and I reached for him.

He smiled and came to me willingly and my heart sighed with happiness. I lay back and he dwarfed me, the warmth of his body settling over mine, the head of his dick nudging my pussy lips apart.

I arched as he slipped inside of me, and he took his time, filling me up so slowly, I very nearly wept with a mixture of joy and frustration.

"Mm, easy baby, just like that," he crooned as he seated himself inside me as deeply as he could go. He brought his lips to mine and we kissed as he barely moved inside of me, touching off a whole new set of amazing sensations.

He brushed my hair away from my face and looked me in the eyes, the intimacy of the moment unparallel in any existence.

"I love you, baby," he whispered and the huskiness of his voice, the gentleness of his tone, it was the sweetest most decadent sound I'd ever heard. The gentle, short, barely there strokes he made inside of me sent pleasure rippling out from my core making my eyes prickle with tears at how sweet and how perfect. He placed his lips against mine and I touched the side of his face, held him to me, and loved him back so fiercely in that moment, gasping out when the kiss was broken, *"I love you, too."*

And I did. From now until forever. How could I not?

Still, there was this low-key worry inside of me, deep down asking, *would it be enough?*

I guess only time would tell…

CHAPTER TWENTY-NINE

SUMMER'S END

*M*arisol…

"Mateo! Be careful!" I cautioned and gave my little brother the hairy eyeball. He grinned impishly at me and kicked his soccer ball across the beach's sand at Tic-Tac who yelled back at me, "Come on! Let the kid be a kid! You're always up his ass!"

I scowled at him and that worry that I would never fully belong or make amends with these guys over interrupting their church meeting that one time returned. Most of the men had gotten over it relatively easy, a few had held out a bit longer but then, there was Tic-Tac… He seemed like he was willing to hold a grudge eternally.

"He'll come around, don't worry!" Little Bird said cheerfully and I heaved a big sigh.

"Who'll come around?" Dahlia asked, dropping into the empty lounge chair between me and Little Bird.

"Tic-Tac," Little Bird said, sweeping her long brown hair over her shoulder, exposing her back to the sun beating down.

We were on the shores of the Pacific, the surf a dull and distant roar down the beach, the water stretching uninterrupted for as far as the eye could see.

It was hot, one of the last days of good weather we were bound to have before the rain and the wet of autumn rolled in. This wasn't an *official* club beach run, just something we had all decided we needed now that Eastern Washington chapter was up and running and we could all breathe a little better.

Abuela had signed over guardianship of my brother to me without a fight and had gone back to Mexico. Julio had called and told me he has all the necessary paperwork waiting and he would pass it along on the next run out that way. He said things were already better. That the air felt lighter and the people were happier than they'd been in a long time.

I was grateful it had all worked out so well. I mean, it rarely did… and as I looked on at Tic-Tac, Derry, Maverick, and Nine kicking the ball around with my little brother, I was reminded that seldom was anything perfect.

"What's he doing?" Dahlia asked, eying the trim blond man over her sunglasses.

"Still giving Marisol a hard time," Little Bird said with a sigh.

"Aw, yeah, he's a stickler for the rules," Dahlia said with a wicked smile of her ruby red lips.

She was dressed totally retro in a black fifties style two-piece swimsuit, her skin shining softly with a sheen of sunscreen making her tattoos almost iridescent in the light of the sun. She eyed Tic-Tac sharply and cocked her head.

"I suppose I owe you one," she said with a sigh, and I turned my head to look back at her. She rolled her eyes at me, but not unkindly.

"Girl, if you're going to be Maverick's queen of this MC, you need to learn how to not take *any* shit off these guys. For example," she craned her neck slightly and called out, "Hey, Tic-Tac!"

"What?" he called back without looking and she turned to me with this look like, *well?*

I sighed, hating confrontation and called out, "I need to talk to you."

"In a minute."

"How about now?" I asked tersely.

He turned from the little impromptu soccer match and demanded, "What's your problem?"

"You!" I cried back. "You're my fucking problem. You and your goddamn attitude. Fucking *get over yourself!* I made a mistake, not sure why the fuck you can't let it the fuck go!"

All activity ceased and the guys all turned.

"I'm not going away," I grated. "So, you better get used to it."

"Bravo," Dahlia said under her breath with a smile. Tic-Tac opened his mouth and Dahlia stepped up, so to speak, and said, "Don't even try it!"

Tic-Tac shut his mouth, turned around and my little brother laughed at him and kicked him the ball. Maverick was grinning from his place on the sand, his sunglasses over his eyes making the emotion in them unreadable but judging by the fact he didn't get in my shit, I had to guess he was some kind of impressed or proud.

I leaned back in my beach chair with a huff in my black bikini and Dahlia handed me a drink.

"To never being a doormat, ladies."

"Here's to being a badass," Little Bird said and held out her plastic Solo cup and we clinked plastic.

"That felt really good," I confessed.

"Had to feel better when you put your grandma in her place," Dahlia said dryly. I nodded.

In some ways it had, in other ways it'd been utterly terrifying.

I had a lot to think about on the beach as the afternoon wound down. We were staying in this odd little hotel made up entirely of vintage travel trailers, this time. Several of the guys manned this huge grill when we got back to it and the liquor and beer was flowing. Mateo had his own trailer near ours thanks to Maverick, and as soon as I got him fed and checked his insulin pump, I got him put to bed.

"Marisol?" he said right before I went to leave the trailer.

"Yeah, buddy?" I asked.

"Am I ever gonna see *Abuela* again?" he asked.

I went back to his bed and sat down beside him.

"I honestly don't know," I told him. "Does that make you sad? I mean, do you miss her?"

He shrugged his shoulders and said, "I like Maverick and the rest of the guys. Their nicer to you than our *abuela* ever was. I don't understand why she hated you so much, it made me sad."

"It's all grown up stuff, Mateo. You don't need to know why, you just need to know she loved you very much, at the very least and it's okay to miss her."

"I missed you too, when you were gone," he said. "A lot more than I miss her."

I smiled and kissed the top of his head.

"You don't have to say things like that to spare my feelings, little bro."

"I know, it's true though."

I sighed.

"You good?" I asked.

He nodded happily.

"I love you," he said and I smiled.

"I love you, too."

I got up and went to the door, halfway out of it he called out to me, "I love you!"

"I love you, too, Mateo. Now, try to get some sleep. We have a long ride back tomorrow then we got to get you ready for school."

He huffed out a sigh, patently unhappy that I was sticking to my bedtime guns and said, "I know."

I shut the door tightly to his little Airstream and went and found Maverick by the firepit.

"Hey, baby." He pulled me down into his lap. I made a noise of protest and said, "I was going to get a drink!"

"What do you want? I'll get it for you." I looked up and Tic-Tac's face was unreadable.

"Jack and Coke," I said softly and he gave a nod.

"He's not a bad guy," Maverick said. "Just a hardass and a stickler for the rules. It's the Army in him."

"He was in the military?" I asked, looking after him as he mixed my drink.

"Yup. Couple of tours, no injuries but he definitely saw some shit."

"I didn't know."

"A lot of us don't advertise our pain," he pointed out. "You certainly did a damn good job of keeping your shit under wraps."

"You got me there," I admitted and looked down into his face. He reached up and tweaked a thumb in a light caress along my cheek.

I laid a hand on the side of his neck and caressed beneath his jaw with my thumb, leaning down to kiss him.

It was never enough to just kiss him with a simple press of lips. It never failed that I would end up wanting more, coming back for more, so I didn't bother to pull back. Instead, I let the kiss deepen naturally, my tongue sliding against his in a sensual dance that ignited things lower in my body.

"Here."

I jumped slightly, the spell broken and looked up. Tic-Tac handed me down my drink.

"Thanks," I murmured.

"No problem."

He walked away and I took a sip, coughing slightly. It was good. Good and *strong*.

"What just happened there?" I asked.

"Well, I do believe you asked to be forgiven and I have to say that looked like a peace offering to me," Maverick said with a grin and I shook my head a bit mystified.

"Boys," I said sardonically, and he laughed.

It wasn't much longer that he bounced me on his knee and said, "What's say me and you go someplace a little more private?" he said.

With a raised eyebrow and a final sip of my drink I asked, somewhat tipsy, "Are you propositioning me?"

He gave an exaggerated nod and said, "Yes. Absolutely."

I giggled and he pushed me up into a standing position off his lap. I got up, handed the cup off to Nine who reached out to take it and

Maverick dipped and came up, hoisting me up over his shoulder like a sack of grain while I shrieked at the unexpected maneuver.

A rowdy cheer went up around us, drowning out my protests as he marched us across the grounds to our own trailer while I cried out, "No, stop! Put me down! Oh, my God, I think I'm gonna puke!"

"You better not!" he cried and swatted me on the ass which was on full display up over his shoulder.

"I am gonna kill you!" I declared and he laughed.

"Can a guy get a last fuck?" he asked, setting me down. The world spun for a moment and I leaned in for a kiss.

"Absolutely," I declared, right before our lips met.

He opened the door to our trailer and practically shoved me up the steps and through. I giggled madly against his lips and lost my breath to his kiss as we both fervently got each other naked as fast as possible.

I groaned when he bent me over the bed, slapped my ass with a great resounding crack that reverberated off of the stainless-steel walls of the small trailer's space, and he rammed into me almost before I was ready.

I arched beneath him, shoving my pussy onto him in offering as he gripped my hips and set the rhythm for a punishing fuck that left us both moaning and gasping.

"You like that?" he demanded roughly. "You like my dick inside you?"

I laughed, a sultry, throaty sound that was wicked in its delight.

"I love it," I gasped. "I love it, now harder!"

He complied, wonderfully so, our bodies clapping together in sharp reports of sound that echoed back at us, our feral cries mingling, our bodies dewy with sweat as we found this special synchronicity that has us flying along that razor's edge of orgasm so hard, so fast, it was even more thrilling than the best wind therapy we'd shared together to date and it seemingly set our souls free like nothing else could.

We switched positions, me on my back, his hands on the backs of my thighs, folding me practically in half, pressing my knees to my chest as he worked his way in and out of my pussy. This position changed the angle somehow, made things not only more intimate, but made it feel as though he somehow went deeper, tightened me up, made it feel as though he filled me to the point of over full and I lived for it.

I gazed into his eyes and gasping, blurted out, "I love you! Don't stop. Please, don't stop!"

"Never, baby, never in a million years," he grunted sharply between thrusts and we were like that for I don't know how long. A minute? Fifteen? An hour?

It didn't matter. All that mattered in these moments was that it was just him and just me and that for however long we could keep this up we were simply *us* and I wanted it to be *us* for the rest of our lives.

Jesus, *fuck*, I loved him.

___

EPILOGUE

___

SOMETIME MUCH LATER...

*F*enris...

Bar was hoppin'. I sometimes bounced at this cowboy bar out in Ravensdale, just north of Black Diamond. I lived out on the edge of Auburn in the Green Valley area, so it wasn't too long of a haul for me and it was something to do on a Friday night when the club didn't have anything going on.

It was a pretty okay gig, a flat rate of pay for the night, cash under the table and it bought some goat or chicken feed for the farm on occasion.

Mostly, it gave me an outlet for some of my aggression when shit was otherwise calm around the club. Nothing like pitching some drunk frat bros or wannabe cowboys out on their ass, or better yet, their face in the gravel lot.

This was one of my pop's first stops when he got out of the joint. His old high school buddy, Mitch, ran the place and always had a job for him when he got out. When my pops started getting up in years, after my sister died, I'd just naturally transitioned into the spot my dad had held down at the door.

He still came in and drank, taking up a stool at the end of the bar to shoot the shit with Mitch while I worked the door.

Not tonight, though. Tonight, it was just me, checking ID's as the citizenry's ladies and gents filed in.

Mitch had been making a killing ever since he'd put in the dance floor and sound system and added the mechanical bull in the corner.

He had a regular Texas-style Roadhouse going on out here, and it was popular.

"Hey, Fen." Bobby, the junior doorman handed me an ID I shone my flashlight on it and double-checked it for him. It was legit. I looked at the picture and up at the girl who didn't look a fuckin' day over sixteen.

"Try not to stay too late, darlin'. Place gets pretty nuts after eleven," I said, handing it back to her. She smiled prettily and blushed and it did absolutely nothing for me.

"I don't know, Lindsay… I don't think this is a good idea," I heard and I looked up into a beautiful set of green eyes, taking the two rectangles of laminated whatever the fuck driver's licenses in Washington were made of.

Lindsay was a brunette, the math told me she was twenty-eight and she looked like a bitch. Her makeup overdone, titties on full display, one of those types looking to hook up and ride a cowboy. She fit right in with the rest of the posers inside. Fake as shit, I had no interest in her or anyone else who came through these doors, typically.

The other license, the name, like her eyes, caught my eye for its uniqueness. Aspen. Aspen Lawson. I handed each lady their license back and let my gaze linger on Aspen.

She was beautiful in an unconventional way – thicker, with some real tits and an ass, a true hourglass figure in a thin sweater that clung to her over jeans and a pair of stylish knee-high boots. She looked cold standing out here waiting to get in. It wasn't exactly a night for going without a jacket, but a lot of girls did. It was warm inside the bar and it was one less thing to have to try and keep track of.

She had these luxurious blonde curls that framed her face, held back by a slim glittering line of rhinestones, some kind of headband that was hidden but for the evenly spaced stones in her hair. Simple, cute, her makeup, if it was there, understated and accentuating her natural beauty.

She was tall, too. Five foot nine, maybe? Still, not too tall when it came to me. I still looked down at her from my six-foot-five height.

"Thank you," she murmured, eyes wide where they met mine and I nodded. She plucked her license from my rough, tattooed fingers and I looked after her as she disappeared inside with her friend.

"Hey, man." I turned back to the half-jock, half-cowboy wannabe who was next in line in his polo shirt and scowled, taking his license from him and skimming it.

"Go ahead," I growled and let him through. I had some difficulty putting the pretty blonde out of my mind…

Hours later, the bar was closing and Mitch came to find me at the door.

"Hey, we got one that's drunk as fuck and can't find her friend."

"On it," I growled and heaved myself off the stool at the door. It'd been a quiet fuckin' night. One near fist fight over a girl, but they'd all been pussies and I'd thrown them out without incident. That'd been it, so far.

I headed into the bar trailing Mitch, and I didn't know what I would find. I can tell you, the absolute last thing I expected to find was the reluctant blonde, Aspen, drunk as fuck in a back-corner booth.

I mean she was *gone*.

It was pretty impressive, actually.

I slid into the booth with her and cupped her cheek.

"Hey!" I called out. "Hey, Aspen!"

"You know her?" Mitch asked.

"No, I just remembered the name for some reason. Not one you see very often."

"Well she's the last one in here, you remember if she came with a friend?"

"Yeah, a brunette, L-something," I answered absently as Aspen groaned.

"Shit, I'll have Becca check the ladies' room but looks like Aspen here got ditched."

"Don't bother, the bitch she came with probably got drunk and fucked off with one of these wannabe cowboys. Do me a favor and call my pops, have him bring the truck."

"You sure?" Mitch asked with an incredulous scoff.

"I'm sure," I said.

I leaned Aspen up against me and sighed. Wouldn't be the first time I'd brought a drunk back to mine and my pop's place to sleep it off, but it definitely was the first time I'd be bringing a woman as pretty as she was home with me.

It took my pops a good half an hour to get there, and he wasn't happy about it.

"What the fuck?" he demanded and I scowled up at him.

"Shut up and get the fuckin' doors for me, old man."

"I am *not*—"

"You ain't doing shit except driving. I'll handle the rest."

He growled a rumbling noise of displeasure and I ignored him. I got her up, unsteady on her feet, groaning. It so wasn't happening. I got my arm beneath her knees and lifted her just as she passed out again. She had some weight to her, and while I wouldn't be able to do this forever, it was a straight shot to the front door and out to my dad's truck where he'd parked it. *Thankfully,* he'd had the presence of mind to keep the passenger side pointed this direction. I went out, Mitch holding the front door for me and put her right into the truck.

My pop's closed the door when he knew she was clear and he wouldn't bang into her.

"Hope like hell you know what you're doing," he said and I nodded.

"Just drive, I'm right behind you."

I waved at Mitch who waved back, and I went over to my bike, mounting up.

The ride home was brisk, and when my dad pulled up, he did it right in front of the door, passenger side pointed the right way. He got out of the truck calling something or other out but I couldn't hear it over the bike. I shut it off.

"What?"

"I said, you clean that shit up! I'm going to bed!"

"Fuck," I muttered.

Sure enough, I opened up the passenger door of his truck and the woman was an absolute mess. The vomit sweet and off-smelling, and I wondered if there was more than just alcohol at play here.

"Come on, darlin'," I muttered and helped her stagger out onto the gravel driveway. "I gotcha."

I helped her into the house, carried her up the stairs and sat her on the john in the upstairs bathroom. She was *out of it.*

I stripped her, got her cleaned up, helped her puke into the tub and spent the better part of an hour helping her into my room and into my bed where she would be more comfortable. Her clothes I put in the laundry across the hall. I got out some aspirin and a fresh clean glass of water and put them on the bedside table for her. Finally, I wrote a long-ass note trying to cover all the bases and left that too.

I still had some proverbial miles before I could sleep, myself. I dragged my ass back downstairs and dealt with my dad's truck, which wasn't that bad seeing as she'd mostly nailed herself.

Finally, after all of that, I dragged myself in and onto my couch.

Tomorrow morning was going to be interesting. That was for sure.

ALSO BY A.J. DOWNEY

The Sacred Hearts MC

1. Shattered & Scarred

2. Broken & Burned

3. Cracked & Crushed

3.5 Masked & Miserable (a novella)

4. Tattered & Torn

5. Fractured & Formidable

6. Damaged & Dangerous

The Virtues

1. Cutter's Hope

2. Marlin's Faith

3. Charity for Nothing

4. Stoker's Serenity

The Sacred Brotherhood

1. Brother to Brother

2. Her Brother's Keeper

3. Brother In Arms

4. Between Brothers

5. A Brother's Secret

6. A Brother At My Back

7. A Brother's Salvation

Indigo Knights

1. Her Thin Blue Lifeline

2. His Cold Blue Command

3. A Low Blue Flame

4. His Wild Blue Rose

5. Her Pained Blue Silence

6. A Cold Blue Call

7. Her Reluctant Blue Cavalier

8. Forged Under Fire

9. Under A Blue Moon

The Sacred Hearts MC - PNW Chapter

1. Over the High Side

Paranormal Romance (with Ryan Kells)

1. I Am The Alpha

2. Omega's Run

3. Hunter's End